Frostworks

Henning Bauer

DEDICATION

To Santhi, without whom I would never have finished.

CONTENTS

ACKNOWLEDGMENTS

Above all, I would like to thank my wife Santhi for her endless patience and for never approving of anything simply because it was written by me. Without her relentless criticism and keen eye for plausibility, this book would have been a lesser story. My deepest gratitude also goes to Dharini Rasiah and Irina Feeney for taking the time to read and review my manuscript.

1 ENCOUNTERS

Paris, February 12, 1968.

Like a furtive caress, a sudden current of cool air passed over Milena's cheek. She looked up from her book. The familiar whisper of chimes, barely audible in the back room, came from the front door. Someone had entered the shop.

She frowned at her watch. Just ten minutes after opening time. She had counted on at least another hour or so to finish the chapter she needed to read, before the first browsers came in. Who could need to shop for clothes so early on a weekday?

With a sigh, she put her book down on the rickety lino table and headed toward the front of the boutique. When she reached the bead curtain that separated the storage shelves from the salesroom, something made her hesitate. She remained still, bating her breath, watching, herself unseen.

A young woman stood by the coat rack, flicking through the hangers. The wind still sighed into the store, its moan rising in pitch as the door slowly closed. Milena saw the draft moving a few strands of the woman's hair. In her left hand, she held a wallet. Something glistened on the slender fingers. Milena's throat tightened. A cinnabar rivulet snaked out from under the woman's sleeve, feeding a drop swelling at her knuckle.

The door clicked shut, cutting off the sough of the wind. The only sound that remained was the sliding of the coat hangers on the metal rail. In the display window, the mannequins stared blankly at the snowflakes that tumbled through the leaden morning light.

The dark drop fell toward the parquet floor and burst on the honey-colored wood. Unaware, the woman continued to inspect the coats.

Milena took a deep breath and stepped through the curtain. The crystal beads produced their usual noise: a gust of rain that came and went in an instant.

The young woman turned around with a gasp. The wallet slipped from her hand and fell to the floor. It was made of tan leather, slick with blood where her fingers had been grasping it. The woman quickly bent down and picked it up.

"I'm sorry I startled you," Milena said.

The woman drew herself up to her full height. Even so, she was shorter than Milena, very slight, fragile-looking. Her skin appeared nearly translucent, her blue eyes striking but only a tinge away from achromatic, her hair not so much blond as drained of color. She hardly looked like she should bleed at all. She brought her knuckle toward her lips as if she meant to lick off the blood. Milena felt her stomach shift. Thankfully, the woman lowered her hand and put the wallet into her pocket. "It's all right," she murmured.

"I was in the back having a cigarette." Milena noticed the stain spreading on the woman's sleeve. On the gray fabric, the color was indefinable. It could have been coffee, or water.

The woman nodded. Another drop of blood fell. She looked at the floor. "I'm the one who should apologize," she muttered. She reached into the clothes rack and pulled out a black canvas coat. "I'll take this one."

As a replacement for her own, the coat was a poor choice. The woman's outfit, if drab, looked expensive. Nothing in the boutique was going to match her style. It probably didn't matter. "I'll also need a shirt. White. Perhaps beige. In a size 34."

Milena mechanically slid the hangers across the shirt rail. It was the same here. No suitable matches for what her strange customer was wearing. "We don't really carry anything elegant. Just trendy clothes. Bright colors, mostly."

"Whatever you have."

Milena picked out two shirts, one beige, one yellow. "I have nothing in white at the moment."

"The beige one."

"Do you want to try it on?"

The woman shook her head. "I need to get back to work."

"You're bleeding quite a bit," Milena said. "How did this happen?"

"I dropped a picture frame. I was carrying it, and I fell. Last night. There was a lot of broken glass."

"I'd see a doctor if I were you. You probably need stitches. Not that it's any of my business."

"I'll be fine. I just need some new bandages from the pharmacy." The woman awkwardly extracted several bills from her blood-stained wallet. "How much for the shirt and jacket?"

Milena dropped the bills in the drawer under the register without touching the red smears on them. Hopefully, the blood would come off. She wasn't keen on having to explain it to Sylvie when she came by to do the accounts later.

The woman hurried to the door, the new clothes carefully draped over her right arm. She tried to twist the brass knob with her left hand, but it resisted her grip. More blood dripped to the floor. "Ježiše Marie," Milena sighed. "Wait."

The woman stopped struggling with the door knob. She did not turn around. "What?"

"I have a first aid kit in the back."

"There's no need," the woman said. She had the air of a panicked animal waiting for the right moment to bolt.

"You're bleeding all over the place."

"I'll be all right." The woman closed her eyes.

"Don't be silly." Milena emerged from behind the counter and gestured toward the chair next to the tiny fitting booth. "Sit down. Please."

The blond woman's stance slackened. At last, she nodded. She dropped the new clothes next to the chair and sat down. Milena locked the door and flipped over the sign that had said "OPEN" from the outside. "I'll be right back." She got the first aid kit from the back room and knelt in front of the chair. "You'll have to take the coat off."

Milena helped the woman slip out of her wool coat. Reaching up from her kneeling position sent a sting into her left shoulder and she winced. The woman gave her a questioning look but said nothing.

Milena felt a convulsion in her stomach as she peeled the woman's left arm out of the coat. The sleeve of her white shirt was drenched in blood. She took a deep breath, unbuttoned the shirt cuff, and rolled up the sleeve. The bandage on the forearm looked expertly applied, but the flow of blood had overwhelmed it. "I'll have to remove that," Milena said. There was no need to make these announcements, but they steadied her. As she lifted layer after layer of blood-drenched gauze, she briefly regretted her offer of assistance. She tried to imagine what she was going to see once the bandage was completely removed. Hopefully, she wouldn't be sick all over the floor.

"Jesus." There were several cuts. At least five. One of them was wider than the rest. Fresh blood was oozing up from it. "What did you do to yourself?"

"I told you."

For a few seconds, Milena struggled with the urge to heave.

"I'm sorry," the woman on the chair whispered.

Milena fought down her nausea and inspected the wounds. All of the cuts were long and fairly deep. None of the minor nicks and scratches you usually got from handling broken glass. None of them intersected. And there were other scars, some long healed. A few extended under the rolled-up sleeve, presumably covering the woman's upper arm. Whatever had caused these injuries had happened more than once.

A man came to the door, looked at the sign, and squinted through the glass. He tapped briefly on the pane. When no one moved to let him in, he walked off. The snow was now falling so heavily that his silhouette seemed to fade as he moved away.

The blond woman looked after him. "You're losing business."

Milena shrugged. She took a small bottle of rubbing alcohol and a wad of cotton wool out of the first aid kit. "This will hurt a bit, I'm afraid."

"I had to dress these cuts in the morning. And last night. I got used to it."

Milena nodded and drenched the cotton with alcohol. "May I ask your name?" When she touched the cotton to the raw wounds, she expected a flinch. She clenched her teeth, imagining the sting of alcohol in cuts this deep.

The woman in the chair didn't move a muscle. Her face was calm, her eyes closed, as if the procedure was soothing her. "Louise," she murmured.

"Louise," Milena repeated. It struck her as an old-fashioned name; at least it would have been in her native Czechoslovakia, where its equivalent wasn't very common. In French it had a more pleasant ring. In between cleaning the cuts, she stole closer glances at her mysterious patient. Slouched on the chair in front of her, Louise looked even smaller, too thin for her height. Faint lines around her mouth and nose made her look withdrawn and slightly haughty. Her lips were delicate, finely curved but too thin to be voluptuous. It would have been hard not to admit that, in her own way, she possessed a certain kind of wan beauty.

Louise nodded toward Milena's left shoulder. "Is there something wrong with your arm?"

"I have a stiff shoulder," Milena said. "An old fracture."

"What happened to it?"

Milena hesitated. Everyone asked, of course. Just not usually within the first ten minutes. Apparently, Louise was less reserved than she looked. "I had an accident, when I was still in school. The shoulder blade was shattered. It never healed properly."

"How awful," Louise said. "Does it hurt?"

Milena shook her head. "The muscles get sore sometimes. Nothing too serious." She braced herself for the usual questions, the usual story. But Louise said nothing more, and she felt grateful for that. "Do you work around here?"

"I work in a gallery on the Place des Vosges," Louise said. "De Benoît's. It's in the south-eastern corner."

"I'm sure I've passed it now and then. But I don't remember the name."

"And your name? Are you Sylvie?"

Milena inspected Louise's forearm. The bleeding still hadn't entirely stopped, but at least the wounds were clean. "Sylvie?" She frowned. "No, Sylvie's my boss. The boutique is named after her. My name is Milena. I'm going to bandage your arm now. I don't know how long it'll take before you bleed through these, and your new shirt and coat. You should see a doctor as soon as you can."

Louise nodded. But Milena knew she was not going to take her advice.

•

Milena filled her plate with tagliatelle and meat sauce and sat down at the kitchen table. "Thanks for cooking yet again."

Pauline had already started eating. "Never a problem," she said.

They had this exchange every time their schedules allowed them to have dinner together, which wasn't often. There were the classes, the jobs, and in Pauline's case, a boyfriend, Alain, who sometimes joined them before he spent the night with Pauline. Whether they ate separately or not, it was usually Pauline who did the cooking. Milena had learned a few traditional Czech recipes from her mother, but she had no illusions about her culinary skills. Even when the dishes turned out well, they were too rich and heavy for Pauline's taste, certainly on weeknights.

"Something strange happened at Sylvie's today," Milena said.

Pauline gave no sign of having heard. There had been a time when this behavior puzzled Milena, and then infuriated her, especially since in the first weeks of their friendship, Pauline had rarely failed to acknowledge her with a word or two, or a smile or a nod, when she spoke. But after more than two years of sharing the apartment, Milena had come to realize that Pauline considered such superficialities unnecessary between friends. When she was unwilling or unable to pay attention, she said so.

Silence, in Pauline's perception, was all that was needed to indicate her readiness to listen.

"This young woman came in. I'd never seen her before. Her left arm was bleeding. She was dripping blood everywhere."

Pauline had pulled her apricot hair back in a tight ponytail. It made her long freckled face look severe, especially when she frowned. "Blood?"

Milena told her what had happened, up to the point when Louise, her arm freshly bandaged and encased in a new shirt and coat, had left the boutique. "My first thought was that she'd botched a suicide attempt. But the cuts were on her forearm, away from her wrist. Almost as if she'd planned on being able to hide them."

Pauline raised an eyebrow. "What sense does that make? It was probably an accident, like she said. I don't know how many times I cut myself on broken glasses at Oriflamme." She held up a palm. "See this one here? Couple of weeks ago. Stupid thing cracked in the dishwater. I reached in there without looking."

Milena winced. "Her cuts looked different. She had lots of older scars, too. Once I got all the blood off her skin, I could see them clearly."

"Maybe she's clumsy." Pauline pushed her plate away and lit a cigarette. She picked three of the previous fall's chestnuts out of the wooden bowl she kept on the kitchen table and began rolling them around in her palm. Her collections were scattered all over the apartment: pebbles, seashells, several years' worth of wine corks. In Milena's own room, a bowl filled with glass marbles sat on the window sill. It had been there when she moved in.

"If you're so intrigued, check in on her," Pauline said. "You know where she works, right?"

"Jesus, I still need to do the reading for tomorrow's lecture."

"Don't tackle it without coffee," Pauline said. "It's soporific."

"Perhaps I'll stop by at this gallery tomorrow, when I get back from Nanterre."

Pauline smiled at the chestnuts moving back and forth in her palm with gentle clacks. "If you want to occupy yourself with someone who's hurting, you should have a word with Jacques."

"He's not in love with me, Pauline."

"Of course he is. He's always around you."

"We're on a lot of committees together. There's always something to discuss, something to coordinate, some meeting to attend."

"Have you noticed the way he looks at you, when you speak at those meetings?" Pauline dropped her chestnuts back in the bowl.

"He's paying attention. As are others."

"He's swooning."

"What's the point of bringing this up again?" Milena started preparing coffee. She made more noise than was necessary. "Even if you were right, you can't reject a man before he's said a single word."

"He'll never work up the courage. Not Jacques."

"Then what's the difference? If you feel something and don't express it, you might as well not feel it at all." Milena ignited the gas burner. "I need to start reading. Can you take care of the coffee?"

"I'll bring you a cup when it's ready," Pauline said. As Milena left the kitchen, she heard her chuckling. "Mon dieu, am I glad I'm not in love with you."

Milena walked down the hallway into her room and closed the door. She picked up the book from her desk, but she did not turn on the light. She sat on her bed, holding the book to her chest, and stared at the winter moonlight trapped in the glass marbles by the window, until she heard the whistle of the kettle in the kitchen, followed soon after by the sound of Pauline's steps in the hallway.

•

Milena pushed open the door to the gallery and stepped inside. A chime jingled above her head. There was no one in the showroom. A door behind the empty front desk led to another room or rooms. She heard a noise of hammer blows coming from there. But nobody appeared.

She looked at the paintings on display. Most of them were old-fashioned, traditional. A gigantic still life of quinces in lurid yellow, a shore with leaden waves, fields with corn flowers, a café scene in the impressionist style. Bourgeois. Unexciting.

The hammering stopped, and a young man appeared in the door at the back of the showroom. He was wearing a quilted coat and was in the process of fastening a shawl around his long neck, covering his mouth with it. Even in the thick winter clothes, he looked lanky. He stopped when he noticed her. The piercing eyes above his rather sizeable nose narrowed in a frown, then widened. He pulled the shawl down, exposing a wide mouth with thin lips, and smiled. "Can I help you, Mademoiselle?"

"I'm looking for Louise," Milena said. "She does work here, doesn't she?"

"She sure does." He glanced at his watch. "I'm afraid she's left to have lunch." He kept staring at her, the smile unwavering. It was irritating. A little unnerving, actually. "May I ask what this is about?"

"I just wanted to say hello," Milena said. "I'll come back at a later time." She started to turn the door handle.

"You can leave her a message, if you want." He gestured at the front desk. "This is where she works."

Her first impulse was to refuse, to leave as quickly as possible. Absurd, she told herself. "All right."

He picked a pen from the desk and held it out to her. Reluctantly, Milena approached him. She wrinkled her nose. He smelled. It wasn't too noticeable, but now that she'd become aware of it, it was impossible to ignore. Not a downright offensive stink, nothing like body odor or worse. Just a stale smell, as though he spent too much time in some place that was never properly aired out. Like a broom closet, or a storage room. Maybe it was the space in the back, where he worked.

She accepted the pen and stepped up to the desk. A silver crucifix hanging on the wall next to it caught her eye. It looked old and tarnished, suggesting that it was, in fact, made of silver.

"That's Louise's," the lanky apparition said. "She likes religious things. Nice, isn't it?"

"If your tastes run toward that." Milena scanned the desk for paper. Nothing there. Before he could offer to help—his eyes followed her every glance and gesture—she took her notebook out of her bag and tore a blank page from it. It occurred to her that nothing would stop him from reading the note. She decided on a few vague words.

How did it go? —M.

She folded the note in half and tucked it under a glass paperweight holding down a stack of unopened letters. The young man was still waiting behind her. At least he kept a respectful distance. "Thank you," she said. "I ought to be going."

"Okay." He escorted her to the door. "How do you know Louise, anyway? Are you in the gallery business? Or a collector, maybe?"

"Not exactly," Milena said. So now the questions were starting. Harmless questions that anyone would ask, perhaps. But coming from him, she resented them without quite knowing why. She felt like she was about to be interrogated.

"I'm just wondering," he said. "Louise never has visitors here, unless they're customers."

"Is that so?"

"As far as I know." He continued to smile, and positioned himself at an angle between her and the door. He wasn't exactly blocking her way, but she would have to move closer to him than she cared to if she wanted to reach the door. "What do you do, then?"

Milena tried to tell herself that he merely meant to open the door for her. But he made no move to do so. "I'm a student. I met Louise in a store." Does that satisfy you, she wanted to add. But who knew, he might be a friend of Louise's. There was no call to be too gruff. Yet.

"A student," he repeated. "What do you study, and where?"

"Sociology. At Nanterre."

"Really?" His eyes widened again, but the smile remained in place. He looked delighted in a foolish way. "Nanterre. There was some trouble down there last month, wasn't there? On a Friday? January 26, I think?"

"I suppose you could call it trouble."

"My boss called it trouble," he said. "Louise's uncle. He read about it in the paper. The police were there, and they sprayed tear gas, right? Were you there when it happened?"

Milena sighed. Why had she told him anything? Now he had a hundred more questions. But it seemed wrong not to answer. What had happened on that Friday was not a secret meeting of a clandestine society; on the contrary, the more people learned about their cause, the better. Excluding him just because he struck her as a bit odd would be unfair, especially since the papers had distorted the facts as usual. "I was there," she said. "I got a taste of the tear gas, too."

"Are you serious? It must be painful."

"It is. Your eyes burn as if they're going to melt out of their sockets, and you can barely breathe. It should make you wonder what kind of people would use it on their fellow citizens."

"No doubt, no doubt." He nodded vigorously. The smile had faded somewhat, lending him an air of greater normalcy. "So you're one of the, what did they call themselves—or rather the paper called them that…" He frowned as if he had to concentrate hard. For a brief moment, he nearly looked serious.

"Enragés," Milena said. She would have preferred to keep her personal affiliations out of the conversation. But she didn't have the patience to wait for him to try and recall what he had read. Besides, what did it matter? This, too, was no secret.

"Yes." The smile expanded to its full width again. "Enragés. They're communists, aren't they? Radicals?"

"In some ways."

"Amazing." He stared at her as though she was some sort of celebrity. "So you fought the police, then?"

"They fought us. We merely defended ourselves."

"I read that some of you threw things at them," he said. "Bricks, rocks, and so on. Did you?"

"Of course some of us fought back," Milena said. "What were we supposed to do?" She moved past him and reached for the doorknob. She had expected him to step back, but he remained fixed in place, forcing her to come close to him. The stale smell hit her again. She'd thought she'd gotten used to it, but in such proximity, it seemed like an entity, enveloping her, stifling her, dispersing the earlier feeling of normalcy. She was overreacting, of course. But the realization didn't help much. "Excuse me. I really need to go. I'll be late for work."

"Oh, I wouldn't want that, of course." He grinned. "Where do you work?"

Milena pretended not to hear. "Thank you for your help." She slipped out the door into the chilly winter air— a relief after his stink—and started walking along the arcade, away from the gallery.

The footsteps came suddenly, without warning, approaching quickly behind her. With a gasp, she flung herself against the nearest wall, back first. A sharp pain shot from her shoulder through her arm and into her hand. Her bag went flying.

It was him. He stood across from her, the idiotic smile still on his lips but looking otherwise bewildered. "Are you all right?"

"You startled me," she said, rubbing her shoulder. She looked at the wall she had crashed into. A strong urge to slap the sheepish grin off his face overcame her.

"I'm sorry." He picked up her bag and handed it to her. "I was afraid I might not catch up with you in time."

She snatched the bag from him. "What do you want, anyway?" She no longer felt the least inclination to be polite.

"You forgot this." He extended a hand toward her. She shrank back but then she realized he was holding her notebook. "It was still lying on Louise's desk."

"Ježiše Marie." Some of Milena's anger faded. She accepted the notebook and dropped it in her bag. "I'm glad you noticed," she muttered.

"That's why I came running after you."

"Of course." She pushed off from the wall behind her. "Thank you. But I really I have to go now." She started walking again.

"Maurice," he called after her. "That's my name. And yours?"

She waved without turning around, pretending not to hear. She could feel his eyes on her back. It took all her willpower not to look over her shoulder to check if he was following her again.

As she turned the corner from the Place des Vosges into the Rue de Birague, she risked a glance in the direction of the gallery. He was gone.

•

"Hey, Milena." Marcel leaned across the table and tapped her on the shoulder. "Milena? Jesus."

"I'm sorry," Milena said. She meant it. She liked Marcel well enough, he was one of the enragés that regularly attended the informal gatherings at Oriflamme. "I didn't hear you." In the noisy bar, it was a plausible apology. The truth was that her mind had kept wandering all day, always back to the encounter at the gallery, to her foolish reaction in the arcade, to the cycle of telling herself not to give further thought to the incident, which really was no incident but nevertheless somehow resisted dismissal. She was exhausted.

"I said, isn't it ironic?" Marcel chuckled. "You know that the Carthusian order got the recipe from Henri IV? Church and royalty worked hand in hand to create your favorite liqueur."

Milena realized that he was nodding toward the glass in her hand. Chartreuse on the rocks. Most of the ice had melted. She shrugged. "That was in sixteen-something, if I remember correctly. Ages ago, in other words."

"It's still made by the monks to this day. You're supporting the church by drinking it."

"I don't mind the church so much." She sipped a mouthful. "As long as the king is out of the game."

"As long as it's neutered, in other words." Marcel grinned and lit another cigarette. "Anyway, is Jacques coming tonight?"

"Maybe. I don't know for sure."

"That surprises me," the young woman sitting next to Marcel said. Jeanne, his new girlfriend. Milena had only met her a few times before. She remembered that she studied ethnology, and that she was involved with the Groupes Anarchistes d'Action Révolutionnaire and their newspaper, Rouge et Noir. Other than that, the most remarkable thing about Jeanne so far was her hip-length hair, smooth and lustrous and black as pitch. "Whenever there's any kind of meeting, I see the two of you together."

"This isn't a meeting," Milena said. The remark irritated her. "Just a few drinks with friends." She ignored the glance that passed between Marcel and Jeanne.

"And dinner," Marcel said. "I hope."

"Wasn't someone else supposed to join us?" Jeanne asked. "Someone from the Sorbonne?"

Milena sighed and nodded. "Jacques said a friend of his might come by with a few people from the Revolutionary Committee for Cultural Agitation." Or was it the Revolutionary Action Committee? It was hard not to lose track sometimes; such was the price, supposedly, of ideological pluralism. "He wasn't entirely certain, though."

Marcel glanced at his watch. "How much longer should we give them? I'm getting hungry."

Milena straightened herself up on her chair and scanned the surrounding tables. At the bar, Pauline was serving drinks to several couples that clearly didn't have politics on their minds. "I don't think they're here." The whole evening was turning out to be a waste of time. "Why don't you two go ahead? I'll stay here in case they arrive, after all. If they do, we'll catch up with you."

"Sounds good. We'll be at the usual place."
Marcel pushed back his chair and smiled. "Perhaps you can support the church a little more as you wait."

"I might do that," Milena said.

•

When Jeanne and Marcel were gone, Milena went to sit at the bar. Pauline was rinsing glasses and hanging them in a rack over the counter. "Why did those two leave?"

"Jacques and his friends didn't show up," Milena said. "Can you pour me another Chartreuse?"

"That's your third tonight. Something bothering you?"

"I don't know." Milena shrugged. "Maybe."

Pauline poured the drink and placed the glass in front of her. "Did you visit your friend with the cut-up arm today?"

"I went to the gallery, but she wasn't there. I left her a note."

"Good," Pauline said. "She can get in touch with you, then."

"I won't be too upset if she doesn't, to be honest."

"I thought you wanted to know what happened to her."

"I do, in a way." Milena hesitated. "But the more I think about it, the more I wonder if it isn't more trouble than it's worth."

"What changed your mind?"

"First of all, think about the way she came into the boutique, dripping blood all over the place. That's disturbing enough. And I'm pretty sure she was lying about how it had happened."

"It's possible," Pauline said. "People often hide the truth when they're in trouble."

"I bandaged her arm and got her into fresh clothes," Milena said. "What more can I do?"

Pauline leaned across the counter. "I admit this could be a lot messier than your safe theoretical masses with their neatly quantifiable problems and predicaments. But this girl might need help, Milena. Isn't that why you left her the note in the first place?"

Milena frowned. "Safe theoretical masses?"

"You know what I'm talking about," Pauline said. "You have a big heart. There's room for the plight of entire nations in there, I know. But up close, people scare you."

"When they come with mysterious injuries, yes."

Pauline began sliding more glasses into the rack above her head. "Whoever doesn't?"

"Suppose I meet her again," Milena said. "Then what? I'll hear her life story, learn all her dark and tragic secrets?"

"Why not? Can it hurt to at least find out what her story is?"

"I wonder." Milena lit a Gitanes. She blew smoke rings at the ceiling while Pauline served a customer at the other end of the bar. The old record player behind the counter churned out some scratchy chanson she didn't recognize. When it was over, Pauline changed the record and turned up the volume. Ne sois pas si stupide, Johnny Halliday demanded.

She had nearly finished her drink when Pauline approached her and nodded toward the door. "That woman over there seems to be looking for someone."

Milena turned around. "I don't believe it. That's her."

Louise stood by the front door scanning the crowd inside the bar. She was wearing another grey wool coat,

darker than the first. Her fingers nearly vanished in the voluminous sleeves. When she spotted Milena, she waved and began making her way across the bar.

"This is a surprise," Milena said.

Louise climbed onto the barstool next to Milena's. "Picon, please," she told Pauline. "Soda, no ice."

Milena lit another cigarette. "How did you find me?"

"I went to your boutique," Louise said. "After work. There was a woman there. She had curly hair and wore glasses. A little older than you."

"Sylvie. My boss."

"She said I might find you here, on Tuesdays. She gave me directions." Louise inspected her drink. "I found your note on my desk."

Milena shrugged. "After I patched you up in the boutique, I couldn't help but wonder how the rest of your day went."

"It went without further troubles," Louise said. "I just wanted to say thank you."

"A note would have been fine," Milena said. "There was no need for you to come all the way over here."

Louise stared at her glass in silence. She turned it between her fingers a few times, then she pushed it away with an abrupt motion and slid off the barstool. "Perhaps you're right."

Milena was surprised by how crushed she looked. "That's not how I meant it."

"I don't want to bother you," Louise said. "I'm sure you have other things to do than listen to me." She dropped a few bank notes on the counter, turned around, and headed for the stairs. Milena sighed. But she made no move to stop her.

Pauline came over. "What the hell is wrong with you?"

19

"She's a little touchy."

"If you don't want to know more about her, that's your decision. But I don't see the need to be so rude. Who knows what kind of trouble she is in?"

Milena looked toward the door, the front windows. Louise had already disappeared. She muttered a curse in Czech, finished her drink, and followed her.

She caught up with Louise near the corner of the street. She was walking fast through the falling snow. When she heard Milena call her name, she turned around and waited. "What do you want?"

"I'm sorry," Milena said. "I was just surprised that Sylvie took the trouble to tell you where to find me."

"She was being nice."

"I know. She was."

"I wanted to say thank you after what you did for me yesterday. But I guess now we're done with each other."

"Don't say that. Come back and have another drink with me."

"I appreciate the invitation," Louise said. "But you don't need to force yourself."

"I'm not forcing myself. Jesus. I'm sorry for the way I treated you."

Louise looked past Milena toward a group of young men standing outside Oriflamme, collars turned up, conversing noisily, expelling spouts of breath into the chilly air. "Are there any quieter bars around here?"

Milena nodded. "I'm sure we can find one."

•

As they turned the corner together, they nearly collided with Jacques. Milena introduced him and Louise.

He apologized for not being at Oriflamme in time; his professor had taken a long time to discuss one of his papers. After that, he missed the train. One thing had led to another. Where were they going now?

"I'm having a drink with Louise," Milena said. "The others went to get something to eat. The usual place. You can probably still catch them."

"I see." Jacques smiled. Snowflakes had melted in his thin brown hair. The wet locks clung to his skull, emphasizing his prematurely receding hairline. Milena felt sorry for him. What if Pauline was right, and he really did have feelings for her? "Or you could tag along with us," she said. Hopefully, he had enough sense to refuse.

"Nice of you to offer." Jacques's eyes darted back and forth between her and Louise. "But I think I'll pass."

"I won't talk you into it," Milena said.

"Right." He kept smiling. "I really need to speak to the others, anyway. Nice to meet you, Louise." He hurried away down the street.

They kept on walking. Louise looked over her shoulder. "You needn't have sent him away."

"He would probably have asked how I know you. Is that something you'd want to discuss in front of him?"

"I don't want to talk about what happened yesterday. With or without him there."

"That's your prerogative." Milena nodded toward a brasserie on the other side of the street. "Let's cross here."

·

Milena extinguished her cigarette in what was left of her oxtail soup. It smoldered in the congealed liquid like a miniature plane wreck crash-landed in a bog. "Tell me about the scars on your arm."

Louise looked up from the croque-monsieur she had carved into tiny pieces over the past fifteen minutes. She had yet to eat one of them. "You agreed to leave that subject alone."

"You said not to talk about yesterday," Milena said. "But I saw plenty of cuts on your arm that were made before that."

"You must be a law student, to split hairs this way."

"Sociology, actually."

"That makes almost as much sense." Louise sawed one of the pieces of her croque-monsieur in half. She pushed it around on the plate for a bit, but she didn't eat it. "Am I to be some sort of case study, then?"

"No," Milena said. "I'm just concerned that something violent happened to you. Anyone would be."

"Nothing violent," Louise said. She finally put the piece of croque into her mouth, chewed for a few moments, and put down her fork. "The ham is too salty."

"Why can't you tell me what happened, Louise?"

"I already did."

Milena signaled the waiter to bring her another glass of wine. "How many picture frames and vases can a person break and fall on? And always with her arm?"

"Try working at a gallery. You'd be surprised."

"I'm sure I would be." Milena sighed and lit another cigarette. "Ježiše Marie," she muttered, frustrated.

"What does that mean?"

"It's Czech. It means Jesus and Mary. Profanity, if you will."

"I don't like profanity." Louise skewered another square of croque, held it up to the light, and put it back on her plate. "Please don't use it around me."

Milena remembered the crucifix next to Louise's desk. Around her neck she wore another one, suspended from a silver necklace. It bore a minute silver Christ, unlike its larger counterpart. "You're religious?"

"Yes. Does that bother you?"

"It's your own personal business. It's not for me to judge."

"I thought communists despise religion," Louise said.

"Who says I'm a communist?"

"Maurice seems to think so."

"The creep who works at your gallery?" Milena couldn't suppress a grimace. "He doesn't even know me."

"He can be a little strange," Louise said. "I know."

"You have your own stories about this character?"

"He's harmless. He told me you were part of a group called enragés. Radicals, he said. Communists. I'm sure he meant no offense."

"And certainly none taken." Milena chuckled. "I see he filled you in on me."

Louise shrugged. "Don't think I interrogated him. But he seemed quite fascinated by your story of the riot at your school. He kept talking about it."

"It wasn't a riot," Milena said. "Just a demonstration that got out of hand."

"I'd call that a riot."

"But we didn't start the violence."

"Then who did?"

"The flics," Milena said. "We were doing nothing wrong, I assure you. But they attacked us. We fought back, naturally."

"Naturally?"

"Wouldn't you?"

"Fight the police?" Louise shook her head. "They represent the law."

"Laws can be unjust."

"Even so, what's the use? They have all the power behind them."

"They do," Milena said. "But power can be challenged. It must be challenged, in fact. That's how it works."

"How what works?"

"Power. It's a bit complicated. Power justifies itself through outside resistance. Some threat it can point to and say, see, you need me."

"And you're the threat?"

"In the eyes of those in power, yes. A minor one, so far, but still."

"Then aren't you supporting the very power you're opposed to," Louise said. "By fighting it?"

Milena smiled. "You catch on fast."

Louise didn't smile back. "I'm not stupid."

"I didn't mean to say you are. Yes, power depends on resistance to strengthen its own position, but if no one offered such resistance, it would concoct one itself, and probably a false one."

"Propaganda, in other words."

"Of a more or less subtle kind," Milena said. "We're not a false threat, however. Nor can we be controlled. And we will bring change, change that power cannot stop."

Louise seemed to consider this. She pushed the croque pieces around on her plate a little more and nodded to herself. "What laws were you breaking, anyway, for the police to come to your campus?"

"None at all," Milena said. "Another student group, a bunch of right-wingers, had threatened a counterdemonstration when we announced ours. They never showed up, but some university official got scared that there would be a fight. A reasonable assumption, of course, considering the brutish mentality of the right. So they called in the flics."

"I see."

The waiter brought a fresh glass of white wine. Milena took a sip. Not too good, not too bad. She could tell plonk from something better, but the finer points of wine appreciation still eluded her.

"So you're from Czechoslovakia," Louise said. "I thought I noticed an accent, but I couldn't place it. Your French is very good."

"Thank you. What else did your friend tell you about me?"

"He's not my friend. He's just a laborer. He works for my uncle."

"If you think I'm a communist, you might want to stop saying things like 'just a laborer' around me."

"I didn't mean it as a putdown," Louise said. "It's how my father would talk." She made a face. "Not that that's an excuse for me."

"He doesn't sympathize with the working class?"

"You have to feel a connection to people in order to have sympathy for them." Louise pushed her plate away with the air of someone who had just consumed a three-course dinner, and enjoyed none of it. She glanced at her watch. Silver, also, Milena noted. "It's getting late."

"Before you go," Milena said. "Just to be clear. About your father's opinions. Do you share them?"

"I didn't share anything with my father," Louise said. "Not willingly."

"Didn't?" Milena hesitated. "Is he—?"

"I haven't spoken to him in six years. Nor do I intend to ever speak to him again."

"May I ask why?"

Louise waved for the check. "I'd rather not end this evening talking about my father."

•

They parted ways on a corner, under a broken streetlamp. Snow like chiffon covered the streets and more was falling. The few tire tracks in the silent street were already disappearing again. Milena looked up into a black sky dizzy with whirling white. She felt unsure of what would be next. They didn't have a real reason to meet again. Perhaps it would be wiser to let their acquaintance end here.

"Will I see you again?" Louise asked.

"I guess it's possible. If you come by the boutique."

"Then it is possible," Louise said. She began walking away.

Milena strode resolutely in the opposite direction. After several yards, she stopped and looked after Louise. As if sensing her gaze, Louise turned around also. It seemed that she smiled, although it was difficult to tell; she was too far away already. She waved, started walking again, and disappeared into the snow.

•

Milena stood under the warm spray of the shower. She thought about switching off the light but decided against it. Darkness would render the shower too comforting, too womb-like to ever want to leave. There was the possibility of Pauline or Alain getting up and wanting to use the bathroom. She'd been lucky enough to come home after they had both gone to bed. A few more minutes, though.

She let the water massage her scalp. On the way home, she'd developed a massive headache. The cheap wine, no doubt. She turned off the water and immediately felt the cold seeping in through the window above the tub. She stepped out of the shower and hurriedly toweled herself off. She glanced at the mirror above the sink. A vague human bust, cloud-like, looked back at her from behind the fogged-over glass. The shapelessness of the reflection unnerved her. She polished the mirror with her towel until she could see herself clearly. A thin layer of condensation began to reclaim the glass. Her features softened, small imperfections in her skin slowly disappeared in a flattering haze. The short black hair, forever refusing to quite settle down on her head, began to appear smooth, pliable, less rebellious.

She took the hand mirror, wiped the larger mirror clear again and turned her back to it. It had it been a while since she had last looked. In the first weeks after her release from the hospital, in Prague, she had stared at the spot every day, as long and often as the pain would allow her the contortion that was required. In the years after that, she had looked less and less frequently, but her wrists still retained the physical memory of how to hold the mirror. It only took her a moment to find the angle. She winced. It was always too sudden.

The scars didn't look like much. One dimple under her left shoulder. The second one was on the shoulder blade itself, longer, darker than the first, a miniature valley in her flesh, forever filled with shadows: the blow that had nearly split the bone in half. The third, right next to it, had finished the job, shattered the scapula, punctured her lung, almost finished her. Complicated wounds. They still were.

She lowered the mirror and returned it to its place on the shelf. Her hand shook. She watched her features fog over once more. Faces faded. Scars endured. There was that to remember.

•

Two Gitanes into her book, Milena heard the front door being tried. She glanced at her watch. She had locked the boutique nearly twenty minutes ago. Aside from the small lamps illuminating the shop window, the salesroom was dark.

She put the book down. "Unbelievable," she muttered. Not even at Sylvie's, well after closing time, was she free from distractions. She cracked open the door and peered through the bead curtain into the salesroom, hoping that whoever had tried the door had realized their mistake and walked off. But a silhouette was still visible behind the 'Closed' sign. A slender silhouette, barely her height, with a halo of blond hair illuminated from above by a streetlamp. Milena hurried across the salesroom and unlocked the door. "What are you doing here?"

"I sometimes take this street on my way home," Louise said. "I thought I saw light in the back."

"We're closed," Milena said. "I like to stay after hours sometimes, to get a little reading done."

"In that case, perhaps I should go. I just wanted to say hello."

Milena considered letting her leave. But they had already played that game. She stepped back and held the door open. "Come in."

Louise crossed the threshold. She looked around the darkened boutique as though she was seeing it for the first time. "Why would you want to stay here to read?"

"It's quiet," Milena said. "At home I'd feel tempted to chat with my roommate or listen to the radio."

"You have a roommate?"

"The woman who was behind the bar, at Oriflamme. Her name is Pauline."

"The tall one, with the red hair?"

"Yes. She's a student, like me. We share an apartment."

Louise thumbed through the glove rack in the dark. "It's hard to have privacy, living with someone."

"I have the place to myself often enough, because of our schedules. But I like her company, actually."

"I lived with my aunt and uncle for a few months," Louise said. "When I first came to Paris. It was difficult, sometimes. Even though I loved them."

"You're not from Paris originally?"

Louise shook her head. "Tours."

"I see." Milena watched her flip through the gloves, then the scarves, all of them colorless in the dim light. "Do you have time to stay a little?"

Louise looked up from her aimless browsing. "If you like."

•

They sat down on the rickety and not entirely clean garden chairs at the old lino table. Louise wrinkled her nose at the chipped Cinzano ashtray overflowing with several days' worth of crushed Gitanes.

Milena pulled her thermos out of her duffle bag. "I have some tea left, if you don't mind sharing the cup."

Louise's fingers found their way across the blistered linoleum to the book lying next to the ashtray. "Critique de la vie quotidienne," she read out loud.

"My professor wrote that," Milena said.

"What is wrong with everyday life, that it needs to be critiqued?"

"Everything needs to be critiqued," Milena said. "Or people will take it too seriously."

"Like religion?"

"Or political doctrine. I don't discriminate." Milena poured the tea into the cap of the thermos and set it down in front of Louise. "Sorry, no sugar."

Louise inhaled the scent of the tea, tried a sip, nodded her approval. "It's good."

"You were talking about your aunt and uncle," Milena said. "Earlier."

"What about them?"

"You said you lived with them, when you came to Paris. I'm assuming that's the uncle who owns the gallery where you work?"

"He does now," Louise said. "My aunt was the one who established it, and made it a success." She watched the dripping faucet over the bare sink by the window. It had been leaking since Milena started working in the boutique, and no amount of force applied to the handles could make it stop. She was no longer consciously aware of the sound. But Louise seemed hypnotized by the rhythmic swelling and plummeting of the drops of water.

"Why did she decide to hand it over to him?"

"She didn't," Louise said. "My aunt was killed in a car accident six years ago."

"I'm sorry."

"I had just arrived in Paris. We were about to go on a trip to England together, and she needed to take care of some last business with a client in Montmorency before we left. On her way there, she had a collision. My uncle said she died instantly."

"Then at least she didn't suffer," Milena said.

"I like to think so." Louise finished the tea. "Is there any left?"

"A little." Milena poured the rest of the tea into the cup.

Louise resumed her observation of the faucet. "I loved my aunt above anyone else. I owe her everything.

The life I have now, my independence. I still cannot believe that she is gone."

"Your parents didn't send you to Paris?"

"No." A twitch flickered over Louise's lips. It was hard to tell what emotion it reflected. "My father was furious when I went to work for Aunt Corinne. If he could have forced me to come back, he would have."

"But it seems to me that you're doing well at the gallery."

"As if that mattered to him." Louise lowered her eyes and inspected the teacup. For a moment, it seemed as if she had forgotten that Milena sat across from her. "All he cares about is the family reputation. Tradition." She took one more sip of tea and slid the plastic cup across the table toward Milena. "That's why he was always at odds with my aunt. He said she was out to undo all his efforts to keep our family name from declining. When he got really angry, he would say that she was a fin de race. Ridiculous."

"I've never heard that expression," Milena said.

Louise sighed. "The end of the line, so to speak. You know how it is, sometimes, when you have families with a long history. Some of the later descendants aren't always—" She grimaced. "Entirely wholesome."

"So it's a more sophisticated way of calling someone a degenerate."

"It's not a category that would apply in just any family, like I said."

"Ah, that's right." Milena smiled. "De Benoît. I keep forgetting that you're nobility."

"You might as well forget it," Louise said. "If there was anything noble left in our family, it died with my aunt."

"How did your father figure that the label didn't apply to him as well as to his sister? They shared the same parents, or didn't they?" Milena wondered if there were any married cousins in Louise's family tree. It was probably too delicate a question.

"I have no idea what his reasoning was," Louise said. "Most likely he felt that his own pretenses of propriety lifted him above such judgments, while my aunt's actions and decisions could only be the result of some kind of hereditary shortcoming. Some nonsense like that."

"May I ask what actions of hers he found so unpalatable?"

Louise straightened herself with such suddenness that Milena thought she was going to pound her fists on the fragile table. "Aunt Corinne was progressive," she said. "She believed that women should have careers, that they should get an education for something more than to impress some future husband's conceited family. And that a woman should marry whomever she chose, regardless of their background."

"I couldn't agree more."

"But you should have heard how my father talked about Uncle Claude, how he went on and on about how horrid it was that Corinne was marrying a commoner."

"A commoner?" Milena smiled. "Ježíše Marie, what is this, the Middle Ages?"

"I'm sure that's what my father wishes."

"I'm beginning to see why you're so at odds with him," Milena said.

Louise gave her a look. For a moment, the slight haughtiness in her features became dominant. "You know nothing about it," she said.

The change was startling. Milena was at a loss as to how she should react. But after a mere instant, Louise's features reverted to their quiet sadness. Milena dug into her duffle bag and extracted her crumpled pack of Gitanes. Only one left. She lit the cigarette and offered it to Louise. "I suppose I don't."

Louise stared at the cigarette as if accepting it would constitute some sort of binding agreement to say more. Milena was about to withdraw her hand when Louise plucked the cigarette from her fingers and took a careful puff. She made a face, coughed, and passed it back. "Tell me about yourself. Your family. Your father. What is he like?"

"I love my parents, plain and simple," Milena said. "As for my father, I worshipped him. I still do, and I always will. All my ideals, everything I believe in, I learned from him. Justice, truth. He worked as a defense lawyer, for people accused of political dissent. One day, he defended the wrong case, or the right one, depending on how you look at it, and his career was over. Perhaps it was inevitable. It happens a lot in my country. But he gave many people hope. And hope always multiplies."

"Are you still close?"

"We used to be. But you know how it is." Milena clenched her teeth and swallowed. "Years go by. There's the distance. Things change."

Louise nodded. "My father is a surgeon."

"That's another way of helping people."

"A way of feeling superior."

"You have nothing good at all to say about your father, do you?" Milena stabbed out the cigarette in the ashtray. She burned her fingertips, and a few butts spilled onto the table. She picked them up and carefully balanced them on the reeking pile. "What about your mother? You haven't mentioned her."

"What's there to say? She was the opposite of my aunt. Old-fashioned. Meek." Louise shook her head. "Well educated, mind you. She has a degree in pharmacy. And what for? She's done nothing with it except maybe to satisfy my grandparents, when my father brought her to meet them."

"It is a shame," Milena said. "To waste an education that way."

"And you, why are you here?"

"I'm sorry?"

"You asked me why I left Tours," Louise said. "But what about you? You loved your parents. They loved you. Why did you go away?"

"There are plenty of reasons for leaving one's home," Milena said. "It's not always about trouble with your parents. For many Czechs, it's politics. For some, there are other reasons, too."

Louise waited. She was watching Milena now, not the faucet.

"My parents sent me here because they were concerned about my education," Milena said. "I had some school-related difficulties, back in Prague. It's a long story."

"I wouldn't mind hearing it," Louise said. "If it's anything you want to talk about, that is."

"Perhaps some other time." Milena studied Louise's face. Against the dark rectangle of the doorway leading into the salesroom, in the light coming from the lamp above the table, she looked radiant. The cigarette smoke hanging in the air softened the contours of her cheekbones. Like the moon on a cold night, Milena thought, haloed by mist. She looked away, cleared her throat, and glanced at her watch. "I really should go."

•

Milena locked the boutique. The snowfall had ceased, but the street was powdered white, and the dark gray sky was bloated with more snow to come. The pepper sting of frost sharpened the night air. Louise took a step away from the door and shivered. "Which way are you going?"

Milena nodded toward the Rue St. Antoine. "That way. Then to the Bastille."

"I'll walk to the corner with you," Louise said. "But I have to go in the other direction, after that."

They walked slowly. The thin layer of snow made the sidewalk slippery. Halfway along the Rue de Birague, Milena felt Louise's hand on her elbow. She couldn't prevent her muscles from stiffening. Louise withdrew. "How is your shoulder these days?"

"The cold always makes it worse," Milena said. "But it's tolerable."

"That's good."

"It was a motorcycle accident, by the way. In case you were wondering."

"I wasn't sure if I should ask."

"Everyone does, eventually," Milena said. "Not that there's much to tell. Someone gave me a ride after a party. It was late, and raining hard. We had been drinking. You can imagine the rest." She had the particulars on standby, as always, for added authenticity. The boy, the name of the street. Even a specific model of motorcycle: an old Jawa 500, built in 1952.

"You don't need to tell me more," Louise said. "Unless you want to."

"Let's leave it at that, then."

Louise nodded. She took a quick step forward and touched her cheek to Milena's, kissing the winter air next to her ear. Just as quickly, she did it on the left side. Milena couldn't suppress a small gasp. Even after three years in France, the gesture still took her by surprise. She cleared her throat. "Good night," she rasped.

They moved apart and stood still for a second, a few feet from each other. Milena gave a small wave with her hand, and walked away.

•

Milena sat on the stairs outside the sociology department. The concrete steps were cold but dry, swept clean of snow. She lit a cigarette and stared off to her right: one steel and glass building after another. A dreary vision of function without form, without style. Students moved through the view like figures dotting an architectural sketch, arranged along vanishing lines that pointed into a future where institutions of learning were not only run like factories, but looked like them, too. No wonder politics and what was wrong with life was all everyone had on their mind here.

Jacques cleared his throat. She had almost forgotten that he was there, sitting next to her on the stairs. She resented the interruption, almost to the point that she considered ignoring him. She'd come to sit here because the cold helped her clear her mind. It also aggravated her shoulder, but as long as she didn't move her arm, she could put the ache out of her mind. Even as a little girl, while the other children were off screaming on their sleds or pelting each other with snowballs, she would be sitting somewhere by herself, waiting for the chill to penetrate her clothes and slow down the clicking and ticking of her thoughts, until she could think without thinking about anything in particular. God knew what her need as a child had been to empty her mind like that. She wasn't even sure why she felt it today. Perhaps with a few more minutes to herself, she could have figured it out. But Jacques had wandered up from somewhere, asked if he could join her—how could she have refused?—and now he undoubtedly wanted to make conversation. She could tell him to leave her alone, of course. He would oblige her, and she'd feel rotten. It wasn't worth it. She sighed. "I'm listening, Jacques."

"Friday evening," he said. "Tomorrow, in other words. Do you have plans already?"

"Nothing, so far. What time?"

"Between six and seven?"

"I should be free by then. Why?"

"I was thinking of having a little get-together at my place," he said. "Nothing organized or anything. Just some nice food, wine, conversation. A change from meeting in cafés and brasseries, in other words."

"Will there be other people there?"

"Of course." He chuckled. "What if there weren't?"

Milena shrugged. "I just want to know."

"I was thinking of inviting some of the newer people," he said. "Like Jeanne, for instance. It'll be a good way for them to get to know us better. I'm encouraging everyone to bring some friends of their own, too."

"Sounds like a good idea."

Jacques got up and brushed the bottom of his pants with his palms. "What do you say we head inside? It's too cold to just sit here."

Milena didn't look up. "I'd rather stay here."

"All right." Jacques sat down again, shivered conspicuously, and checked his watch. "Ten minutes until the seminar starts."

Milena nodded. He was making a bit of a nuisance of himself. Still, it was hard not to feel guilty. Jacques didn't lack backbone. He was articulate. He could convince, lead, and organize people. He headed or was involved in several committees on campus, and she'd seen him hold his own in any number of fierce arguments and debates. That was the Jacques she admired, the friend she could rely on. Not the Jacques who became acquiescence personified as soon as he was alone with her. When he was like that, it was difficult to believe that Pauline was wrong about him, and if Pauline wasn't wrong, a major mess was in the offing. Milena closed her eyes and took a deep breath.

Whatever she had come out here to contemplate, it certainly hadn't been Jacques's feelings for her.

Jacques buttoned up his jacket. "Something on your mind?"

"There's always something on my mind, Jacques."

"Are you sure I can't convince you to mull it over indoors, where it's warm?"

"I can't think in there," she said. "It's too warm."

"I don't mean to split hairs, but considering our seminar room is well heated, your thought processes certainly don't seem sluggish in class."

"That's a different kind of thinking."

"I see." He hesitated, shivered a little more, shuffled his feet. "So what is it? What's bothering you?"

"I don't think it would interest you very much," Milena said. He'd yanked her out of another drift. There seemed to be no way she could stop her thoughts from wandering back to—at least this had become clear now—the evening before. She certainly had no intention of telling him that. Maybe this was as good a time as any to talk about what Pauline suspected, since he kept insisting that she come up with something.

"Try me." He smiled. "You may find I'm interested in many more things than you expect."

It was the kind of corny thing Milena had hoped never to hear from him. She mumbled a curse in Czech, remembering too late that he had asked her— and that she had told him—on numerous occasions what some of those phrases meant.

He kept smiling. "That bad, is it?"

Suppose she simply asked him if it was true, if he had feelings for her? It should be acceptable; they were both rational beings who prided themselves on their ability to solve any interpersonal problem in the framework of an open discussion. But she knew it would change things, no matter how much they might reassure one another that it did not. There were limits to an intellectual approach. Perhaps that was what irritated her about the idea of love: it came with severe discursive limitations. Unless, of course, you loved someone back. "It's about a friend of mine," she said. "Family problems."

"The little blonde that was with you Monday evening? What was her name again?"

"No. You've never met." Milena wasn't sure why she lied. It troubled her that the fib came so quickly, so naturally, without a reason clearly formulated in her mind.

"Really? I thought I knew all of your friends."

"Not all of them." His presumption was irritating, in spite—or because—of the fact that, until a couple of days before, he would have been entirely right. Milena felt an instinctive need for a world that was inaccessible to him. Hence the lie.

"You want to talk about it?"

She shook her head. "It's rather personal."

"Not if I've really never met her," he said.

"So you just assume it's a woman?"

"Ah," he said.

Milena couldn't tell if his smile was real or a mask quickly put in place to cover up his disappointment. She was already weary of this new need to second-guess his gestures, his expressions. "We should head up to the seminar room."

Jacques sighed, nodded, and followed her to the elevator.

•

After the seminar, Jacques stayed to attend the office hours of one of his professors. Milena hurried away toward the station. She boarded the train into the city and settled into her seat. Listening to the rhythm of

the tracks, she began to feel peaceful, drowsy. She let
her head sink against the window pane and dozed off.
Suddenly, an ocean of gold surged into the darkness
behind her closed eyelids. She squinted into the
brightness and saw that the train had emerged above
ground. The clouds had opened up, and sunshine
warmed her face, her scalp. She closed her eyes again.
The glass of the window no longer felt hard and cold. A
sensation took shape in her mind, of Louise's forehead, of
the soft blond hair, nestled against her temple. She sat up
straight, blinking. Across the aisle, a young man was
leaning against the window, much like she had been
doing a moment earlier, but snoring loudly. Opposite
him, an elderly lady was reading the paper. From time
to time, she glanced disapprovingly at the snorer. She
noticed Milena watching them, smiled, and rolled her
eyes.

A moment later, the train plunged underground
again.

•

When Milena ascended the stairs to the Place de la
Bastille, the sun had yielded once more to heavy clouds.
She bought a crêpe—ham and cheese, her favorite lunch—
from one of the stands outside the restaurants along the
Boulevard Beaumarchais. It was a detour; normally she
took the Rue Saint Antoine. She didn't reflect on her
choice until she stood in front of the gallery. Through the
glass door, she saw Louise standing behind the front desk,
going through papers or letters. Just as Milena decided to
keep walking, Louise looked up. Milena opened the door
and stepped inside. What else could she have done?

Louise watched her approach across the
showroom. She put down the papers.

"I'm on my way to work," Milena said. "I didn't expect to see you here. No lunch?"

"I take short lunch breaks. Sometimes I don't go at all."

"How is your arm?"

"The cuts are healing. They itch a little."

"Are you still wearing bandages?"

Louise nodded. "I'm not sure if it's necessary. But I'm still afraid, after what happened. The customers would be shocked, if they saw me with blood on my clothes. Not to mention my uncle."

"Do you have anyone to help you with the bandages?"

"I live alone," Louise said.

"More reason to be more careful." Milena heard the creak of a chair being relieved of a person's weight somewhere in the back rooms. Louise cast a quick glance over her shoulder. "Don't talk about this in front of my uncle, please."

A tall man emerged through the door at the back. Milena judged him to be in his mid-fifties. He strode briskly to Louise's desk, frowning at a sheet of paper as he walked. His eyebrows were thick and black, unlike his graying—though full—hair, and the eyes underneath looked soft and careworn. He was slim, without even a trace of a paunch, and carried himself with excellent posture. Milena found him rather handsome. He smiled briefly when he noticed her. "Good afternoon, Mademoiselle."

"Uncle Claude," Louise said. "This is Milena, a friend of mine."

"Really?" He sounded oddly the way Jacques had, when Milena told him she had a friend he hadn't met before. "A pleasure to meet you."

"Likewise," Milena said. She couldn't resist a feeling of immediate sympathy with this man, in light of the condescension Louise's father had supposedly directed at him, even though with his impeccable suit and tie he appeared more like the textbook example of a bourgeois businessman than a downtrodden commoner.

"Milena," he repeated. "You are Russian, Mademoiselle?"

"Czech."

"Ah, yes. I thought it was something Slavic." He exchanged a few hushed comments with Louise. Twice, he flicked an index finger at the paper in his hand, producing a sharp noise. When they were done, he excused himself and disappeared through the back door, but not without taking another look at Milena. The invisible chair creaked again, then there was silence.

"I'm afraid I have some phone calls to make," Louise said.

"I need to head over to Sylvie's, anyway."

For a few seconds, they stood awkwardly, Louise behind the desk, Milena in the middle of the showroom. Louise looked down at the letters she had been holding, shuffling through them as if she was searching for something. It was a little off-putting. "I'll see you," Milena said. She spun on her heels and headed for the door.

"When?"

Milena stopped, turned around. Louise was still not looking up. But she had stopped shuffling through the letters. Perhaps what she had really been searching for was the courage to ask this simple question. Grudgingly, Milena felt herself soften. "Do you have plans for tomorrow night?"

•

The next evening, Louise walked into Sylvie's minutes before closing time. Milena was behind the counter, balancing the register. "I'll be done in a minute."

Louise nodded and began to aimlessly look through the clothes.

"Your uncle seems nice," Milena said.

"He is."

"I wasn't quite sure how to address him. If the name of the gallery, de Benoît, is your aunt's, then what is his?"

Louise picked a bright red suede vest out of a rack. "Gabbard."

"Your aunt never took his name?"

Louise frowned at the garment and put it back. "She didn't believe a woman should have to give up who she is. Uncle Claude respected her choice."

"That's commendable of him." Milena wondered if he'd had much choice in the matter. Had Louise's aunt ultimately been unwilling to give up her aristocratic name?

"She caused my father no small amount of anguish," Louise said. "I don't know what galled him more, a woman refusing to take her husband's name, or the thought of a de Benoît becoming a Gabbard."

"What a dilemma." Supposedly, there were people to whom such problems were utterly real. "But what about the gallery? Did your uncle ever think of renaming it, after her death?"

"Never. The gallery, the name, it's all part of her memory. He wouldn't dream of erasing that. Nor would I, if it were for me to decide."

Milena pushed the cash drawer shut. The bright ring of the register reverberated through the still air. "Why didn't you want me to mention your arm in front of him? Doesn't he know?"

"I wish he didn't," Louise said. "I tried to hide it from him, but apparently he noticed something when I left the gallery that morning. Now he won't stop worrying and asking questions. I didn't want you to remind him of the whole thing."

"What kind of questions?"

"How it happened, am I telling him the whole truth, and so on and so forth. I suppose he imagines I nearly bled to death or something like that."

"I'm surprised he doesn't know the details as it is." Milena reached through the bead curtain and flicked a switch. The boutique went dark except for the small lamps illuminating the shop window. "Didn't this accident of yours happen at his gallery?"

"It happened in the evening. He wasn't there."

"And all the other times? He never happens to be there when you break something?"

Louise stood still between the display stands that suddenly contained only clothes as gray and colorless as her own. "There haven't been that many other times, really. Just one time that my arms got lacerated very badly. It was a huge pane of glass, for a larger painting."

Milena slipped on her coat. "We should go." She paused by the door. "Even so, are you sure your uncle isn't right to be worried about you?"

Louise shrugged. "Nothing serious ever happened. And I don't want him to think I keep breaking things."

"I see." Milena opened the door. A blade of cold sliced into the air between them. "We don't want to be late."

·

They walked briskly toward the Rue St. Antoine. So far no snow was falling, and the air was sharp and clear. Louise hooked her hand into Milena's elbow, and quickly, with a stammered apology, withdrew it. "It's all right," Milena said. "The pavement is a bit icy here and there." The hand returned, a cautious touch of gloved fingers.

"Where does Jacques live?"

"Just a couple of blocks from here."

"Not bad for a student," Louise said. "The rents aren't cheap in this area."

"I think his parents help him out financially. He doesn't like people to know, of course."

"Too bourgeois?"

Milena smiled. "I can't say I'd refuse, if I could afford a place around here. It's not like it would change who I am. But some people say your credibility suffers."

"My apartment is tiny," Louise said. "And it's on a tiny street. There's a bistro next door, and when I open my bedroom window, I have to smell their food."

"You live close by?"

"Near the intersection of Rue Rambuteau and Rue du Temple. Close enough to be expensive."

They hurried across the busy Rue St. Antoine.

"But you're a professional," Milena said. "That's different. Jacques is a student, and a very vocal critic of the bourgeois establishment."

"You don't seem to hold it against him."

"No, but with the communist party portraying us as spoiled brats every chance they get, being funded by well-off parents is a bit of a stigma. It's stupid, of course. I guess some of them would prefer a fascist from a poor family to a middle-class intellectual."

"One can be privileged and still feel sympathy for those who are not," Louise said. "It's not unheard of."

"Unheard of enough, unfortunately," Milena said. "That's why the Marxists say that university students, who are justly considered to be privileged, cannot have a genuine interest in the plight of the working class. The

Gaullists, of course, say the same thing, with slightly different arguments. In their eyes, we are ingrates, soiling our own nests by questioning the very order from which we benefit. Either way, privilege is equated with complicity with the establishment."

"I find it hard to believe that the right and left both should have so much common ground," Louise said.

"They're two sides of the same coin. Both have a stake in the existing system."

"But that still doesn't answer my question. Why should the privileged take an interest in the working class?"

"The universities are no less a part of society than the factories are," Milena said. "We're all fish in the same river. What is done upstream is felt downstream."

Louise pursed her lips. She began to make a response but the sudden rasp of an engine cut her off. Milena turned around. A scooter came speeding up the street behind them. Instead of passing them, it slowed down and matched their pace. Milena was about to challenge the helmeted rider when he flicked up his visor, revealing the foolish grin of Louise's co-worker, Maurice. "Where are you two headed?"

Milena struggled to suppress her resentment for him. She bit back a sharp retort and decided to let Louise handle the conversation.

"We're visiting friends of Milena's," Louise said. "They're having a party."

"Oh?" Maurice brought the scooter to a halt, forcing them to stop walking as well. "Can I come?"

Milena couldn't contain herself. "What gives you that idea?"

Louise touched her hand and squeezed it briefly. "No, Maurice. Of course not. It's for Milena's friends only."

"Oh, I see." The fatuous smile wavered. Suddenly, he scowled. "You're friends now, you and her."

"We have to go, Maurice."

"I'm your friend, too," he said. "And friends can bring along friends of their own to parties, can't they?"

"We work together, you and I," Louise said. "But that's all. I told you that before."

He stared sullenly along the street. "I've known you much longer than she does."

"Jesus Christ," Milena said. "We don't have time for this."

Louise nodded. "We should go." They started walking again.

He remained where he was. "Some other time, okay? Louise?"

Louise shook her head and kept walking.

"He better not be following us," Milena said.

"I don't think he would do that."

Milena turned around. Maurice was still there, one heel on the curb to balance himself, staring off into space, looking sulky. "What is he thinking, trying to invite himself along like that?"

"I know," Louise said. "I'm sorry."

"I'm not saying it's your fault."

Louise sighed. "It is, in a way. I went out with him, once, a couple of weeks after I came to Paris. I knew nobody here, aside from Uncle Claude. I thought perhaps Maurice could be a friend."

"But it didn't turn out that way?"

"He got the wrong impression."

"Men are good at that."

Louise hesitated. "He walked me home, and when we got to my door, he tried to kiss me."

Milena heard the engine of Maurice's scooter howl in the distance. She was relieved to see him drive away in the opposite direction.

"I wouldn't let him, of course," Louise said. "But he thought I was just being coy. In the end, I had to threaten that I would tell Uncle Claude, and that he would get fired if he didn't leave me alone."

"He doesn't seem to entirely have gotten the message."

"He still tries to ask me out, now and then. It is awkward for me, but as long as he doesn't do more than that, I don't have the heart to make him lose his job. I simply make sure to avoid situations where I'm alone with him."

"It's none of my business, of course," Milena said. "But I think a man should be able to take no for an answer."

Louise shrugged. "I can't control what goes on in someone else's head."

"Six years and he still keeps asking? To me, that sounds like a bit of a fixation."

Louise smiled. For a moment, she did appear coy. "Hard to understand, isn't it?"

"That's not what I meant." Milena cleared her throat. Was Louise fishing for a compliment? "It's just that, after so long a time, without encouragement—"

"I certainly never encouraged him," Louise insisted. "If that's what you're implying."

"I'm not."

"I'm sure normally he would have put me out of his mind long ago. But I'm always there, right in front of him, at work."

"Like a constant temptation," Milena said.

Louise nodded. "Exactly."

"I can see that, I guess."

Louise smiled again. She looked pleased, as if she had just won an argument. They walked like this for a while, Louise looking strangely content, Milena puzzling over her reaction.

"We're almost there," Milena said. "Just a few more blocks."

•

Jacques looked surprised when he opened the door. "You may remember Louise," Milena said. "I thought she might be interested in meeting some of my anarchist friends."

Jacques smiled, but he seemed uncomfortable with the joke. "Louise, yes. Of course I remember." He motioned for them to come inside. "We met Tuesday evening, near Oriflamme?"

Milena stepped into the apartment, and into Jacques's living room. Louise followed her. No one else was there. "Are we early? We came directly from work."

"No, no," Jacques said. "That's not it. Actually, the others aren't coming."

"Excuse me?"

"Several people canceled to attend some event at the Sorbonne. Apparently it was announced just this morning. I decided to call everyone and tell them we'd meet some other time. You're the only one I wasn't able to reach."

Milena raised an eyebrow. "I can't believe Pauline didn't call me to tell me about this."

"I tried to reach Pauline myself," Jacques said. "But I couldn't get a hold of her."

"We should leave then. I'm sure you have things to do."

"Nothing that can't wait," Jacques said. He glanced quickly at Louise. "Why don't you stay for a drink, at least?"

"I wouldn't want to impose," Louise said.

He hesitated for a moment, as if mulling over his options. "It's perfectly fine. Please, make yourselves comfortable." He took their coats and disappeared into the back of the apartment. "I'll be right back."

Milena let herself drop on the leather loveseat that accompanied a larger sofa and motioned for Louise to join her. Louise sat down and took a look around. "This is a chic apartment," she said. "Does he live here alone?"

"He does."

"You've been here before?"

Milena nodded. "He holds these meetings pretty often. Of course there's usually at least a dozen other people around."

"You've never been alone with him here?"

"I'm sure this evening was supposed to correct that. If there was an event at the Sorbonne, I'd have known about it."

Louise glanced toward the door. "You think he's lying?"

"Yes."

Jacques entered the room. "What can I get you? A Cinzano, perhaps, or some pastis?"

"Pastis sounds good," Milena said.

They sipped their drinks and smoked a few cigarettes. Milena spoke little. More and more, she wished she had refused to stay altogether.

Jacques did his best to keep up the small talk by asking Louise about her job at the gallery. Milena found his efforts to make his unexpected guest feel at ease rather redeeming. Perhaps it was possible to pretend that she believed his ridiculous story, and to forget whatever intentions he might have had. What were those, anyway? Did he love her? Want to sleep with her? Did things like that go away, if one chose to ignore them? No, they would need clarity, and they would need it before the evening was over.

Jacques turned to her. "I'm surprised you didn't go to Berlin, for the Vietnam congress. Unless of course you're planning on still heading there tomorrow. I'm taking the train early in the morning, myself."

"I was going to go," Milena said. "But Sylvie begged me to help out at the boutique tomorrow. The regular girl got sick. I couldn't say no. She's put up with so many of my sudden absences already."

"That's too bad. We could've taken the train together."

Milena shook her head. "I would have gone with Dany, anyway. He and a couple of the others are taking a car together and sharing a hotel room in Berlin. He offered to squeeze me in."

"Squeeze you in?" Jacques's lips curled. If it was meant to be a smile, he wasn't quite managing it. "Interesting choice of words."

"Is it?" Milena raised an eyebrow. "I'm confused, Jacques. Are you jealous of Dany, or of me?" It was a cheap taunt, but she couldn't resist.

Jacques blushed. "I'm just surprised. I didn't think you knew him that well."

"Who is this Dany?" Louise asked.

"Daniel Cohn-Bendit," Milena said. "He studies sociology, like me. We have the same advisor. He's sort of a spokesperson for the enragés, if there can be such a thing."

"He'd be the first to reject the notion," Jacques said.

Milena nodded. "He's smart, charming, and extremely eloquent. The kind of person who can take on the authorities in their game of rhetoric, and beat them at it."

"People are calling him Dany Le Rouge now." Jacques pointed at his own thin curls. "Hair color and politics. It's a pun."

"And an irritating one, in my opinion. It sounds like a nickname for a pirate."

"Maybe." Jacques shrugged. "I have a feeling he enjoys the connotation." He winked at Louise. "But you see, our Milena is rather sensitive to the possibility of anyone belittling the great orator."

"My admiration for Dany is purely intellectual," Milena said. "I'm capable of distinguishing between appreciation and infatuation. Are you?"

"I'm afraid I've never heard of him," Louise said.

Jacques gestured toward her with his cigarette. "What happened to you there?"

Louise frowned. "I'm sorry?"

"Your arm," Jacques said. "I couldn't help but notice—I hope I'm not being forward or anything."

"Oh, that." Louise hastily tugged at her shirt cuff. Milena caught a glimpse of gauze. It wasn't bloody. But it was on her right arm. Not the left she had bandaged at the boutique two days earlier.

"I had an accident with a Stanley knife," Louise said. "I had to open a number of shipping crates."

"I didn't know that was part of your responsibilities," Milena said. Louise glanced at her and quickly looked away.

"Damn sharp, those things," Jacques said. "I remember one time when I had a job in a warehouse—"

"Please," Milena interrupted. She'd heard the story of his injuries before. The working class hero. "Enough with the talk of blood and lacerations."

"Fine." Jacques smiled and finished his drink. "How about another one?"

Milena shook her head. "Let's not draw this out more than necessary."

"Draw what out? Drinks with friends?"

"This little charade of yours." Milena put her glass down. "There was no event at the Sorbonne, Jacques, any more than there ever was a meeting planned here at your apartment."

Jacques cleared his throat. "I don't quite follow."

"I was at the boutique all day. I gave you the number a long time ago. Not to mention that it's in the phone book."

"Goodness, Milena," he said. "I had so much on my mind, that didn't even occur to me. I kept trying your apartment."

"Pauline was at home. I called her myself around noon. And by the way, how come you didn't invite her?"

Jacques smiled briefly at Louise, then at Milena. He had the air of a boy caught in a prank, trying to get by on charm but already aware that it wasn't going to work. "Are you saying I orchestrated this whole evening?"

"Please," Milena said. Here then, was catharsis. Or catastrophe. "Don't make this more awkward by trying to play me for a fool."

"Excuse me." Louise stood up. "Where is the bathroom?"

•

"You're making your friend uncomfortable," Jacques said.

"Don't try to hide behind her, Jacques."

"It's not fair to drag her into this. To her, I mean."

"You should have thought about that when you invited me under false pretenses."

"How was I to know you were going to bring her along?"

"I'll consider that a confession," Milena said.

"Jesus Christ, Milena. Is it a crime, wanting to spend some time alone with you? Considering you brought unexpected company, I think I'm handling myself well enough."

"The only thing that was unexpected tonight was for us to be the only people here," Milena said. "Why didn't you just tell me you wanted to see me alone?"

"Because I know you, Milena. You never make time for this sort of thing. I wanted to surprise you."

"Catch me off guard, you mean."

"Yes," Jacques said. "Because I think you're one of those women—those people—who will never give a feeling a chance unless it does catch them off guard."

"And here I am, stumbling into your arms."

"That's not what I expected. I just wanted for us to talk about something other than politics, for once. I wanted to see a different side of you. And show you a different side of me."

"You did," Milena said. "You lied to me." The silence dragged on after that, for seconds, maybe minutes. She felt dizzy. Too much pastis. Too much emotion. Louise and her cuts, Jacques and his hidden affections. "So what else did you have planned for tonight, Jacques?"

"Come on, Milena. The less said. At this point, anyway."

Louise returned from the bathroom. There had been no water running, no sound of flushing.

"Sit down," Jacques said. "We're back to normal."

"Actually, I think perhaps I should go."

"Please. There's no need for anyone to leave."

"No," Milena said. "She's right."

Jacques sighed. "I'll get your coats."

Milena stared at the carpet while he was out of the room. "I'm sorry I dragged you into this mess," she said.

"Would things have been different, if I hadn't come?"

"I wouldn't have stayed," Milena said.

"Are you sure?"

"I'm not in love with him, Louise. Is that so hard to understand?"

Louise made a subtle motion with her chin. Milena looked over her shoulder. Jacques stood in the door, holding their coats. "No," he said. "It's not."

"I'm sorry, Jacques."

"It's all right." He chuckled behind tightened jaws. "I figured there was a fifty-fifty chance I'd be hearing something like that tonight."

"You overestimated your odds," Milena said. She caught Louise's eyes widening at the cruel remark. "I'm not trying to rub salt in your wounds, Jacques. But we need to be clear on this once and for all, if we want to have a chance to continue to be friends." She took her coat from him.

He helped Louise into hers. "Is that going to be possible?"

"That's up to you."

"Of course it is." The chuckle again. He was doing his best not to be bitter, and failing. "What exactly do I need to do?"

"Don't make it seem like I'm dictating terms to you."

"Do you want to go on like before or not, Milena? I need to know how to handle myself, if that's really what you want."

"It is," Milena said. "For my part. Perhaps you need some time to decide if you want to respect that, or go on making a mockery of it."

He walked them to the door. "Can I just ask you one last thing, before I consign this evening to my memories as nothing more than a glass of pastis with friends?"

"Go ahead."

"Do you ever think about love, at all?"

"You've had too much to drink, Jacques. Good night." Milena touched Louise's elbow, and together they hurried down the dimly lit staircase.

•

They stepped into the street, and into a snowstorm. It took Milena a few moments to get her bearings in the strong wind. She pulled her wool cap tightly over her ears, extended her elbow for Louise to hold on, and started walking. They had moved several steps away from the door before she thought about where each of them needed to be going. "Aren't you headed the other way?"

"I'll walk with you," Louise said.

"In this storm? You're crazy."

"I don't mind it," Louise said. "But I can turn back, if you don't want me along."

"It's not that," Milena said. Snowflakes kept blowing into her face, under the brim of her woolen cap, getting caught in her lashes where they hung for a blink or two before they melted. She linked arms with Louise. "I don't want you to get sick on my account."

"I'll be fine."

There was the matter of Louise's new bandage. Milena decided not to bring it up. Louise knew that she had seen it. If she was ready to talk about it, she would. She felt a touch of wetness under her left heel. She'd picked the wrong boots.

"Is there someone else?" Louise asked.

"Someone else?"

"In the place Jacques wants to be. With you."

A gust of wind leaned into them, driving a swarm of snowflakes into Milena's face. She nearly lost her balance. Louise pressed close, steadying her. "No," Milena said. Sullen and bleak, the word instilled in her a need to say more. But there was nothing.

"Has there been anyone, ever?" Louise's blond hair, protruding wildly from underneath a black beret, was studded with ice crystals. Milena thought of a fairy tale she had loved as a girl, a story about a little boy who is taken to the Snow Queen's palace where he must solve an impossible puzzle made of shards of ice in order to regain his freedom. "Not in a while," she said.

The snowfall grew denser. Milena could barely see from one streetlight to the next. Beyond the circle of light underneath each lamp post they passed, the world was somber and immaterial. They would go on walking like this forever, from streetlight to streetlight in a city made of wind and snow. Every now and then a car passed them, a somber bulk pushing twin cones of light through the storm.

"I need a cigarette." Milena pulled Louise into a doorway. She searched her purse, her pockets, until she found a pack of Gitanes. But it was empty. "Do prdele," she muttered. "That's Czech for 'shit,' in case you're wondering."

Louise looked inside her own purse. She had one cigarette left in a slender pack. "Do you mind sharing it?"

"You know I don't."

Louise lit the cigarette and watched the snowflakes hurtling past the doorway. "I love this weather," she said. "Storms, snow, rain, all of it. In my building, in the attic, I often stand under one of the windows—they're the kind you push up, that stay horizontal when they're open. I go there when it rains, and listen to the drops hitting the glass over my head. Snowflakes, too. You can hear them if you keep really quiet."

"You're a little odd," Milena said. "No offense."

Louise shrugged and continued to take little puffs of the slim cigarette. Now and then the wind threw itself into the doorway and sent the ashes flying into her face. "You never answered his question," she said after a while.

"Whether I think about love?"

Louise stuck the cigarette between Milena's lips. "Do you?"

Milena took a furious drag. The tip of the cigarette lit up sizzling, sending their shadows twitching across the wall of the doorway. She sensed the moisture of the filter as her lips squeezed it. "Rarely."

"I do," Louise said. "From time to time."

Milena passed the cigarette back to Louise. "And is there anyone?"

Louise put the cigarette to her lips and shook her head. A thin stream of smoke issued from her nostrils. The wind snatched it away.

"But there was?"

"Not so far." Louise threw the cigarette into the wind. It trailed a shower of sparks. She looked suddenly tired. "I'm cold," she said. "Perhaps I should head home, after all."

"Perhaps."

They stepped out of the doorway, back into the wind.

"Good night," Louise said.

They kissed each other on the cheek. First one, then the other, then the first again. Louise's nose brushed against Milena's. It broke their rhythm. Her lips landed on the edge of Milena's mouth. She let them rest there for an instant. Milena could smell her breath, and her own, mingling with it: tobacco and a faint scent of anise. She took a step back. Louise stood across from her, unreadable, the Snow Queen presenting her impossible puzzle.

Without a word, Milena wheeled around and hurried through the storm toward the Bastille.

•

In the dark, in her room, sitting on her bed, she tried to put things into perspective. Except for her boots, which she had kicked off by the door, she was still fully dressed. The chill of the blizzard lingered in her coat. Her left sock was wet, and her knees smarted. In her haste to run away from Louise, she had slipped and fallen on the Métro stairs. Pauline, fortunately, had already been asleep when she got home. Perhaps Alain was with her, but Milena hadn't seen his shoes in the hallway.

She peeled the drenched sock off her foot, let her coat slide to the floor, and lit another cigarette. The storm threw its embrace around the building. Inside the walls, the timbers sighed and whispered. Invisible cats pawed softly at the window pane. Louise was right: when you were very still, you could hear even snowflakes.

She watched the smoke curl toward the ceiling: pale and dead, a burnt-out soul drifting through silence, already cold.

It had been an accident, plain and simple: two pairs of lips, numb with cold, missing their mark in the night, in the storm, in the freezing wind. Nothing more. They could go on as if nothing had happened, just like she and Jacques would. The irony. Perhaps there was such a thing as karma.

She put out the cigarette and closed her eyes. It took her a long time to fall asleep, and when she did, she dreamed of snowflakes and puzzles and the wind embracing her with fierce but slender arms.

•

Pauline joined her for breakfast. Alain was not there.

"How was the meeting at Jacques's?"

"There was no meeting." Milena summarized the previous evening for Pauline. "It was a ruse to be alone with me."

"I suppose that explains why I wasn't invited," Pauline said. "What happened?"

"Not much. I brought Louise."

"The girl from the gallery? Why?"

"Jacques had told me he wanted people to bring friends. I guess he never expected me to have any."

"I wish I could have seen his face when he opened the door."

"He invited us in for drinks, actually. In the end, I had to call him on his little scheme."

"With Louise there?"

"I wanted to be done with all the nonsense," Milena said. "She understood."

"And Jacques?"

"His feeling's are hurt. But he'll live. We agreed to pretend nothing happened."

"Then you're both naïve." Pauline finished the rest of her coffee. "I should take a shower. By the way, did you ever find out how she got those injuries?"

"She had a few accidents. Broken glass, box cutters. I guess it's bound to happen, in her line of work."

"Mystery solved," Pauline said as she walked out of the kitchen. "I told you, she's probably clumsy."

"Yes," Milena murmured. The sound of the faucets being turned came from the bathroom, followed by running water. "Mystery solved."

When she heard Pauline close the bathroom door, she went into the hallway and picked up the phone.

•

They walked across the Place des Vosges together. Snow lay thickly on the Square Louis XIII, weighing down the branches of the trees, blanketing the statue of the king on his horse and the silent fountain in the center of the park. The air was still. It was mid-afternoon, but judging by the leaden light filtering through the clouds it could have been early morning, or near sunset.

"I didn't expect to hear from you so soon," Louise said.

"Last night was something of a disaster. I thought I'd make up for it."

"It wasn't your fault," Louise said. "And it wasn't so bad, in the end."

Milena closed her eyes, exasperated. How was she to take that? Just when she'd gotten rid of the uncertainties between her and Jacques, the same thing was starting with Louise. "Perhaps. I did get a chance to clarify a few things."

"I'm sorry about what happened later," Louise said. "When we said good night."

Milena cleared her throat. "I didn't think anything of it."

"You looked upset."

This is my chance, Milena thought. A few well-chosen words, and all the ambiguities would go away. "We need to take the St. Paul Métro," she said. "Then we'll have to switch lines a couple of times."

•

It was cold on Montmartre. Between the time they boarded the Métro and the time they emerged at the Abbesses station, a sharp wind had sprung up. They leaned over the stone railing at the foot of the basilica and took in the view of the city. The light was failing fast. All over Paris, windows began to flicker in the dusk. Louise slipped her hand around Milena's arm. Milena tried to relax. "I can't believe you've never been up here," she said. "You've been living in Paris for six years and you've never experienced this view?"

"It's far from where I live," Louise said.

"Even farther from where I live. But I went everywhere, in the first weeks after I came here. The Eiffel tower, the Louvre, the Père Lachaise cemetery, you name it. I explored the entire city. I still do."

"All by yourself?"

"Yes," Milena said. "I didn't know anyone in the beginning." She turned around to look at the basilica. "This of all things I would have thought you would go visit."

"I feel out of place in churches."

"That's a strange thing to say, for a Catholic girl. You mean you've never gone to confession?"

"No. My mother went, now and then." Louise shivered and stepped away from the stone ledge. "Let's walk a bit." After a few steps, she nodded toward the cathedral. "Do you know anything about the history of the basilica?"

"Nothing much, I'm afraid."

"Saint Denis, the patron saint of France, was beheaded here in 250 by the Romans," Louise said. "They subjected him to various kinds of torture, but God protected him from all harm and pain. After they finally executed him, he rose up, picked up his head, and walked all the way to what is now Saint-Denis."

"That's quite a walk from here, even with one's head still in place."

"I suppose you don't believe in miracles," Louise said. "But these stories aren't jokes to me."

"I'm sorry. I just find it hard to accept, that a man would walk so far without his head on his shoulders."

"It was God's will," Louise said. "He sent an angel to lead him."

"I suppose it's all a matter of faith."

Louise nodded. "In more than one way."

"Please don't think that I'm intolerant toward religion," Milena said. "It's simply something that doesn't have much of a place in my life."

"Because of your politics?"

"There's that, too."

Louise remained silent for several paces. Her eyes were on the view below. But Milena knew that her thoughts weren't on the city. "You can't have been born a Marxist."

"Of course not," Milena said. "Like the majority of Czechs, my parents are Catholics."

"Didn't they try to raise you in their faith?"

"We don't always follow our parents in everything, or for all of our lives."

"I know," Louise said. "But faith can give so much meaning to life."

"Too much, sometimes. It doesn't make sense to me, to accept the hand of God behind everything."

"I admit, it can be hard. Especially with the bad things."

"Yes," Milena said. "Especially with those."

They rounded the northern end of the basilica. Behind the gray clouds, the winter sun was setting. Of the few visitors that came at this time of day, this time of year, none lingered this side of Montmartre. They were alone in the shadows behind the church.

"Do you think Jacques will continue to be your friend, after last night?"

"I can't avoid seeing him," Milena said. "It will be awkward. Things like that don't go away."

"You're angry at him for having feelings for you."

"His feelings are about him, not me," Milena said. "Pure narcissism. He saw something in me, or thought he did. But it was just his own reflection."

"Isn't that how love always begins? Eventually, you learn to see more and more of the other person. That's when infatuation becomes love."

"Fine. But if you knew that your infatuation was unrequited, what would you do?"

"Nothing, of course. What's the point of sharing something with someone who wants no part of it?"

"Exactly my point," Milena said. The fact that for once Louise had said what she expected her to say reassured her. "It's about discipline. People always think that it's harder to be the one being rejected, but that's not true. If someone confesses their love for you, and you don't want it, you stand helplessly before the mess they made. And why did they do it, if they knew better? It's a self-indulgent, aggressive act. That's why I'm angry at Jacques. What I would have done, in his position, is to take control, grind down my feelings, block them, forget about them, act as if nothing—" She stopped herself. "You get the idea."

"I think I do," Louise said.

"I've launched into a lecture. I'm sorry."

"People can't help falling in love, Milena."

"But after two years of knowing someone, wouldn't you be able to tell whether it is mutual or not?"

"I would know much sooner," Louise said.

They came around to the front of the basilica again. They sky was almost completely dark. Myriads of city lights glittered below them. The wind was icy.

"We can't stay much longer," Milena said.

"Do you have to be anywhere?"

Milena shook her head. "I'm freezing."

"You could have dinner with me," Louise said. "I made a cassoulet with duck, two nights ago. My mother's recipe. There's quite a bit left."

"You cook?"

"I'd get by on tea and bread, if it were up to me. But my uncle feels I need to gain weight. So once a week I make something heavy and rich. I can't eat more than a little of such food without getting sick. Usually I end up bringing him most of it. But he was invited by clients for several dinners in a row this week."

"Cassoulet with duck," Milena murmured. A snowflake landed on her cheekbone. Then another, on her nose. She shivered. "I don't think I've ever had that."

"I have some wine, too. Or we could find a restaurant, if you want something different."

Milena felt the cold crawling into her sleeves, making its way down her collar, nesting between her shawl and her skin. "No," she said. "I'll come."

·

As with every house or apartment she entered for the first time, Milena was immediately aware of a characteristic smell. Christmas, she thought. She recognized the scent left behind by extinguished candles. There was something else, too, harder to identify but equally linked to the holidays in her memory: a faint aroma of duck fat.

On a small rack by the door, she saw the light gray overcoat Louise had worn when they first met. The outlines of the blood stain were still faintly visible on the left sleeve.

"I'll go heat up the food," Louise said. She disappeared through a door at the other end of the hallway.

Milena hung her coat and shawl on the rack and followed Louise. She passed an open door and peeked inside. The living room, evidently. It was small and extremely tidy. No scattered books, no clothes hanging over the back of chairs. A few tastefully placed paintings adorned the walls: an ocean landscape, a portrait of a young girl in the Flemish style, and, puzzlingly, a reproduction of Bosch's Ship of Fools. No television set. She heard the sound of a gas burner being ignited and walked across the hallway into the kitchen. Louise stood by the stove, stirring the cassoulet in a large iron pot. In a corner, next to a small window, stood a table with two chairs. In the middle of it sat a squat red candle, a book of matches beside it.

Milena leaned over the pot. "Smells delicious."

"There are glasses in the cabinet," Louise said. "If you want to set the table."

Milena opened the cabinet. Not much in the way of dishes and glasses. Exactly two of everything. "You don't entertain much, do you?"

"Not often," Louise said. "In the beginning, after I moved into this apartment, Uncle Claude came by every weekend. He still comes, but only once a month."

"How long have you been living here?"

"Almost six years."

"That long? Didn't you say you lived with your uncle for a while?"

"Only for a short time," Louise said. "After my aunt died, I stayed for a few more months, because I didn't want him to be lonely. Eventually, he helped me find this apartment."

"Wouldn't he rather you'd have stayed with him?"

"He suggested it. He has a very large apartment in the Sixth, in Saint-Germain-des-Prés, with plenty of room. It used to belong to my aunt, of course."

"Of course."

"But I needed my privacy," Louise said. "He understood. And after all, I still see him every day at work."

Milena placed two wine glasses and two plates on the table and sat down. The window had fogged over. She wiped one of the panes with her sleeve. She saw black roofs, bare treetops, and here and there a brightly lit window. The courtyard, presumably. As she watched, scattered snowflakes began tumbling against the glass, emerging out of the dark and vanishing again, like sea creatures peeking into the portholes of a submarine. "Should I light the candle?"

"If you like," Louise said.

Somewhere in the apartment, a phone rang. Louise handed the wooden spoon to Milena and nodded toward the pot. "Stir it gently."

Milena maneuvered the pieces of duck meat around in the stew. She tried hard not to listen to Louise talking in the hallway but short of whistling or singing a song, there was little she could do to prevent herself from overhearing. It didn't take her long to realize that Louise was refusing some sort of invitation. After a minute or so, she returned to the kitchen and took the spoon from Milena.

"Maurice?"

Louise nodded. "Perhaps I will have to talk to Uncle Claude, after all."

"Maybe," Milena said. "But if all he ever does is ask you out once in a while..." She let that dangle, unsure why she felt so forgiving all of a sudden. "That is all he ever does, isn't it?"

"It bothers me more than it used to, these days." Louise frowned. "I don't know why he doesn't go after somebody else already."

Milena smiled. "Who's to say he doesn't do that, as well?"

"He just doesn't seem the type," Louise said. "He's never mentioned a girl in all these years, not once." She touched the spoon to her lips. "Give me your plate."

It was a strange meal. Louise turned off the light and they ate by the flicker of the candle. A cool draft moved through the kitchen. The candle flame twitched and periodically erupted in thick exhalations of smoke. Somewhere in another room, Milena heard the rattle of a window.

The cassoulet was as delicious as it smelled, and extremely rich. Louise stopped eating after a few spoonfuls. She sipped her wine and watched the snow. Milena noticed the bandage on her right arm, the edge of it just visible under her cuff.

Louise turned away from the window. Their eyes met. Milena glanced at the exposed gauze. She said nothing.

Louise pulled her sleeve down. "We should go to the attic, when you're done."

"The attic?"

"Remember what I told you, last night? About listening to the rain and snow, under the window?"

"You want to go up there, now? It must be freezing."

"No colder than Montmartre," Louise said. "We'll put on our coats. Unless you think it will bother your shoulder."

"It's not that." The cold draft moved through the kitchen with renewed force, nearly extinguishing the

candle. The distant rattling grew more insistent. Milena
put down her fork. It made a bright noise as it hit the plate,
a single note of a clarity that clashed with the unsteady
light. She tried to think of reasons to refuse Louise's
suggestion. "It's just such a strange idea," she muttered.

"You showed me a beautiful view today," Louise
said. "I want to return the favor."

•

A single naked light bulb dangled in the middle of
the attic, at the end of a wire that descended out of the
blackness between the rafters. Louise did not switch it on.
She navigated the dark space by what light came from the
lamp in the staircase outside the attic door. Milena made
out several windows in the slanted roof, dim milky
rectangles, each admitting a mere suggestion of light.
Louise took her by the hand and led her to one of them.
She pushed it open with a rusty lever. A few handfuls of
snow fell onto the uneven floorboards. The lamp on the
landing shut off with a resounding click, and they stood in
near darkness. Louise moved toward the attic door with
the surefootedness of long use—Milena could barely see
anything when she looked away from the aperture above
her head—and closed it without a sound. With equal speed
and quiet, she returned to the window. Snowflakes came
drifting into the attic, settling and melting on their faces
and in their hair. The window was not very wide. They had
to stand closely together to both look out at the same time.

Across the white roofs of Beaubourg, Milena saw
the silhouette of Notre Dame in the distance. Snow
whirled about them in every direction. It was as if they
were standing in the middle of the sky. "You were right,"
she said. "It is beautiful."

"Listen."

Milena became aware of a faint sound on the window pane above their heads, a tapping so delicate she only barely heard it. "The snowflakes," she whispered. Louise nodded.

They stood there for a long time. After a while, Milena felt Louise's forehead against her cheekbone. It was a familiar sensation; she had dreamed this touch while dozing on the train from Nanterre to Paris two days before. Warm skin, soft, covered by cool strands of fine hair. Milena's throat turned thick and hot. She had come for this, of course. She had called Louise in the morning, had accepted the invitation to share the cassoulet, had agreed to the peculiar suggestion of visiting the attic, all so she could stand here and feel Louise's head resting against her own. Just one more moment, she thought. One more moment, before I end it. But she didn't say anything. There was only the attic window, the whisper of the snow hurtling out of the fathomless sky, and Louise standing still and very close beside her.

•

The next morning, Milena tried in vain to catch up on her studies. Pages of text turned into hieroglyphics under her eyes and then went blank. She turned on the radio to find some classical music, got lost in the static between the stations, and listened to it for what felt like hours. Outside, the world kept ticking on, distant, muffled, indifferent.

She decided to take the Métro to the Parc du Champ de Mars. Perhaps a walk in the crisp winter air would help clear her head. The hush that had settled on the city—or was it just her own life?—was only briefly interrupted, during her ride on the Métro, where she sat near a group of chattering and laughing children.

The Eiffel tower loomed with surreal clarity against the slate-grey but snowless winter sky. Even in the chilly weather, the park wasn't wholly deserted. A few families were taking walks, and Milena encountered several couples as well, arms linked under heavy clothing. But all in all, a sense of dormancy enveloped the park.

She sat down on a bench. The wood was hard and chilly against her thighs; she could feel the cold creeping up her spine, her neck, into her skull. In front of her feet, a tidy path ran in either direction. On the other side of the park, across the snow-white lawn, she saw a solitary man move at a trot under the black branches of the bare trees, dragged by a gigantic mastiff determined to be elsewhere. She watched the peculiar tandem until man and dog, still moving at their absurd pace, disappeared behind a hedge in the distance. Once they were gone, no other living being remained in sight. The air was still. On the rime-covered lawn, nothing stirred. It might have been a solid expanse of ice, of emptiness, all the way to the trees on the far side. She closed her eyes and slowly drew the icy air into her nostrils until it filled her lungs. She saw a frozen river before her, and trees on the far bank. Trees, and a bench, and two girls sitting on it, laughing.

Across the years, a hand reached for hers. She didn't push the memory away. It was nearly impossible, in this season, not to think of their last walk together, at least once.

They had ventured toward the middle of the river, one leading the other, leaving the crowd of skaters and mummed strollers behind. The ice began to crackle under their feet. For a moment, it seemed possible, acceptable, to stay and let it continue. A sharper crack came, a shift they could feel more than hear: the final warning. They hurried back to the embankment and sat down on a bench, breathless, laughing at the absurdity of courting the black stream that ran underneath the ice. But it had been a joke to only one of them.

She almost sensed a presence sitting beside her, almost heard a voice, felt a touch. She forced herself not to whisper the name. When you did that, ghosts took shape and began to whisper back. And then…

The wind breathed gently onto her cheek. She was no longer aware of any chill. How sweet it would be, to turn to ice after all, to sit like this forever.

·

After a restless night of unremembered dreams, she woke up with a fever. She had spent hours on the park bench in the Champ-de-Mars, without being aware of it. By the time she finally walked home the cold had penetrated her bones, and refused to leave again.

A dull throbbing heat engulfed her head. Her skin felt clammy. She could hardly breathe through her nose, and the inside of her chest itched with what she knew would develop into a cough. She blew her nose, muttering curses. Food wouldn't have any taste, and cigarettes were out of the question. On top of it all, Monday was the day she worked full time at the boutique.

She called Sylvie's home number. No one answered. She would have to go to the store. Maybe by the time she got there, she would be able to reach Sylvie. She looked for Alain's shoes by the front door. If he was there, and if he had come with his car, he might drive her to work. He had done it in the past, it was on his way. But the shoes weren't there.

At the boutique, Milena called Sylvie again. This time she picked up. "Try to make it through the morning," she said. "I'll find someone to cover for you in the afternoon."

At a quarter to twelve, Milena stood in the Rue de Birague, shivering in her thick coat, half delirious, free to go home. She pulled her green wool cap over her ears and began to walk toward the Place des Vosges.

When she reached the gallery, she saw no one at the front desk. The lanky assistant might be in the back, of course. She still wasn't sure why he made her so uneasy. The way he asked questions, perhaps, or the way he kept pestering Louise. She checked her watch. Almost noon. Louise might have left for lunch already. It would be foolish not to stop by and say hello merely for fear of encountering Maurice. Let him give all the inquisitive looks he wanted, ask all the questions he could think of. She could always tell him to mind his own business.

Milena pushed open the door. The chime sounded as she entered, but no one came to the front. She waited and listened. She heard indistinct noises somewhere inside the gallery, but other than that, nothing stirred. She turned around to leave again when she heard footsteps. Louise's uncle appeared in the door leading into the showroom.

"Mademoiselle?" He smiled politely. Milena mumbled his name, a greeting. "Milena, is it? Louise never mentioned your family name, I'm afraid."

"Beranovà," Milena said. The noises in the back room ceased for a moment. When they resumed, they seemed more deliberate, almost careful.

"Louise is not here," he said. "I assume you are looking for her?"

"I thought we might have lunch together. Did I miss her?"

"She didn't come in today." He descended the four stairs and stopped a few feet away from her. "She called this morning to tell me she was unwell."

"Unwell?"

"She said she had a cold." It was obvious from his tone that he doubted this explanation. "Nothing serious, I'm sure, but I can't help feeling a little worried about her. She's never missed a day in all the time she's been working for me. Not that I am so strict or demanding, mind you. It's just the way she is."

"I'm sure it's nothing," Milena said. "It's the season, after all." She decided to walk over to Louise's apartment to check on her. She was about to tell the uncle that she would do so—after all, he would undoubtedly be relieved—but something stopped her. She couldn't tell what it was; the fever made it hard to think clearly.

He nodded. "I shouldn't keep you, Mademoiselle."

The cold air outside was welcome at first. It soothed her hot face, her simmering thoughts. But as she traversed the Square Louis XIII, she began to feel a chill. Every few steps, the sensation swelled to a tremor that shook her entire frame. She knew that going anywhere but home, to her own bed, as quickly as possible, was a mistake. But she kept walking west, toward the Rue Rambuteau.

·

She had to ring several times before the door opened. It was no longer just a matter of seeing Louise. Her temperature was very high, and the walk from the gallery had exhausted her; she needed to rest. Climbing the three flights of stairs to Louise's apartment was a struggle. She stopped on the second landing, incapacitated by a fit of coughing. From above, she heard Louise's voice calling her name. When she looked up, she was peering over the railing. The staircase wobbled under Milena's feet. She took a deep breath and tackled the final flight of stairs.

Louise led her into the living room. She pulled the green cap off Milena's hair and sat her down on the sofa. "I'll make some tea," she said. Before she left the room, Milena saw that the bandage on her left arm was thicker than before. A few dark spots were visible underneath the layers of gauze. Her right forearm, too, was still bandaged.

Milena listened to the sounds coming from the kitchen: running water, the clatter of cups, the gas stove being ignited. The next thing she heard was the whistle of the kettle. She had nodded off.

Louise sat down next to her and poured the tea. She had put on a white cardigan with sleeves that nearly covered her knuckles.

"I looked for you at the gallery," Milena said. "Your uncle said you had called in sick. He's worried."

"Of course he is. Did he send you?"

"No. I decided to come here as soon as he told me you were at home."

"Why?"

"I was worried, too." Milena nodded toward Louise's arm. "With reason, it seems."

"It started bleeding again." Louise sat straight, without looking at Milena, balancing a saucer in her hand. "For some reason, it's taking very long to heal."

Milena sipped the tea. It was dark and hot, but aside from a hint of astringency, she tasted nothing. "I wish I didn't have to see you with those bandages all the time."

"Did you tell my uncle that you were coming here?"

"I told him I was going home. He seemed quite concerned about you."

"He didn't believe me about having a cold?"

"I don't know. Either way, I wouldn't be surprised if he paid you a visit after work."

"He probably will." Louise sighed. "Another excuse for him to check whether I haven't managed to cut my own throat yet. I know he means well, but I'm getting a little tired of it."

"You can't blame him for worrying." Milena put down her cup and leaned back into the upholstery. She felt the fever at work inside her body. She could hear her own breath inside her head: rough like escaping steam, rhythmic, hypnotic. Her eyes fell shut again.

She felt Louise's hand on her forehead. "I'll take your temperature."

The springs of the sofa shifted. For a while, the room was silent. Minutes went by. Hours, perhaps. Something cold and metallic touched Milena's lips.

"Under your tongue," Louise whispered.

Another vague stretch of time later, Milena felt the thermometer being pulled out of her mouth. She heard Louise mutter a number. "Good God, this is too high."

"I have to go home," Milena said. She tried to sit up but she couldn't find the strength. Had she spoken the words out loud, or merely thought them? She wasn't at all sure.

"You're in no shape to go anywhere," Louise said. "I may have to call a doctor."

Milena half opened her eyes. "He could look you over, too."

"I don't need a doctor."

"Neither do I. Just some rest."

"You can stay here."

"Out of the question," Milena said. In truth, she found the idea of remaining on the couch, of not having to move or even speak, more and more appealing. She shivered. "It's cold in here."

"I'll get you some blankets."

"If I stay, I'll only get you sick as well."

"I've never had a cold in my life."

"No wonder your uncle isn't buying your story," Milena said. But Louise had already left the room.

•

Milena woke up to the touch of fingers in her hair. Someone whispered her name. For several moments, she didn't know where she was. "Louise?" The room was dark. She saw light coming from the hallway, outlining the rectangle of the half-closed door. "How long have I slept?"

"Hours," Louise said.

Milena realized that she was drenched in sweat. Everything that touched her body made her feel sore. Her scalp felt raw where Louise's fingertips caressed it.

"You're burning up," Louise said. "If the fever doesn't go down tonight, I will have to get a doctor."

"I need to call Pauline," Milena said. "She'll wonder what happened to me."

"You can do that later. I need to move you to my bed."

"Your bed? Why?"

"My uncle is on his way," Louise said. "He just called. He doesn't need to see you here like this."

"I'll go home. I can take a taxi."

"There's no need." Louise slipped an arm under Milena's shoulders. "I already put on fresh sheets for you."

"That seems like a waste," Milena murmured.

Louise wrapped the blanket around her and walked her into the hallway. The light hurt Milena's eyes. They passed through a door into a dark room, darker than the living room where she had slept. She had a vague sense of being helped out of her clothes and into a fresh dry night shirt. Then the darkness tilted around her, and she found herself lying on cool linen. A down comforter enveloped her, equally cool. The sensation was soothing and chilling at once.

"Sleep," Louise's voice told her. "I'll come check on you when he's gone."

Within seconds, the sheets lost their coolness. Milena drifted off into the undulating heat inside her head. Once, she thought she heard voices, but they were no more than a murmur weaving through fitful dreams before fading again.

•

Milena opened her eyes to dim light. She saw the ceiling: a grey expanse interrupted here and there by cracks and cobwebs. It had to be dawn. The air around her was cold, she could feel it on her face. But her body was warm under the immense down comforter. The fever had run its course, leaving her exhausted, spent. Her breath still felt hot leaving her nostrils, passing over her cracked lips, as if somewhere inside her, a fire was still burning. It hurt to swallow.

It occurred to her that at this moment, no one she knew had any idea where she was. She felt pleasantly lost, secluded. She could let days pass this way, curled up in Louise's bed, absolved by the sickness from the need to make decisions, to take any action at all.

She heard the wind prowl around the house with soft moans. In some other room, the unseen window still rattled. Where was Louise?

Milena sat up. She was suddenly very thirsty. The room around her, the objects in it, were shadowy outlines, like details in the background of a charcoal sketch: hinted at but not fully realized. Behind the bed was a window. Heavy dark curtains were drawn over it. The wind picked

up with a sudden sigh. Was it snowing outside? She lifted
a corner of the curtain. Frostworks covered the window
pane, letting in faint morning light but no vision except for
what filtered through their own patterns. And they were
lovely, all the more beautiful for their impermanence.

She pulled the curtain to one side. The room came
into focus. It was small. Aside from the bed, she saw an
old-fashioned armoire, a tiny dresser, and a night table.
Her clothes hung carefully folded over the backrest of a
wicker chair. Only the chartreuse wool cap was missing.
On the night table, she found a glass of water and a stack
of linen handkerchiefs, neatly folded. Louise had placed
them there sometime during the night, no doubt. Milena
greedily drank the water. When she put the glass down she
noticed the other objects on the night table. Candles, a box
of matches. A Bible with a vermillion silk ribbon to mark
its pages. There was a picture, too, a miniature painting in
a gilded frame, of a stern female figure identified as Saint
Geneviève. An icon, undoubtedly an antique of sorts. Next
to it sat a small lacquer box, black and unadorned, with a
tapered lid, like a miniature reliquary. She wondered what,
if anything, might be inside, but she resisted the temptation
to open it. Instead, she picked up the Bible. As she sat up,
she noticed a large crucifix hanging in the shadows above
the bed, glinting with a faint hint of gold or bronze. An
emaciated Christ was suspended from it, his body pale as
bone except for the dark red of his wounds.

She parted the thin sheets of India paper at the
bookmark. The Bible was a beautiful edition, with
flourished initials marking the beginning of each chapter:
quite unlike the utilitarian little copy she had opened and
closed for the last time on Christmas Day 1960, eight years
ago, before hurling it into the Vltava.

The pages fell open to the first book of
Corinthians. Milena felt a sting in her heart. She
remembered every verse, every word. The passage wasn't

a dialogue, but it had become one, once, years ago, on a winter's day in Prague, read in turns in the seclusion of her room.

Though I speak with the tongues of men and of angels, and have not love, I am become as sounding brass, or a tinkling cymbal.

And though I have the gift of prophecy, and understand all mysteries, and all knowledge; and though I have all faith, so that I could remove mountains, and have not love, I am nothing.

With a soft clap, she closed the Bible between her hands and shut her eyes firmly against the tears.

And though I give my body to be burned, and have not love, it profiteth me nothing.

As she put the Bible down on the night table, she knocked over the small lacquer box. The lid came off, and its contents spilled onto the dark wood.

It was a milky shard of glass, about the size of a book of matches but triangular in shape. She picked it up. It was thin, and had a slight curve. There was no telling what kind of object it had once been part of. It didn't look like a relic in the ecclesial sense. The sight of it, the feel of it between her fingertips, made her uneasy. She put it back into the box, replaced the lid, and stretched out on the bed. She stared at the ivory Christ on his ancient cross. Someone knocked very softly on the door. She closed her eyes.

.

She felt the weight of Louise sitting down on the edge of the bed. Milena watched her through half-opened lids. Louise was looking at the night table. Had she noticed that the objects on it had been moved?

"Good morning." Milena was startled by the rasp that was her voice.

"I have to leave for work soon," Louise said. "How are you feeling?"

"The fever's gone."

Louise placed a palm on Milena's forehead. She nodded. "I left a thermos with tea in the kitchen for you. And I made some porridge. All you have to do is warm it up."

"How did it go with your uncle last night?"

"He said the air in the apartment smelled of illness," Louise said.

"You can thank me for that."

"I hope you don't think I enjoy lying to him." Louise moved her hand from Milena's forehead and started caressing her hair.

"Please stop that," Milena said. "My hair is disgusting. I've been sweating all night."

Louise withdrew her hand.

Milena sat up. "You could have told him that I was here. He knows we're friends, doesn't he?"

Louise nodded.

"Then why did you make a secret of me last night?"

"He knows you're just a friend." Louise lowered her eyes. "But I am no longer sure if I do."

"Really? Then what am I, Louise?"

Louise got up and walked to the door. "Stay as long as you want. Or at least until you feel better."

"You didn't answer my question."

"Only you can answer that," Louise said. "And you should, before we see each other again."

Stunned, Milena watched her leave the room. Moments later, she was alone in the twilight with the silent saint, the faraway Savior, and the sighing wind.

•

Milena made her way to the bathroom. The small slanted window above the tub rattled softly in the wind. The sound had become calming, like a familiar voice. It was colder in the bathroom than anywhere else in the apartment, and she freshened up in a hurry, without waiting for the water to run warm. After she got dressed she made the bed, a pointless exercise considering Louise would have to launder everything. She sat in the kitchen, sipping the tea from the thermos. On a shelf she spotted a tin labeled Kenilworth Ceylon, probably a pricey blend. She had a bowl of the porridge with butter and black cherry confiture that Louise had put on the table for her. Unfortunately, the fine food was wasted on Milena's deadened taste buds. She finished the tea. The hot liquid soothed her throat and chest, but she still felt perfectly miserable.

Briefly, she contemplated staying. The prospect of the Métro trip to Levallois, of telling Pauline where she had been—even if she didn't ask, it seemed unthinkable not to volunteer some explanation—was exhausting. She was tempted to climb back into the cozy feather bed, to leave the world in the dark about her whereabouts and abandon herself to Louise's care for just one more day and night. Milena pictured her, getting up while it was still dark outside, quietly making tea and cooking porridge. She felt suddenly like crying.

With a sigh, she stood up, rinsed the cup and plate, and got her coat from the bedroom. She searched for her wool cap, without success. Perhaps she could borrow something from Louise. She checked the coat rack by the front door for hats. She found her cap hanging there, incongruously green amidst Louise's drab coats.

•

The Métro trip home was dreadful. On the cold platform, waiting for the train, the chills started up again, and there seemed no end to them. When Milena finally closed the apartment door behind herself, she was unsure how long it had taken her to get home. Her wrist watch said ten forty-five, but she no longer remembered at what time she'd left Louise's place. The climb up the drafty staircase, the train ride before that, everything seemed hazy, dreamlike. She was freezing and sweating at the same time.

From inside the apartment, she heard Pauline's voice. "Milena?"

Milena found her sitting on the red sofa in the living room. On the table next to her stood an empty coffee bowl. A cigarette smoldered in an ashtray. The only sound in the room was the clacking of Lucite bracelets Pauline kept picking out of a bowl and dropping again. In her other hand was an open paperback. Milena couldn't see the title. "You're home," she said.

Pauline picked another cluster of bracelets from the bowl, held them for a few moments, and let them fall. "You've been gone for a day and a night."

"I'm sorry. I should have called."

"You look terrible. You sound terrible." Pauline extinguished the cigarette. "I was worried last night. I had no idea where you were."

"I'm not feeling well, Pauline. I need to lie down."

"You do that. Do you want anything?"

"Tea, please."

"What kind?"

"It doesn't matter."

In her room, Milena drew the curtains and got into bed. She had dozed off by the time Pauline brought her the tea in a large brown mug. She sipped it carefully, inhaling the steam rising from the cup through her swollen nasal passages. Pauline sat down on the rattan chair by the window and watched. "Good God," she said. "You're sick as a dog."

"I'm sorry I didn't call."

"It's all right. As long as you were in good hands."

Milena thought of the bandages on Louise's arms, of what they concealed, but also of her featherbed, of the glass of water on the night table next to Saint Geneviève and the Bible, and of the hot Ceylon tea in the thermos. "I was," she murmured into the steaming mug.

"Friends of yours?"

"A friend of mine, yes," Milena said. "I had no intention of staying the night, naturally. But I was too sick to leave. My temperature went up all of a sudden."

"That's sweet of them, to take care of you."

"Yes. Very."

"Anyone I know?" Pauline sat facing the window, caressing a single glass marble from the bowl on the sill between her long fingers. She would let the question go if Milena chose not to answer, and move on to something else, or she would tell Milena to get some sleep, as if nothing had been said, and leave the room, quietly closing the door. It was the way she was: attentive, thoughtful, offering friendship in her own unobtrusive way, applying a light touch that didn't make itself felt except when it was needed. Milena felt a sudden rush of affection for her, a desire to tell her everything. But that would take more courage than she could muster, for now. "No," she said. It wasn't strictly a lie. Pauline had only met Louise once, and never exchanged a word with her. "And it was just a friend." She handed Pauline the empty mug and wrapped herself in her comforter. "In case you're making assumptions."

Pauline smiled. "I wasn't." She took the mug and stood up. "Now go to sleep, and get better."

A moment later, Milena heard the sound of the door being closed, gently, with the softest of clicks.

•

The phone rang three times on Wednesday morning. The first time, it roused Milena from some troubling dream she immediately forgot. She let it ring until she remembered that Pauline had left early in the morning to go to Nanterre. It rang again shortly after. It was Sylvie, who wanted to know how she was and when she could come back to work. Perhaps Friday, Milena told her.

The third time it rang, about an hour later, Milena had just made herself some tea and was on her way back to bed to try to read a little. She considered ignoring it. But she knew she'd be wondering for hours who it might have been. What they needed, she thought as she reached for the receiver, was a cable long enough to extend into her room.

It was Louise. "How are you feeling?"

"Better," Milena said. "Thank you again for everything."

"It's nothing. I was wondering—"

Milena heard a muffled voice in the background. Maurice? No, the uncle. Louise exchanged a few brief sentences with him. There was a pause of several seconds before she spoke again. "I was wondering if I should come by to see you. To see if you need anything."

"That's all right," Milena said. "I'm feeling better, like I said."

"Okay." Another pause. Milena strained to hear the male voice in the background again. She heard nothing, only a soft sound that might have been Louise breathing. "I figured your room mate is probably helping you," Louise said. "But I thought I should ask, all the same."

"She's at the university, actually. She won't be back until the evening. But I can manage."

"That's good. I'll see you when you come to work again, perhaps."

"Perhaps," Milena said. "Thank you again, Louise." She hung up.

She went to her room and sat down on the edge of her bed. She took a sip of tea. A hint of taste was coming back. She heard her clock ticking. Second after second dragged on. Nearly twelve. The telephone conversation kept repeating inside her head.

Thank you again, Louise.

The words sliced her heart in two. Was that really all she had to say?

She got up, nearly spilling the tea as she set the mug down on her desk. In the hallway, with the draft from the front door playing over her naked feet, she dialed the gallery's number. She misdialed once, cursing. The second time it was busy. When she heard the ring tone on her third attempt, she muttered a prayer: Please let Louise still be standing by the front desk, let her answer and not, by some chance, the uncle. It seemed to take forever until someone picked up; in truth, it rang barely two times before she heard the receiver being lifted and then, thank God, Louise's voice.

•

Milena sat on her bed in her robe, watching the snow drift by the window. She had slept, or tried to sleep, through most of the afternoon. She was tempted to try and smoke a cigarette. But her cough was painful enough without doing something so foolish. She thought of the sound the snowflakes had made, on the window in Louise's attic.

At six, the knock on the door came.

Louise kissed her on the cheek, softly, but not with the briefness of the common custom. Milena swallowed hard; a dull pain blossomed in her throat and surged into her ears. She touched her lips to Louise's cheek in return, hastily, poorly aimed, near her ear. Nothing was simple any longer.

"I brought you something." Louise produced a small jar from her purse.

Milena smiled. "Honey?"

"Spruce honey from Vosges. Take it with tea, or with warm milk. It will soothe your throat."

They sat down in Milena's room, Milena under her comforter, Louise at the foot of the bed.

"When will your friend be back?"

"Seven. Perhaps seven thirty."

Louise slipped her shoes off and pulled up her legs, hugging her knees. It was a strangely casual pose for her. She stretched out a hand and touched Milena's ankle under the comforter. "Should I make tea?"

"Just sit with me." In spite of the hours of forced indolence that lay behind her, Milena felt drowsy. A few times, she nearly fell asleep again. At one point, she thought she heard Louise quietly humming a melody. It sounded at the same time vaguely familiar and utterly foreign. Perhaps it was an old French lullaby. But it might just as well have been a dream.

"It's almost seven," Louise said.

Milena sat up. "Let me walk you to the door."

"I can find my way out."

They fumbled an embrace in the middle of the bed. Milena's stiff shoulder made it more awkward. The last time she'd held someone, the bones had still been whole. She felt Louise's nose brushing hers, cool, icy almost on her hot skin. "Don't," she whispered.

Louise averted her face. Helplessly, Milena caressed her forearm, tracing the bandages under the fabric with her fingertips. Without a word, Louise got up. She took her coat and slipped into it as she walked out of the room. Distantly, Milena heard the front door fall shut. She made no attempt to fight her tears.

·

The next morning, after breakfast, after Pauline had left once again for Nanterre, Milena sat down by the telephone in the drafty hallway and dialed the elaborate sequence of numbers required to reach Prague. The monthly call. It rang many times before someone picked up. She said hello. There was a pause. That terrible, heart-breaking pause she dreaded every time she made the call. A rustling sound, then her mother's voice, flat, weary. "How are you?"

"I'm fine," Milena said.

"You don't sound good."

"It's just a cold. How is tatínek?"

"The same as always. He gets bored."

"No chance yet for him to return to work?"

"Not the work he loved," her mother said. "You know that."

Milena strained for things to say. She knew that Pauline always had a collection of little notes ready when she called her parents in Marseille, things to tell them that she jotted down beforehand at all odd times. Milena had considered doing the same, but it would have been a futile exercise. The conversations with her mother never changed.

"Have you found a good doctor yet, Milena?"

"My shoulder isn't bothering me that much," Milena said. "Besides, they've done all they could do for it."

"You know that's not what I meant."

"I'm fine."

"Are you still living with that woman?"

"Pauline," Milena said. "Yes. I couldn't afford the rent, by myself."

"You should have stayed with Karel and his wife."

Milena sighed. Cousin Karel and his wife and their three kids, out in Orly. They'd taken her in for a few weeks, but when she left to live in Paris, as soon as she could manage it, they had been as glad to see her go as she was to be gone. "Or I could sleep under a bridge."

"Don't be ungrateful," her mother said. "Without them, where would we have sent you?"

"I don't need to impose on them anymore. I've made many friends since then."

"What kind of friends?"

"All sorts. Most of them are students, like me. I've told you all this before."

"Have you met anyone yet?"

"I meet lots of people all the time."

"You know what I mean."

Milena's mouth went dry. She swallowed. "There might be someone."

"Does he have a name?"

"I have to go, maminka. It's an expensive call."

Silence. The line crackled. Tiny voices wove in and out of the electronic noise, bits of distant conversations, laughter. Why can't our talks be like that, Milena thought.

"I want you to go see a doctor, Milena. I keep telling you this. I worry about you."

"I don't need a doctor."

"If you have trouble finding one, your father has friends that may know someone in Paris."

"There is nothing wrong with me," Milena said.

"You keep saying that. But you have to face reality. You have to let someone help you."

"That means different things to you and me."

"You can't stay the way you are, Milena." More crackling and distant voices. Second after second slipped away into the static. "Or you'll be alone for the rest of your life."

"I need to go," Milena said. "Give my love to tatínek." She hung up. For a long time, she stayed on the chair by the phone, watching the dust drift through the pale morning sunlight that filtered out of the kitchen into the hallway.

·

Milena returned to work at Sylvie's on Friday afternoon. She still felt shaky but her throat no longer hurt. In the evening, when it had gotten dark outside and she had only an hour left to work, she sat down in the back room with a book, a spoon, and the jar of spruce honey. Her sense of taste was returning. She closed her eyes and let the delicate flavors spread over her tongue.

Closing time came. She locked the boutique and walked up the Rue de Birague. At the entrance to the Place des Vosges, she stopped. The freezing wind sighed through the archway behind her. She leaned against one of the piers, sheltered her lighter with her palms, and lit a cigarette. The smoke hit her lungs like a fist. She coughed, threw the cigarette away, and stepped it out. Her shoulder began to lock up. Which way to go? Suppose she just remained where she was, with the wind whistling past her ears. But life demanded decisions, movement.

You can't stay the way you are.

She pushed away from the pier and headed across the Place.

•

Louise stood in the door to her apartment, looking puzzled. "Milena?"

Milena remained at the threshold, out of breath from her ascent up the three flights of stairs, and the two more cigarettes she had tried to smoke on the way.

"Please come in," Louise said.

Milena shook her head. She leaned against the doorpost. "I came to talk about the other night. Wednesday evening."

Louise lowered her eyes. "That was my fault. I should apologize."

Milena traced Louise's jaw with her fingertip. "You don't have to."

Slowly, Louise looked up. Milena leaned forward until her nose brushed against Louise's, the way it had happened two nights before. Their lips almost touched. "I can't promise you anything," she whispered. She closed her eyes and kissed the corner of Louise's mouth.

Louise stood perfectly still. Milena could hear her breathing. Almost imperceptibly, she returned the kiss.

The lamp in the staircase went out with its sharp snap. Only the light coming from Louise's hallway remained, warm and copper-colored. They stood on the threshold, holding one another, carefully, as if they were each afraid they might bruise the other. Which was still possible, of course.

2 SECRETS

Paris, April 8, 1968.

Milena sat in the back room of the boutique, alone, a book resting open in her lap. A cigarette smoldered, mostly turned to ashes, on the oversized Cinzano ashtray. She had never again enjoyed smoking since her fever in February, but she refused to take the opportunity and quit. The constant dripping of the faucet was drowned out by the sound of raindrops tapping on the window above the sink. She felt like going to sleep.

The bells over the front door rang. She glanced at her watch. Almost closing time. She put out the cigarette, quickly consulted the mirror she kept in her purse, and stepped through the bead curtain into the salesroom. She expected to find some well-dressed young woman, or group of women, stopping by for a bit of browsing on the way home from some job in the area. Or Louise, perhaps. They hadn't made plans to meet, but still, she might have decided to come by.

The customer wasn't a woman, nor young. Standing in the middle of the store, looking very much out of place, was Louise's uncle, Claude Gabbard.

He smiled when he saw her enter. "Mademoiselle Beranovà. Good evening."

"Good evening." She had seen him frequently during the past couple of months—whenever she picked Louise up at the gallery—but to say that they were well acquainted would have been an exaggeration. For him to seek her out at the boutique was somewhat bizarre.

"It's all right to be surprised." He looked around, glancing at the racks and shelves of trendy clothes and accessories. "I don't suppose you get many older gentlemen as customers."

"We get male customers of all ages," Milena said. "They're usually shopping for gifts. I have to help them, of course."

"Of course. I did come to enlist your help with just that, as a matter of fact."

"You're looking for a present?"

"It's for my niece," he said. "I had to ask her to stay at the gallery a little longer today. She has been working very hard. I'd like to make it up to her somehow."

"That's thoughtful of you." Milena stepped around the counter. "I'm just not sure if we have anything that would complement her style."

"She has very particular tastes, I know." He sighed. "Much like her aunt."

Milena became aware of an alcoholic odor on his breath. She couldn't identify the smell. Something herbal and actually rather unpleasant.

He absently picked through a basket of Indian glass bangles. "Something like this, perhaps."

"You may want to take a look at our necklaces. We have some sterling silver chains that could be paired with any pendant."

He moved to the plastic tree that served as a display stand and inspected the necklaces and bracelets suspended from its branches. "I suppose you're thinking of crucifixes, Mademoiselle?"

"That does seem to be the kind she prefers."

"Religion," he murmured. "I don't know why a young girl would be so preoccupied with it." He looked up. "Her aunt wasn't, you know. It was the one thing in which Louise did not follow her."

"There are benefits to faith," Milena said. "It can be something beautiful, even."

He smiled. "My niece told me that you are surprisingly tolerant of religion, for someone leaning, shall we say, to the left."

"Did she?"

"I agree with you, of course." He picked up a long double necklace made out of mahogany beads interlaced with sunstones. "Faith can be a wonderful thing. If it isn't abused, or twisted to some perverted purpose."

"You won't be able to add a pendant to that one," Milena said.

He let the mahogany beads run through his fingers, as if he was counting a rosary. "You've gotten to know her fairly well, haven't you?"

Milena shrugged. "We go out together a couple of times a week. Cafés, dinners. The movies, now and then. That's about the extent of it."

"It's the most time I've seen her spend with anyone, since her aunt passed away." He stopped playing with the beads. "I care about her a great deal, Mademoiselle. I'm glad she has found a friend."

Milena was unsure how to respond. Should she welcome his approval? Be on guard against an intrusion? "You make it sound like some unprecedented occurrence."

"To the best of my knowledge, it is."

Milena looked at the wall clock above the counter. "I'm going to close shop." She locked the door and flipped the sign hanging in front of the glass pane. "You're welcome to keep looking."

"You don't think my niece has difficulties forming connections with people?"

"I didn't see a problem."

"I'm concerned about her, Mademoiselle."

The suddenness of his admission took Milena off guard. "Concerned?"

"Louise is like a daughter to me. My wife and I, we never had children."

"I'm sorry to hear that," Milena said.

"I won't pretend that I ever gave much thought to such matters, myself. Nor did my wife, when she was still alive. But now that Louise is part of my life…" He hesitated. "I would be devastated if anything were to happen to her."

"What makes you think you have reason to be worried?"

He looked directly at her. His gaze was gentle; pleading more than searching. "You haven't noticed anything, Mademoiselle?"

Milena averted her eyes. "I have to balance the register."

"Of course." He cleared his throat. "I think I'll take this." He followed her, the necklace dangling from his hand. After he had paid and accepted his change, he remained by the counter, still fiddling with the beads. "I'm afraid my niece may have tried to take her own life, Mademoiselle."

"My God." So that was what he suspected. No wonder he had been questioning Louise about the incident with her arm. "What gives you that idea?"

He slipped the necklace into his pocket, as if now that he had made the decision to speak his mind, there was no more need for anything to occupy his hands. "One Monday, about two months ago, Louise left the gallery very suddenly. She claimed that she had run out of cigarettes. Shortly after, she returned wearing a different shirt and coat."

"That would be odd."

"She told me she had spilled coffee on herself, forcing her to purchase a change of clothes, rather than go home and change, which would have taken too long."

"But you didn't believe her?"

"I saw blood," he said. "On her hand, when she left the gallery. I have no doubt about it."

"You don't assume she tried to cut her wrists behind the front desk?" Milena's thoughts raced. How long could she avoid telling him what she knew of that morning? Was there even a reason to keep her knowledge from him?

"Of course not. But suppose she did injure herself during the few minutes she had been at work, in the course of some minor accident. She would have had no reason to hide the fact from me. I must therefore assume that the injury had in fact occurred earlier, under circumstances she did not wish to recount."

"Sound reasoning," Milena said. "I imagine you confronted her about it?"

"I did, when she returned," he said. "She told me some story about having broken something at home the night before, how she did not want me to worry about her, and so on and so forth. I didn't have much choice but to accept her explanation, which was frustrating to say the least."

"I can imagine," Milena murmured.

"I've been keeping a close eye on her ever since. But she always notices, and she is very resentful of such attention. At one point, she even threatened to quit her job and go away, if I didn't leave the subject alone."

"But why would you think she wants to kill herself? If I may ask."

"My niece has had a difficult past," Gabbard said. "That is all I can tell you, for the moment. But you must have noticed it too, the sadness about her. How lonely she is. She is different from other young women, Mademoiselle."

"I did get that impression."

"I wouldn't dream of intruding on your friendship with her, if I didn't feel so helpless. Discussing the matter with Louise is impossible. I fear she may indeed leave, if I press her. But what if she makes another attempt, and succeeds?"

"There is no reason to worry," Milena said. "Your niece is not trying to kill herself."

He looked at her, eyes wide. "How do you know this?"

"I dressed her wounds, that morning. Those new clothes, she bought them here. It's how we met."

"That would explain how quickly she returned," Gabbard said.

"She was bleeding all over the place," Milena went on. "Naturally, I asked what had happened. She gave me the same explanation she gave you, about some glass she had accidentally broken the night before. I convinced her to let me patch her up."

"But it must have been a serious injury," Gabbard said. "For her to bleed so badly."

"She had some nasty cuts, but nowhere near her wrist or any veins. Nothing like what you would expect to see after a suicide attempt, I assure you."

"Are you certain?" His expression wavered between skepticism and a visible desire to believe her.

"It's not very complicated, Monsieur Gabbard. Either one cuts those veins, or one doesn't."

"I suppose." He nodded. "I admit I had hoped that, having befriended her, you might be able to provide—" He interrupted himself. "I hope you can forgive my approaching you in this way, Mademoiselle. I was desperate."

"I understand. Like I said, you shouldn't worry."

"If you are right, it would be a tremendous relief," Gabbard said. He took a business card out of his wallet and placed it on the counter. "Allow me to give you my private number, Mademoiselle. Just in case."

Milena made no move to take the card. "In case of what, Monsieur Gabbard?"

"As I said, my niece has had a difficult past." He exhaled an invisible cloud of the strange herbal odor. His body seemed to shrink in the process. "And she tends to keep her troubles to herself."

Milena finally recognized the aroma of his alcoholic breath: Gentiane. She had tried it once, a long time ago with Pauline. The smell seemed less unpleasant now that she had identified it. She nodded and picked up the card.

"Do not hesitate to call me anytime," he said. "If you have questions. If you simply need to talk."

Milena kept her eyes on the spidery letters and numbers hand written on the card. "Thank you," she said.

She unlocked the front door to let him out. She remained standing in the doorway and looked after him until he rounded the corner of the Rue de Birague and the Rue St. Antoine, and disappeared into the rain.

•

The next day, she met Louise in the evening. They had a quick dinner before visiting a theater in the Marais to catch a showing of 'Morocco' since Louise had a weakness for old Marlene Dietrich movies that Milena neither shared nor comprehended. Fortunately, she turned out to be equally fascinated, if often bewildered, by the experimental Nouvelle Vague films Milena insisted on seeing every once in a while.

After the movie, Milena walked her home, to the small street where Louise lived, up the stairs, to her door. It was a routine that went without saying by now.

They stood in the doorway, close to each other but ready to separate at the sound of a door being opened, a key being turned somewhere. Then the kiss, always the same as the first time: careful, never exploring too much. Perhaps they could go on like this forever, safely, without asking questions, in the half-light on the landing that, for a few minutes, became their entire world.

Milena touched Louise's arm. As so often, she felt bandages under the fabric. They disappeared periodically, but they always came back. The explanations were variations on a now familiar theme. Accidents. Cuts that wouldn't heal. After so many weeks, the stories were hard to believe. Time and again she told herself that she was going to press Louise for the truth, no matter the consequences. Just not tonight. Tonight was too precious; it always was.

"Come by on Saturday," Louise said. "I only work till noon."

Milena nodded. "I'll be there."

Then the way back down the stairs, as usual: a descent into silence, and shame.

•

When Milena came to the gallery on Saturday, Louise wasn't there. She stood in the empty showroom for a minute, listening for any noise. Nothing. She called Louise's name. In response, she heard the creak of a chair in the back. Louise's uncle appeared in the doorway. He looked more careworn than usual.

"Louise told me to pick her up for lunch," she said.

"I'm sorry, Mademoiselle. She left."

"Is something wrong?"

He walked to the front desk and took a piece of paper out of a drawer. It was covered in closely spaced handwriting. "This arrived today," he said. "It's a letter from Louise's mother."

"I didn't know Louise corresponded with her parents."

"She doesn't. Her mother writes now and then, to inquire about Louise's well-being. Occasionally she asks me to try and persuade her to get in touch." He dropped the letter back into the drawer. "Louise never reads a single one of these. I read them to her, or tell her the gist of what they contain." He smiled wearily. "She has little choice but to listen, when she's at work, you see."

Milena smiled back mechanically. "Why don't her parents simply come to Paris to talk to her? I'm sure if she saw them face to face—"

"It wouldn't move her," he said. "They did that, once, shortly after she left Tours. They came here, to the gallery. Louise left screaming in a rage. Her father went after her, pleading with her to listen. She made such a scene that the police got involved. Francois was almost taken into custody."

"Francois?"

"Her father. Louise's mother wrote this letter on behalf of him." He exhaled a heavy breath. No smell of

Gentiane, this time. "He's dying. She writes that it is only a matter of days. And that he is asking for Louise."

"I'm terribly sorry," Milena said. "Is that why she left so suddenly?"

"If only that were true," he said. "I conveyed his request to Louise, naturally. She refuses to go. We had an argument, and she left. That was about twenty minutes ago."

"How can she not go to him? No matter what differences they may have, he is still her father."

"May I ask, Mademoiselle, exactly what you know about these differences, as you call them?"

"Nothing too specific," Milena said. "She resents his conservative views, especially regarding women. I can certainly see why she would have left home, when her aunt offered her the possibility."

"But is that enough cause for her to refuse her father's dying wish?"

"My guess is that there's more to it."

He nodded. "A great deal."

"I'd like to try and hear it from herself," Milena said. "At a time like this, she may be willing to tell me her reasons."

"I understand. But please be careful, Mademoiselle. I don't want her to get the impression that you and I spoke about this."

"Of course." She reached for the door handle.

"She may not be at home," he said. "In the past, whenever she was upset, she would go to the quays and watch the Seine for hours. She used to do the same thing in Tours, along the Loire."

"That's a lot of riverfront to cover."

"Start at the Quai Henri IV, south from here. It's closest. Work your way west along the bank. With any luck, you'll find her."

•

Somewhere between the Pont Marie and the Pont de Sully, along the Quai des Celestins, Louise stood leaning on the wall that overlooked the embankment. It had begun to rain. Her blond hair hung in strands, dripping at the ends. She didn't look up when Milena approached and stood beside her, shielding them both with her huge indigo umbrella.

"You'll catch your death of cold out here," Milena said.

Louise only shrugged.

They remained like this for several minutes, silent, while the rain drummed incessantly on the nylon canopy above them and ran off the edges in strings of silver.

Milena nodded toward the Seine below them. "This past winter, I was certain it would freeze over."

"I've never heard of it happening in my lifetime," Louise said.

"In Prague, in cold winters, the Vltava freezes over occasionally. You can walk across the ice, even skate in places."

"That sounds very nice," Louise said. "And a little frightening, too."

"It could be. I remember one winter, being on the river. Close to the center, the ice began to groan and crackle under our feet. We withdrew very quickly to the bank."

"Who was with you?"

"A girl I knew." Milena fished her cigarettes out of her purse. She lit one, inhaled, and started coughing.

Louise picked the cigarette from her fingers and dropped it into the wet dirt at the bottom of the wall. There was a brief hiss as it went out. "Why don't you quit already?"

"Your uncle told me about your father," Milena said.

"I'm sorry I didn't wait for you at the gallery."

"Why won't you go to Tours, Louise?"

"I don't want to see him. He can't force his will on me."

"Ježiše Marie. He's dying. He just wants to see you. It's not about forcing his will on anyone."

"It's always about that, with him."

"If you let this last chance go by, you will regret it for the rest of your life," Milena said.

"I can live with one more regret."

"What is it that you can't forgive him?"

Louise closed her eyes. A spasm passed over her mouth, a twitch as of some brief but intense pain. "I won't go to him. Just accept that."

"Nothing is beyond recall. Not among family."

"Some things are."

"I don't want to believe that."

"Of course not. Why should you? You have nothing but love for your father."

"I do," Milena said. "And not a day goes by that I don't wish I could tell him that."

"What are you talking about? Your father is still alive, isn't he?"

"He's alive, yes." Milena's fingers crept toward her purse, eager for another attempt at a cigarette. She forced herself to dismiss the impulse. "But for the past eight years, he's refused to speak to me."

For the first time since Milena had joined her at the quay, Louise turned to look at her. "Why?"

•

"Her name was Katarina," Milena said. "The girl who was on the ice with me."

"A friend?"

Milena shook her head. "Not exactly."

"Katarina," Louise repeated. The syllables rose from her lips like a benediction. "Such a beautiful name."

"She killed herself the next day." Milena let her eyes go out of focus on the water. "It was Christmas Eve. She returned to the river early in the morning, before sunrise. She walked to the middle and waited for the ice to break underneath her."

Louise muttered something in a liquid French Milena couldn't understand. Perhaps it was a prayer, this time.

"She suffered from severe depression," Milena said. "She was deeply religious. And she was in love with me. I'm not sure which was worse."

"Did you love her?"

"Love?" The word tasted like a mouthful of dust. "We were both seventeen, Louise. Children, practically. One kiss, barely, that's all that had happened between us. Whatever you want to call it, I tried to end it."

"Is that why she drowned herself?"

"I did it to help her," Milena said. "She had gone to confession, and been told that she had to repent, and fight what she felt. I wanted to make it easier. But it was useless. With or without me, she couldn't deny herself."

"But to take her own life? That is a mortal sin, far more grave than anything that may have been between you and her."

"She didn't think of it that way, when she went out on the river that morning," Milena said. "When the ice broke, it was God's doing, not hers. She was seeking his judgment. Although I am sure that she waited long enough, and walked far enough, to meet the fate she felt she deserved."

"How do you know that?"

"The day before, when we walked to the middle of the river together, to where the ice was starting to be too thin, she said that perhaps we should let it be God's judgment of us. If the ice carried us, she said, it meant God had forgiven us. But when the ice began to crack, she hurried back to the bank with me. I fooled myself into thinking it had all been a joke."

"Anyone would have assumed that."

"I shouldn't have."

"You can't blame yourself for what happened to her," Louise said. "Even if you had taken what she said seriously, what could you have done? Tell her parents that she was suicidal because she had feelings for you?"

"Why not?" Milena shifted her shoulder. It hurt from holding the umbrella. "They found out anyway, in the end."

Louise took the umbrella from her. "How?"

"She'd kept a diary." Milena rubbed the stiff shoulder and winced. The damaged bones were doing their part in bringing her memories back to life. "Her parents read it after her death, looking for answers. And they found them. Along with my name."

"What did they do?"

"I assume they let her brother read the diary as well," Milena said. "The first day after the Christmas holidays, he ambushed me at school. He stabbed me three times in the back with a scratch awl."

"Oh, mon Christ," Louise muttered.

"I had no idea what was happening," Milena said. "I was face down in the snow, which was turning red all around me. I couldn't breathe. I thought I was dying. I was told later that if one of the teachers hadn't been there to drag him off me, he would have killed me. I don't doubt it. I woke up in a hospital bed, shot up with morphine. My father was sitting next to me, holding my hand. He asked me if it was true, what he had heard. I nodded. It hurt terribly to move my head, even with the morphine, and it seemed to take a hundred years. Somewhere far away, I felt his hand letting go of mine. That was the last time he ever spoke to me." She exhaled a jet of steam into the cold air and wiped the few tears away with her sleeve. She was surprised she hadn't wept more. Perhaps the worst stories were like drowning in freezing water: after the initial plunge, you quickly turned still and rigid. "Now you know why I don't want to see God's hand behind everything. I prefer to think of God as a distant observer, a force that set everything in motion and now just watches the world unfold, without judging us who live in it."

Louise swallowed. "Maybe he does both, in a way that we can't understand."

"Then it's a waste of time for us, trying to make sense of it," Milena said. "Can we start walking?"

·

They walked arm in arm along the Quai, past the Île Saint Louis. Ahead of them, a corner of the Île de la Cité was visible through the rain.

"I was in the hospital for a long time," Milena said. "In the meantime, the school decided to expel me. For my own safety, they claimed. I suppose that was true, in part. Katarina's brother had many friends."

"Did your mother react the way your father did?"

"She didn't stop talking to me," Milena said. "But only to send me to various psychiatrists. My condition, as they called it, meant a diagnosis of mental illness. As you and I both now know, they didn't manage to cure me."

Louise gave her a wavering look, as if she was unsure whether she should smile at the remark.

"My father called a few favors and got me into another decent school, but word about me was already out. Communist bureaucracy isn't big on privacy. I was mocked, taunted, and inevitably threatened. A few times, I was beaten. Luckily, I was only a year away from graduation. I toughed it out. As soon as I had my diploma in hand, my parents sent me abroad."

"So they did it to protect you."

Milena nodded. "Katarina's brother wasn't going to be in the reformatory forever. His parents had already informed my father that he had vowed to finish me off as soon as he got out."

"At least they warned you," Louise said.

"I doubt it was entirely for my benefit. For one thing, they didn't want to see their son incarcerated for murder. But they probably also felt that I deserved to live in fear. I still can't bear the sound of someone running behind me on the street. I always think it's him."

They stopped again, and watched the barges go by on the pewter-colored river. "So here I am," Milena said. "Aside from a few close relatives, no one knows I went to France. Every month or so, I call home to tell my parents that I'm alright. If my father picks up, he hands the telephone to my mother without a word."

"That's very sad," Louise said.

Milena shrugged. "No sadder than your story, I'm sure, or any number of others."

"What made you tell me about all this? And why now?"

"I don't know. To show you that I'm not just a naïve idealist, that I know a thing or two about family tragedies, about wishing for someone's forgiveness. Or maybe I'm tired of keeping secrets. Maybe both."

"And now you expect me to give you mine, in return."

"I don't expect anything. Only for you to consider carefully what you're doing. Some chances don't come back. Your father's running out of time."

"It makes no difference to me."

"If my father wanted to see me, whether he was dying or not, I would go," Milena said. "Even after eight years of silence. I would go to him right this minute."

"So would I, if silence was the worst I had seen from my father."

"What did he do to you, Louise? What is so hard to forgive?" Milena waited. But Louise remained silent. "I won't press you any more. But if you ever want to talk—"

Louise cut her off. "You will press me," she said. "Perhaps not now, but other times. In your own way. I know you well enough by now. You can't abide unanswered questions."

"Funny," Milena said. "Because for more than two months now, that's what I've been doing."

Louise looked at her. "What are you talking about?"

"Your bandages. No one has that many accidents."

Louise turned away again. "I do. And I told you before, my skin heals slowly."

Milena sighed. One secret at a time. "Don't you think it would help to talk?"

"And how would it help? Did it make your shoulder whole again, to talk about what happened to you?"

"It didn't undo the past," Milena said. "But I feel the weight of it a little less."

For several minutes, Louise watched the river. Making up her mind, Milena hoped. She wasn't sure how much longer she could stand in the rain like this. The umbrella kept them dry, but she was beginning to feel chilly and miserable. Still, if Louise decided to speak, it might be worth coming down with another cold. Who knew, perhaps she would be laid up in the down bed under the watchful eyes of Saint Geneviève again. The prospect wasn't entirely unpleasant.

"When I was five years old, my brother drowned," Louise said. "My father was responsible."

The words didn't register with Milena at first. "You had a brother?"

Louise nodded. "Frédéric."

"Ježiše Marie. I had no idea. I'm so sorry."

"I don't really remember him," Louise said. "I was too little at the time. But I think of him often. I remember that he was very affectionate with me. A little rough sometimes, I think. At least that's what my father claimed, later on. But he was a boy, after all."

"How old was he?"

"He was fourteen when he died. Nine years older than me. He would have been thirty-three years old this February."

"And why do you blame your father? What happened?"

"It was just so unfair." Louise's lips tightened with disgust. "My father never had patience with Frédéric. He was—" She made an aimless gesture. "My aunt said Frédéric was very perceptive. But he was a little slow. My father had no patience with him. He would beat him for the smallest things he did wrong."

"Your aunt told you this?"

"As with most things my parents didn't want me to know," Louise said. "If it hadn't been for her, I doubt I would ever have found out what really happened to Frédéric. My parents told me he'd run away, and made sure that no one told me otherwise."

"I'm sure they only meant to protect you," Milena said.

"They meant to never tell me the truth. They didn't want me to know that Frédéric's death was my father's fault."

"Just how was it your father's fault?"

"The night that Frédéric died, my father was after him to punish him for breaking something," Louise said. "My aunt said he was furious, and that Frédéric was terrified."

"How does your aunt know all this?"

"She was visiting when it happened," Louise said. "She tried to stop my father, but he wouldn't listen."

"What did your brother break that was so important?"

"Does it matter? It never took much for my father to give him a beating." Louise made a face as though she was about to spit on the ground. "He was ashamed of him. Ashamed of his own son."

"So what happened next?"

"My parent's house is on the Loire river," Louise said. "We had a small pier back then, and a rowboat. Frédéric took it out on the river. It was found washed ashore the next day, without the oars. The police said the boat had foundered, and that he had drowned."

"What you are describing is a terrible accident," Milena said. "A tragedy. And yes, your father shares a measure of responsibility, but—"

"A measure of responsibility? He might as well have drowned Frédéric with his own hands!"

"Your father didn't mean for this to happen, Louise."

"It was his fault," Louise said. "Nothing you say can change that."

"But you don't even remember what happened that night. You're condemning your father on someone else's account."

Louise's eyes narrowed. "Are you saying I should mistrust my aunt?"

"Of course not." Milena sighed. "Did you ever talk to your mother about what happened?"

"What for? She would never have spoken out against my father. Even with her own son dead." Louise snorted. "There. That's the kind of woman my mother is."

The kind of woman who still writes letters asking about her daughter's well-being, Milena thought. But what was the use of pointing out what Louise herself knew and chose to ignore?

"So now you know," Louise said. "Does that satisfy you? Or do you need me to flay more such dreadful memories open for you?"

"I can understand the way you feel," Milena said. "But I still urge you to go to your father. If nothing else, do it for yourself. For closure, and perhaps peace. Your own peace."

"As far as I'm concerned, my father died when I learned the truth about what happened that night." Louise turned to go. "I've already made my peace with that." She handed the umbrella to Milena and started walking away.

Milena watched her take a few steps into the rain. Perhaps it was time to accept the fact that the compassion she felt for Louise's father came out of the longing she felt for her own. Perhaps Francois de Benoît was the monster Louise made him out to be. Perhaps he deserved to die alone, abandoned, estranged from his only living child.

And yet.

It bothered her, for some reason she could not yet determine, that Louise's aunt seemed to have been so eager to make sure Louise was aware of her father's tragic mistake. By her judgment alone, he had been cast down into the pit of his daughter's hatred. Her own brother.

Milena thrust her free hand into her pocket and followed Louise with the umbrella. Between her fingers, she felt the card Claude Gabbard had given her.

•

To Milena's surprise, no maid received her at the door to Gabbard's apartment the next day. The address he had given her was exclusive enough, and the apartment nothing short of luxurious with its ivory walls and antique furnishings. But he himself opened the door, led her into his living room, and gestured at a highly polished dining table made out of some dark wood. "Please sit down, Mademoiselle Beranovà."

Milena took a seat on one of six expensive-looking but rather uncomfortable chairs. She hung her coat over the intricately carved backrest. "You can call me Milena."

Gabbard smiled graciously. "Would you like something to drink? Tea, perhaps, or coffee?"

"Coffee would be nice."

"Very well." He disappeared into a hallway.

Milena heard kitchen noises: running water, cabinet doors, dishes rattling. No maid, then. Perhaps Sunday was her day off, or he had sent her away on account of her visit. She craned her neck to look out of the window into the tree-lined street. The room overlooked a corner of the Boulevard Saint-Germain and a smaller street Gabbard had indicated as the Rue Grégoire de Tours. She saw branches with young green leaves through which the gray pavement below was visible. Pedestrians with umbrellas moved underneath the trees.

After a few minutes, she heard the sputtering of a percolator.

Gabbard returned with a silver coffee pot and cups of fine bone china. He made one more trip to the kitchen to fetch a small plate of madeleines. Milena decided that he possessed the adroitness of a man accustomed to waiting on his guests himself.

They sat for a few awkward minutes sipping the strong coffee and eating the pastries. Milena tried to break the ice by talking about Proust's tea-dipped madeleine. Gabbard maintained his gracious smile and admitted that while he had heard the expression, he had never made it far enough into the author's labyrinthine prose to discover the story behind it. "I'm afraid I'm not entirely aware of what it is you study, Mademoiselle. I assume literature is your field, then?"

Milena shook her head. "Sociology."

"Ah, yes. That makes more sense. My niece did mention you were rather political."

"I wouldn't say being political makes less sense for a student of literature," Milena said. "I have quite a few friends who study literature and are very engaged."

"Of course," he said. "I forget that everything is, in the end, political. Even art."

"Especially art."

"You wouldn't think it listening to some of our clients," he said. "I understand you're at Nanterre? With whom do you study, if I may ask?"

"Professor Lefebvre," Milena said.

"Henri Lefebvre?" He raised an eyebrow. "He's quite well-known."

"I am aware."

"I read an essay of his in the paper a while ago. Rather interesting. He's a Marxist, isn't he?"

"To a degree." Milena felt wary. In spite of the gentleness of his inquiries, she found it hard to imagine that he might sympathize with leftist thought. Political debate would be a bad way to get comfortable with one another. "He is rather out of favor with the Communist party, these days."

"I see. And why is that?"

"Disagreements on doctrine," she said. "Or rather, the very idea of doctrine. The left can be as inflexible as the right, Monsieur Gabbard."

"I am sure of it. Ideologies are often no different from religions, in that regard. But as for Professor Lefebvre, he's a non-conformist, then?"

"In a manner of speaking, yes." Milena moved to help herself to more coffee, but he quickly reached for the silver pot and refilled her cup.

"I can see why you would work well with such a man. My niece has described you as a bit of a, shall we say, revolutionary."

"I'll take that as a compliment."

"And no doubt it was meant that way. You see, her aunt, my wife, was very much like you in this regard."

Milena raised an eyebrow. "Was she?"

"Not in every detail," Gabbard said. "But she, too, was trying to break away from tradition, from what was accepted and proper in her family."

"Much to her brother's patriarchal dismay, I understand."

Gabbard smiled. "That is perhaps an oversimplification. I know Louise highlights her father's insistence on the traditional role of women, a view she perceives to be quite repressive."

Milena crossed her arms in front of her chest. "As do I."

"Believe me, Mademoiselle Beranovà, I sympathize. I could not have been married to Corinne if I did not. But in all fairness it must be said that Francois's efforts were not simply aimed at limiting the freedom of female family members. His primary concern was the reputation and standing of the de Benoît family."

"The preservation of a conservative and increasingly obsolete status quo, in other words."

"Please try to understand, Mademoiselle. In his way, Francois was doing his best to reconcile his family with our changing times. He knew that the past was slipping away. The time when the de Benoîts had owned tracts of land and sizeable fortunes was long gone. There had been some financial ineptitude in the past, a certain gambling great-grandfather, and all sorts of signs of decline."

"If you're evoking the plight of nobles coming to terms with their diminishing status in a modern world, don't expect sympathy from me, Monsieur Gabbard."

Gabbard shook his head. "On the contrary. What I am trying to tell you is that Francois realized full well that if he wanted to preserve his family's status, it would have to be based on personal achievements, merit, and contributions to society, rather than reliance on a name or other things associated with a bygone age. Whatever shortcomings of character one may attribute to him otherwise, by pursuing the medical profession, he chose prestige as well as a worthy cause."

"I have mixed experiences in that regard," Milena said. "But what's the point of telling me all this?"

"To show you that all is not so simply black and white where Louise's family is concerned, Mademoiselle. Much as I loved my wife and admired her free spirit, I also know that not all of her pursuits, particularly in her youth, were idealistic and unselfish. Some where probably even reckless."

"A matter of perspective," Milena said.

"Undoubtedly." Gabbard smiled again. "We don't need to go into detail. Let me simply say that when Louise makes it look as though her father was the guardian of an old order, attempting to lay shackles on his progressive sister as she tried to break free from it, it was in reality just as often a matter of Corinne, shall we say, acting wild while he was working to preserve the de Benoît family name."

"You're sure you don't want to get into the details about this?" The idea that Louise's aunt had been more troublemaker than feminist paragon piqued Milena's curiosity. It was the first definite indication that the distrust she felt for the woman might be justified.

"I'm not privy to them, to be honest," Gabbard said. "Neither Francois nor Corinne were ever very clear on the kind of things that caused strife between them when they were younger. But I've heard enough to give either of them the benefit of the doubt vis-à-vis the other's incriminations."

"Quite unlike Louise." Milena picked up her newly-filled cup and peered into the dark brew. An undulating reflection of her face stared back at her. "Which brings me to the reason I came to see you. You probably remember that I meant to get some answers from Louise about her strained relationship with her father."

"Strained is an understatement," Gabbard said. "But I assume you found that out for yourself."

"She blames him for the death of her brother. Frédéric."

Gabbard folded his hands underneath his chin. "And were you satisfied with this explanation?"

"I wouldn't be here if I was," Milena said. "The boy's death was an accident. I can see how their father was indirectly responsible, but he could hardly have meant for his son to drown."

"Then you believe that, given the present circumstances, Louise should be able to set her rancor aside."

"Of course I do," Milena said. "The man is dying, for Christ's sake. He made a mistake, a terrible mistake with tragic consequences that must have been as hard to bear for him as for Louise."

"Harder, I imagine. He lost his son that night. Louise didn't even learn of the accident until she was much older."

"I just can't help but feel that there is something else to this story." Milena took the last madeleine and dipped it into her coffee. "Something Louise is not telling me."

Gabbard took a deep breath. "There is, Mademoiselle. And it is not easy to tell. Not for my niece, obviously. Not for me, either."

The madeleine disintegrated between Milena's fingers. The crumbs sank and disappeared in her coffee. "You know her true reasons for ignoring her father's last request?"

He nodded. "Sometimes I wish I didn't."

Milena felt something slithering inside her stomach, like a snake waking up and uncoiling with slow but unstoppable determination. Gabbard studied her face as if deciding whether she was strong enough to hear what he had to tell. "Louise undoubtedly told you that the reason her father meant to punish Frédéric was that he broke something."

"She didn't specify what it was."

"I suppose she said that it didn't matter, because Francois would beat Frédéric for just about any offense or misbehavior?"

"Those were her words," Milena said.

"The boy didn't break anything." Gabbard's features were suddenly hard, his eyes steely. "No, he saw something. Something that he wasn't meant to see, something that frightened him. And he was caught seeing it."

Milena clasped her hands in her lap to keep them from trembling.

Gabbard didn't wait for her to ask the obvious question. "Frédéric came to Louise's room that night. I understand he had great affection for his sister, and would always check on her before going to sleep himself. But this time, he found his father in the room." His jaws worked in an effort to maintain control of his voice. He wasn't entirely successful. "Doing what no father should do to his daughter."

The snake in Milena's insides reared up, spat, and struck. Venom spilled into her mouth. "Jesus Christ," she croaked.

Gabbard kept looking at her. His hardened gaze broke, and his eyes began to shimmer with moisture. "If there is a God," he murmured through clenched teeth, "he had business elsewhere that night."

•

Somehow, Milena managed to get her squirming stomach under control. She felt numb, as if her body from the neck down had turned into dead wood. She tried to imagine Louise as a little girl. "She was five years old, for Heaven's sake."

"Five years," Gabbard repeated. "It defies comprehension."

"But how do you know all this?"

"My wife. She used to visit her family often during those days. She was there when this happened. In fact, Frédéric came to her room that night, seeking protection from his father. He told her what he had seen, as best as he could describe it, and that he was afraid that Francois would kill him for it."

"Do you think he would have?"

Gabbard shrugged. "Who can say? Corinne said when Francois entered her room, shortly after, he certainly had the air of someone capable of committing a murder. She asked him what the boy had done, but he was unwilling to explain himself at the time, as you may imagine. Corinne tried to keep him from seizing the boy. They got into a brief scuffle, and Frédéric slipped out of the room. Francois ran off in pursuit, but he never found him. It was the last time anyone saw the boy alive."

"What about Louise? Did your wife check on her?"

"Of course. After Francois had run out of the house to find Frédéric, she immediately headed to Louise's room. Her mother was there, comforting her. She assured Corinne that the girl was merely suffering from nightmares and a stomach ache."

"So she covered up her husband's crime." Milena exhaled noisily. "That seems consistent with Louise's description of her."

"She may not have known about it. Louise was never able to say what happened to her. Even later, all she remembered was a terrible belly ache, and not being able to breathe." A look of physical pain distorted Gabbard's features. "Corinne's theory was that Francois had pressed a pillow over her head to keep her from screaming, and that she may even have lost consciousness."

Milena hissed a stream of invective in Czech.

Gabbard looked puzzled at first, then he nodded. "As I said, it defies comprehension."

"So this monster rapes his own daughter," Milena said. "Then he terrifies his own son into running off and drowning—"

"He tried to escape down the Loire," Gabbard interjected. "By boat. The police found the boy's handkerchief on the pier. That's how they knew. Louise must have told you."

"How is it that your wife didn't ask the police to investigate what the bastard did to his daughter?"

"The situation wasn't as simple as that," Gabbard said. "You have to understand this family."

"I think I'm beginning understand them well enough."

"For a boy to disappear without the authorities getting involved is unthinkable, no matter how closed-off a family may be."

"Degenerate is what you mean."

"Please, Mademoiselle. I understand that you are upset." He made an aimless gesture with his hands. "Believe me, this story makes me as sick with revulsion as it does you. But let us not forget that my niece and my wife are de Benoîts, as well. Would you damn them along with their relatives?"

For one black second, Milena wasn't sure what to answer, what to think. How well did she know Louise? Could she assume that she was not as rotten as the rest of the de Benoît clan, if only in a less pernicious manner? She got close to bolting from her chair and leaving the apartment, leaving this entire nauseating tale behind. An instant later came a sting of shame. Whatever troubles plagued Louise were not of her own making; she was a victim. And she needed help. "I'm sorry," she said. "Please go on."

"As far as Frédéric's disappearance was concerned, police involvement was inevitable," Gabbard said. "As for the other matter—"

"Louise paints your wife as a strong woman who had firm convictions," Milena interrupted. "How do you justify her failure to alert the police to what her brother had done to Louise? Was it just so much easier to sweep that under the familial rug?"

Gabbard stared at the tabletop as though searching for something hidden underneath the polished wood. "Do you have any idea how difficult such things can be to prove?"

"Are you joking?" Milena strained to keep her voice down. "This was practically minutes after the rape had occurred!"

"And I assume you imagine the officers could have just walked into the de Benoît residence and examined the girl based on Corinne's accusations? It would have been her word against Francois's." He shook his head. "No, Mademoiselle. Hours, if not days would have gone by before anyone competent would have examined Louise. If an inquiry would have been undertaken at all."

"So your wife just figured it wasn't even worth trying?"

"One thing you must know about my wife," he said, "is that she was never given to emotional outbursts, to impulsive action. Had I been in her place, I would have thought and acted much like you would have, I assume, and confronted Francois. But Corinne always thought ahead."

"Ahead to what? To leaving her perverted brother untouched and free to keep abusing his child?"

"That is exactly the crucial point," Gabbard said. "Corinne knew that open accusations might not achieve anything except a final and irreversible break of relations with her brother, and subsequently, destroy her chances to continue seeing, and protecting, her niece. You cannot fail to see that Louise was going to need an ally."

"An ally who did nothing," Milena snorted.

"Not so," Gabbard said. "You see, Corinne may have judged police involvement at the time to be of little use, something I believe she was right about. But that doesn't mean Francois wasn't afraid of a scandal."

Milena frowned. "I'm not following."

"Tours may not be a village, Mademoiselle. But Louise's father is sufficiently well-known there in certain circles, due to his esteemed position at the hospital. After Frédéric's death, speculation was rampant. Even the most benign interpretation of the circumstances had to involve, at the very least, suspicions of criminal neglect. If rumors of incest and rape had been added to this…" Gabbard turned up a palm toward Milena as if inviting her to finish the sentence.

"She could hold the threat over his head indefinitely." Milena was beginning to appreciate the aunt's aptitude for long-term strategy, even if the cold rationale of it disturbed her.

"Like the proverbial sword of Damocles," Gabbard said. "Corinne kept visiting, every Christmas and every summer, and sometimes in between. Any sign of Francois repeating his crime, or even simply trying to keep Corinne away from Louise, and she would have brought scandal down on his head. As you can see, her way of handling matters was far more beneficial to Louise in the long run."

"But over the years, the power of her threat must have diminished. People forget. Even rumors and suspicion fade. Especially since she held no real proof."

"Very true," Gabbard said. "But you forget Louise grew up. My wife spent as much time with her as she could, and the girl trusted her like no one else in her family."

"She mentioned that, in fact."

"They went on little trips together in the summer. Usually for a week or so, just the two of them. Francois could hardly object, after all. Nothing happened in Louise's life that Corinne would not know about, I assure you. And as she grew older, she was essentially on stand-by to corroborate any accusations Corinne would have made against Francois. He realized this far too late."

Gabbard smiled grimly. "Even a decade after that terrible night, Corinne and Louise's testimony combined would still have destroyed him. Perhaps not in court, but certainly socially and professionally."

"Then why didn't they do it? He deserved it."

The smile faded from Gabbard's face. He looked suddenly old and tired. "I think Corinne meant to. But she died before she could carry out her plan."

"She shouldn't have waited so long," Milena said.

"She had to. Louise turned eighteen on January eighth, 1962. After that, no matter what happened, her parents could no longer force her to stay with them. Unfortunately, the accident that claimed Corinne's life occurred only three weeks later."

"I see. I am sorry."

"So am I, Mademoiselle." He folded his hands in front of his face again. "So am I."

In the silence that followed, the only noise Milena heard was the sound of rain drops beginning to tap, with increasing urgency, on the window pane behind her. Daylight was slowly failing. Shadows began to fill the room.

"I should go," Milena said. "This is a lot to think about."

He nodded. "Entirely too much, I fear. Allow me only one more question before you leave, Mademoiselle."

Milena pulled her coat from the backrest of her chair and slipped it on. "Go ahead."

"Louise is unaware that I know this story. And I doubt that she meant for you to hear it. In a way, I have invaded the trust that is between you and her."

"I won't bring any of this up with her."

"And your friendship? Does knowing what I told you change anything?"

Milena stood up. She held on to the chair. Still shaky. Her stomach, too, felt unstable. She shook her head, or thought she did. Nothing seemed entirely real.

•

Gabbard walked her across the darkening room to the hallway. He flicked a switch. The sudden illumination made Milena blink. When she had first entered the apartment, she had been too apprehensive to pay attention to the photographs that covered the wall above a chest of drawers. The pictures were set in small frames of all shapes and colors. Several were old family pictures in fading sepia shades. A few were in color. There were also a number of black and white images of more recent date with sharp, crisp contrasts. One of these immediately caught her eye. It showed a tall woman in an elegant black dress, standing next to a moss-covered garden urn mounted on a tall pedestal. Her right hand rested on the shoulder of a stone faun clinging to the side of the urn, as if she was holding the creature back in its effort to scale the vessel. The woman's posture was straight, almost regal, and she smiled at the photographer with a self-assurance that bordered on hauteur. Her eyes resembled Louise's, although her gaze was far more guarded, and her hair was longer and darker. Milena guessed that she was in her mid-thirties.

"I forget what year that was taken," Gabbard said. "Sometime before we got married, at any rate."

"This is Madame de Benoît? Your wife?"

"You've never seen her picture? I would imagine Louise must have at least a few."

"She's never shown me any," Milena said. "She was very attractive."

"There was something about her," Gabbard said. "A presence. You couldn't quite describe it." He smiled faintly as he gazed at the photograph in its bronzed frame. "I believe she is in her garden here, in Montmorency. She owned a house there once. She sold it several years before we met."

"I don't think I've ever seen a faun like this before," Milena said. In truth, the creature's expression was nothing short of hateful. Its posture, too, was strange: the goat legs were coiled underneath its body as if it was about to launch itself, curved horns first, at the onlooker. It looked less like a playful nature sprite than a demon. But Corinne de Benoît's hand, so nonchalantly resting on the figure's shoulder, made the faun appear small and impotent, it's fierce malevolence rendered inert stone by the power of her touch.

"The urn was sculpted after Corinne's own specifications," Gabbard said. "I think she was still in art school when she designed it."

Milena's skull began to throb as if it wanted to split along the sutures. She had a momentary vision of her head popping open like some sort of seed pod, scattering her thoughts into the air like a cloud of pollen. All she wanted at this point was to be back out in the street, inhale the fresh air, and find a bistro where she could get some water and an espresso or two. "I've taken up far too much of your time, Monsieur Gabbard."

"Not at all," he said. "I cannot thank you enough for coming."

Milena hurried down the stairs. She was on a landing two floors below when she heard his door fall shut.

•

For about half an hour, Milena sat under the awning outside a small café on the Boulevard Saint-Michel and stared into the rain glittering in the streetlights. A jumble of raincoats and umbrellas slipped past her, blurry ghosts in the somber street, hurrying in a million directions. She had come here to straighten out her thoughts, but so far she wasn't succeeding.

The waiter set another espresso down in front of her, along with the tab, and politely informed her that he was about to finish his shift. Milena paid for the coffee. She sipped the fresh espresso and the bitterness of it hit her as though she tasted it for the first time in her life.

No wonder Gabbard thought Louise might have tried to kill herself. How one could live with a past like hers, bear the weight of it with you every day, everywhere you went, without being able to talk to anyone about it, not even someone close to you—it had to be a very lonely version of hell. But Louise wasn't trying to end her life, Milena remained convinced of that. Aside from the nature of her wounds, the diligence with which she tended to them, and the care she took to ensure they remained invisible, there was the fact that she considered suicide a sin. But there had to be a connection all the same. Between her past, her constant injuries, and her faith. Especially Saint Geneviève.

Milena drank the rest of the espresso all at once, without thinking. It scalded her tongue. The pain sobered her. Suddenly, she understood.

•

It wasn't until Monday evening that Milena had a chance to go to the university library. A long wait that she shortened by closing the boutique an hour early.

She knew the location of the stacks she accessed regularly by heart; a glance at the call number was usually enough for her to get an approximate idea of where to look for the volume she wanted. The Religious Studies section was another matter. For the first time in years, she had to consult the floor plan.

Half an hour later, she was so deeply immersed in the text she had sought that she didn't take note of the footsteps approaching her desk until they stopped next to it. She looked up and saw Marcel standing beside her, smiling. "Catching up on some reading?"

"As you can see."

"It's been a while since I've seen you." He crouched next to her table. "Since anyone's seen you, really."

"I was busy over the weekend," she said. "You know how it can get."

"True, true. But there was a meeting of the UJCML on Thursday that I would have thought you'd definitely attend. Unless you were there and I didn't see you for some reason."

"I decided to miss it. I'm not that partial to Maoism, as you know."

"Which is why I figured you might show up and say a few words."

"Maybe next time," she said.

He nodded. "Lots on your mind these days?"

"What is this, Marcel? I skip one meeting of an organization I don't even support and everyone gets concerned?"

"No," he said. "But you didn't show at Oriflamme on Saturday evening, either."

"Shit." She sighed. "I completely forgot." She knew she was blushing. She'd been with Louise, until well after midnight, recovering from their long and exhausting walk and even more exhausting talk on the banks of the Seine.

"Don't worry about it," Marcel said. "We all have lives to live, right?"

Milena didn't know what to say. In the life she had intended to live, you didn't forget about meetings.

"Besides, you weren't the only one," he said. "Jacques didn't come, either."

She gave him a look. "What does that have to do with me not being there?"

"Nothing, of course." He pursed his lips. "Well, actually, I wonder."

"Wonder what? I have to read this, Marcel, and they'll be closing soon. If you want to say something, say it."

"I don't think I've seen you and Jacques in the same room in months," he said. "To be honest, I got the feeling that he didn't come on Saturday because he expected you to be there. Did you have some sort of falling-out or anything?"

"Why don't you ask him that?"

Marcel stared off along the rows of tables for a few moments. He looked at her again and wrinkled his nose. "I did."

"So what did he say?" Milena gestured at the book in front of her. "Don't make me drag every single word out of you, Marcel."

"All right. He told me you didn't turn out to be who he thought you were, and that I should leave it at that."

"Then perhaps you should."

He smiled. "I had a feeling you'd say something like that. It's just a little awkward for me—I should say for us, really, this affects Jeanne, too, and Pauline, I imagine—because we're friends with both of you."

"I can't help that," Milena said. "But just so you know, I never gave him any false hopes. He developed certain ideas all on his own."

"I have no trouble believing that."

"And he'll get over them all on his own, too."

"Well, let's hope so." Marcel stood up and rubbed his knees. "Anyway, are you coming to hear Laurent Schwartz speak on Wednesday? Ought to be interesting."

"I'll be there. Definitely, this time."

"Great. I'll see you then." As he turned to go, he glanced at the book on her table. He grinned. "The stories of the Saints?"

"It's for a paper," she lied. "I just need one reference for a footnote."

"Why don't you check it out?" he said. "Then you can read it as you sip your favorite church-manufactured liqueur."

"Very funny. But it's non-circulating."

"Ah, too bad. Until Wednesday, then."

"Until Wednesday." She waited until he disappeared between the bookshelves. Then she continued to read.

•

On Wednesday, Milena barely managed to squeeze through the crowd that spilled out of the auditorium. There was no room left to sit inside. She spotted Pauline standing by the wall at the back and made her way toward her. Everywhere around her, students were arguing, trying to make themselves heard over the confusion of voices. She could pick up shreds of conversation in passing: the proposed reforms, the consequences one believed they would have—devaluation of degrees, selective admissions, the end of free education, of academic freedom, even.

She was familiar with all of these issues; she had been laboring for months to increase awareness of—and opposition to—the government's reform plans among her fellow students. Consequently, there could be no question as to why she was attending a talk by a proponent of these reforms. But after her conversation with Marcel, she couldn't shake a nagging feeling that part of the reason for her presence here today was the need to prove to everyone, most of all herself, that her dedication to the issues at hand had not wavered.

She cleared her path through the crowd a bit more aggressively than necessary, as if she could push her unwanted thoughts out of the way along with the people in front of her. She had to mutter numerous apologies before she reached the spot where Pauline was standing.

The chaos in the auditorium enveloped the stage at the front as well, where one person after another tried to get the attention of at least part of the assembly. It was difficult to follow the exchanges. Milena gathered that a general consensus had begun to emerge not to let the scheduled speaker speak at all.

"But that's ridiculous," she said into Pauline's ear. "What are they afraid of? That Schwartz will open his mouth, cast some sort of spell, and charm us all into supporting the reforms?"

"Who knows," Pauline said. "I just want to hear why a man like him would back them in the first place."

Milena shook her head. "I still have a hard time making sense of that." Laurent Schwartz, celebrated mathematician, former Trotskyist, co-signatory of the 'Déclaration des 121' against the war in Algeria along with Sartre and Simone de Beauvoir, an act that had cost him his position at the École Polytechnique, and a vocal opponent of the Vietnam war—why would such a man speak out in favor of so technocratic and socially divisive a project as the Fouchet reforms? "The least we can do is hear him," she said. "Out of sheer curiosity, if nothing else."

"Definitely," Pauline said. "We can always send him to hell afterwards."

"Afterwards, yes. But if we get into the business of flat out silencing unpopular opinions, we're no better than our opponents."

Pauline tapped Milena on the elbow and nodded toward the entrance. "There's Jacques. And Marcel."

The two men stood by the door, casting about for a spot to move to. When they saw Milena and Pauline, Marcel smiled and waved. Jacques made eye contact with Milena, gave a brief nod, and looked away. Pauline gestured for them to come over. Jacques said something into Marcel's ear, Marcel nodded, then Jacques began to squeeze through the crowd, in the direction of the stage. Marcel shrugged at Pauline and followed him.

"Jesus," Pauline said. "Jacques is still smarting?"

Milena nodded. "He's been avoiding me since that evening at his apartment."

"Perhaps you should tell him that you're seeing someone. It might make it easier for him to accept that you said no to him."

"So a woman needs to be in a relationship before her word carries weight?"

"That's not what I meant," Pauline said. "I meant for his sake. Psychologically."

"Besides, I'm not seeing anyone."

Pauline opened her mouth to say something, but the noise in the room rose in pitch and cut her off. A surge of activity swept through the crowd, and a large number of students climbed up on the stage. Everywhere in the room, people rose to their feet. Milena stood on tiptoes trying to see what was going on. She caught glimpses of a slim man with close-cropped white hair, wearing a dark suit, approaching the podium. He tried to speak but was immediately shouted down. After a few minutes of this, a young man motioned to be heard. She recognized the crown of red curls and the jovial smile of Daniel Cohn-Bendit. The crowd began to quiet down.

Milena turned to Pauline. "You can tell Jacques what you want, of course. If you think it'll help him get back to normal. That's best for everyone involved, isn't it?"

Pauline nodded, but it was hard to tell if she was really listening.

Still smiling, Dany suggested that Laurent Schwartz be allowed to speak, and that one would decide afterwards whether he, and everything he had come to say, was rotten or not, a proposal which was met with widespread approval.

•

The next day, in the afternoon, Milena paid another visit to Gabbard. Once again, she sat in the rigid chair at the somber table. There was no coffee, this time. Gabbard had been about to pour his evening brandy when she called, and had waited for her to arrive before taking it. His well-assorted bar included Chartreuse. A glass of it stood in front of her now, untouched. They exchanged a few brief and perfunctory remarks on politics and Laurent Schwartz's position on the Fouchet reforms. After that, Gabbard sipped his brandy and waited for her to speak.

Milena decided that there was no more need for dancing around things. "I think I know the truth about Louise's injuries."

Gabbard froze in the middle of swirling his snifter. It rested in his palm, motionless except for the brandy that continued its undulations inside the glass. "The truth?"

"There is something I didn't tell you," Milena said. "What happened that day, when you saw the blood on her hand, was not an isolated incident."

"Good God," he said. "I was right, then."

Milena shook her head. "Louise was not trying to kill herself, Monsieur Gabbard. The incisions on her arms were made with care, away from the veins."

"Made with care? By whom? By herself?"

"I see no other possibility."

"Then how can you judge this to be anything else but a suicide attempt?" For the first time, an expression of vexation passed over Gabbard's face. "Especially considering she bled so heavily. Through her coat, for Heaven's sake."

"Many cuts bleed badly without being fatal," Milena said. "Let's also not forget that Louise is a devout Catholic. To her, suicide is a sin."

Gabbard's expression regained some of it characteristic mildness. But he still looked frustrated. "I'm beginning to wonder if my niece's original version of events is not the most plausible one, after all."

"Normally, I would agree," Milena said. "But when I removed her bandages, I saw that her arms are covered with cuts and scars. Not just the ones that were bleeding that day. Some of them must go back years and years."

"You mean she has done this before?"

"Many times. And she is still doing it. I keep seeing new bandages on both of her arms. She tells me that her skin heals slowly, forcing her to wear them for long periods of time. In truth, they come and go."

Gabbard frowned. "In all the time I've known my niece, I never once saw her bare arms, not even in summer. How come you were able to notice these things?"

"You know how women are. We're not quite as careful around each other as we are around male relatives."

"Did you ever ask her why she keeps having these injuries?"

"It's always a different version of the same story. Accidents at work. Broken glass, box-cutters, that sort of thing."

"But that's absurd," Gabbard said. "The only remotely dangerous tool my niece regularly uses at the gallery is a letter opener. She never works with the art directly, nor does she do any of the packaging. That's what my wife hired Maurice for."

"Your wife? I didn't realize he's been at the gallery for so long."

"Oh, yes. Corinne hired him at least five or six years before Louise arrived in Paris. I still held Louise's current position at the time."

"Be that as it may," Milena said. "The fact is, I accepted her explanations so far. I'm not proud of it. I should have pressed her for the truth, but I was too afraid to alienate her."

"Don't be too hard on yourself, Mademoiselle. Remember that she threatened me with quitting her job and leaving if I kept asking her questions. You had little to gain by pushing her."

"I should have done it no matter what," Milena said. "I feel like a coward."

"But if you doubted her explanations, and at the same time you do not believe in suicide attempts, just how do you account for those injuries?"

"It all has to do with God," Milena said.

Gabbard stared at her over the rim of his snifter. "With God?"

"I suspected that Louise was inflicting these wounds on herself on purpose. I just couldn't for the life of me imagine what that purpose was. Until you told me about her past."

Gabbard put down his snifter without drinking from it. "You will need to explain this to me, Mademoiselle."

"There is a picture Louise keeps in her apartment," Milena said. "An icon of Saint Geneviève."

"I am familiar with the icon," Gabbard said. "I gave it to Louise as a present, on her nineteenth birthday. It came out of a collection an older client of mine offered for sale several years ago, which comprised some thirty or so icons, all in all. It is quite valuable."

"Why this particular one?"

"Louise chose Saint Geneviève at her confirmation," Gabbard said. "When she was twelve years old. I think she was always interested in her, even before that. But what does this have to do with her injuries?"

"Do you know anything about Saint Geneviève, Monsieur Gabbard?"

He thought for a moment, then shook his head. "I do seem to recall that she is the patron saint of Paris, but that's all. I don't have any particular enthusiasm for such things, I am afraid."

"I don't either," Milena said. "Nevertheless, I went to the library on Monday and consulted the Legenda Aurea. The Lives of the Saints."

"A voluminous tome, I'm sure."

"It's full of stories of martyrdom and suffering in the name of God, as one might expect. I wanted to know why Saint Geneviève is so significant to Louise. Part of her story is pretty morbid." Milena took a sip of the Chartreuse. The flavors of the liqueur expanded in her nose and on her palate like a fiery vapor. A moment later, the warmth filled her stomach. She took another sip, then she put her glass down. No point in getting tipsy. "Among other things, Saint Geneviève is known to have averted the sack of Paris at the hands of Attila. I guess that's what gained her the status of the city's patron saint."

"I do recall hearing that story, now that you mention it."

"But it's hardly what attracts Louise to this figure." Milena pulled her notebook out of her purse. "I wrote down a couple of passages from the text that I found significant." She slid the opened notebook across the table toward Gabbard.

He frowned at her handwriting for a moment and began to recite the first sentence. "This holy maid did great penance in tormenting her body all her life, and became lean for to give good example." He looked up. "I'm not sure if I understand, Mademoiselle."

"Saint Geneviève spent a good deal of time in Tours exorcising foul spirits from the bodies of demoniacs with holy oil and prayer," Milena said. "One quote I found in that context made my skin crawl. It's underneath the one you just read."

Gabbard recited the next passage, tracing the text with his finger as he read. "Anon after, it happed as she was in orisons in a corner in the church of Saint Martin that—" He paused, his frown deepening. "That one of the singers was so sore vexed with the enemy that he ate his members."

"The man sought Saint Geneviève's help," Milena said. "She subsequently managed to drive the foul spirit out of his body and free him from the demonic taint he suffered."

"But what is the significance? Many saints performed exorcisms, Mademoiselle. Just as there must have been others who mortified their own flesh in a quest for purity."

"Of course. But this one did her godly work in Tours. And her icon stands on the night table of a young girl from that city who repeatedly inflicts mysterious injuries on herself." Milena decided not to mention the lacquer box with the white shard of glass in it. The thought of it made her feel ill. "A young girl who, at least once in her past, was subjected to the closest thing to a demonic taint I can imagine. There's your significance."

"Jesus Christ." Gabbard sat back in his chair. "She is trying to cleanse herself?"

Milena nodded. "Your niece is living through hell in an endless bid for salvation."

•

Gabbard emptied his snifter and poured himself another brandy. Milena slowly sipped what was left in her glass and let him reflect on her findings.

"It makes sense," he muttered. "Dear God, it makes sense."

"Yes, that part does make sense." Milena finished her Chartreuse. He offered to refill her glass, but she waved him off. "But one thing does not. Not to me, anyway."

"What do you mean?"

"The demon in this story, the fiend who is responsible for your niece's suffering, is her father."

Gabbard swallowed. "It would certainly seem so."

"Then how can you, knowing her story, urge Louise to reconcile with this monster? You want her to set aside her memory of the crime he perpetrated against her, and console him on his deathbed? How can you seriously believe her father deserves such mercy?"

For a long time, Gabbard looked at her without saying a word. Milena held his gaze. Eventually, he faltered and directed his eyes at the shiny wood of the tabletop. He still didn't speak.

"I don't really expect an answer." Milena reached for her coat.

"Please, Mademoiselle."

She sat and waited, coat on her lap.

"There is a chance that my wife's account of the events of that night may be untruthful," he finally said. His expression looked strained like that of a man undergoing physical torment.

"What on earth are you talking about?"

Gabbard got up. "I'll be back in a moment," he said.

•

Milena stared at the sheet of paper he placed in front of her. About half a page of text, type-written. At the bottom was an arabesque scrawl that, in spite of all its intricacies, she was easily able to identify as the signature of Francois de Benoît. She recoiled. "What am I looking at?"

"A letter Francois sent to my wife shortly after Louise left Tours and came to live with us," Gabbard said. "Corinne had told Louise what her father had done to her only weeks before. I found it among my wife's papers after her death. Please read it."

Reluctantly, Milena scanned the lines of jagged typeface. Louise's father hadn't wasted a word. The letter warned Corinne that he was going to make use of certain documents at his disposal—he seemed to assume that she knew perfectly well to what he was referring—to destroy her reputation and her marriage. The final sentences were so unexpectedly poignant that, for an instant, Milena's revulsion toward the man wavered.

'You have poisoned my child against me,' he wrote. 'I know now that she is lost to me, and that the damage your lies have caused may never be undone. But do not think your triumph will come to you without a toll. Only the thought of the pain it will cause Louise and Claude to find out whom they have trusted so many years makes me hesitate. But you should pay the price of your betrayals. Burning for burning. Wound for wound.'

"Exodus 21, 25." Milena looked up. "Very dramatic. But nothing more than the ravings of a criminal trying to cast his accuser as a liar."

"It would seem easy enough to take that stance."

"You don't seriously believe there is anything to this?"

"I admit that the tone of his letter gave me pause when I first read it," Gabbard said. "I even tried to contact Francois to ask for an explanation."

"And?"

"Let the dead rest. Those were his only words before he hung up on me. I wrote Louise's mother to see if she would tell me more, but unsurprisingly, she refused. She repeated the same words, in fact."

"What did you expect?" Milena snorted. "He obviously never had anything in hand. This letter is nothing but an attempt to intimidate your wife. He was obviously furious that she finally told Louise the truth about him."

Gabbard fiddled with his snifter. "But what if?"

"Look, I understand if it bothered you that he might know some embarrassing secret about your wife," Milena said. "But even if he did, it wouldn't change anything."

"I resigned myself to that notion, in the end," Gabbard said. "What choice did I have, after all? Francois was not talking to me, and Corinne was dead. Whatever had happened to Louise lay in the past, unchangeable, the damage done. But what you told me today changes everything."

Milena frowned. "How so?"

"Because the past is not dead, Mademoiselle. If what you said is true, my niece is reliving it again and again, maiming herself, bleeding, never escaping the shame of what was done to her. Isn't it worth considering even the slightest chance that the past may not be what she thinks it is?"

"Are you suggesting we should pretend Louise's father never raped her, simply because he claims your wife made the whole thing up?"

Gabbard shook his head. "Of course not. But what if Corinne, for whatever reason, distorted the truth?"

"The attack Louise suffered was no invention," Milena said. "She may have been too small to remember the details, but you yourself said that she remembered enough."

"Pain, and a sense of suffocation, yes. But such impressions could have been left behind by some other event, some sort of draconic punishment, a bad beating, anything."

"I can't believe you're even considering this," Milena said. "This is insane."

"No, it isn't." Gabbard voice betrayed the strain of trying to ignore the heat in Milena's tone. "Think, Mademoiselle. What would be the worse defilement, in the eyes of a young girl with strong religious feelings? The idea that her father battered her, in whatever intemperate fit of rage—or to believe that he forced himself on her?"

Milena closed her eyes. She massaged her forehead. "Why would your wife want Louise to believe such a thing, unless it was the truth?"

"Corinne and Francois had many quarrels," Gabbard said. "God only knows how much bad blood there was between them."

"So your wife would ruin her niece's life by telling her such a monstrous lie, all in order to get back at her brother?" Milena opened her eyes and looked at Gabbard. "Are you prepared to accept the possibility that the woman you married was capable of that?"

"I am, Mademoiselle. If it means we could help Louise."

"I hate false hopes," Milena muttered. But she already felt her heart clutching at this one. It was possible, after all. Louise's memories of what had happened to her were vague and incomplete. When her trusted aunt filled in the gaps years later, what reason would she have had to doubt her?

"We have nothing to lose," Gabbard said.

Milena took a deep breath. "If your wife's account of what happened was untrue, why didn't Louise's parents ever try to tell her their version of things, whatever it was? I imagine that's why they came to Paris."

"Of course they tried. Francois pleaded with Louise to listen to him, telling her that he was innocent. She wouldn't hear of it. I'm sure later on they sent her letters explaining it, but she destroyed them unread, no doubt."

"And that's why this letter is meaningless." Milena nodded toward the piece of paper lying on the table between them. Neither of them seemed willing to touch it. "It was his word against your wife's back then, and it continues to be so. Louise would believe nothing he says or writes. I'm far from giving her father the benefit of the doubt, but even if you and I were to do so, it makes no difference."

Gabbard nodded. "Unless there is something to these documents he mentions."

"And what could that possibly be? Some awkward secret or other about your wife? They were siblings. They must have known thousands of embarrassing things about each other."

"He talks about the pain his revelation would cause to me as well as Louise," Gabbard said. "And he hints that we would find our trust in Corinne betrayed."

Milena made a dismissive gesture. "Of course he would write things like that. He was furious at her."

"But what if, Mademoiselle?" Gabbard leaned toward Milena; for a moment, she half expected that he was going to grab her by the shoulders and shake her. "What if he had something in hand, something palpable and irrefutable, something that would call Corinne's trustworthiness into question in such a way that even Louise would have to begin doubting her?"

Milena looked into his eyes. "As would you."

He sat up straight again. "The truth wants strong followers, Mademoiselle."

"Gustav Meyrink," Milena muttered. Part of her mind puzzled absently over when she had last read any of his stories.

"We could open my niece's eyes," Gabbard said. "Make her receptive to other versions of the past. We might be able to lift the taint she sees in herself, and end her suffering."

Milena nodded. She was exhausted. Entering the world of Louise's family, even in thought, was like a bloodletting. The de Benoîts seemed to be one rotten apple after another from the same rotting tree. She reminded herself that Louise had sprung from the same line. But didn't her solitude, her suffering, and her sadness redeem her, make her pure? She liked to believe so. A bitter smile took shape on her lips, shielded behind her hands. What a very Christian conception of things. Old habits did die hard. She inhaled deeply and drew herself up in her chair. "Then you have to contact your brother-in-law one more time, Monsieur Gabbard. We must find out what he was referring to in the letter you showed me."

"I don't look forward to trying," he murmured. "Especially not at a time like this."

"There could not be a better time," Milena said. "He may be eager to set things right, now that he's at death's door."

"He may simply wish to take the whole affair to his grave."

"Tell him what is at stake." Milena slipped into her coat. "Tell him that the truth may bring Louise to him. What else matters now? And if he won't or can't talk to you, try her mother. But you better hurry." She got up. "I can show myself out."

Milena left him sitting by the window. She looked back once before she left the room. He remained at the table, hands folded before his chin, as if in prayer.

As she passed through the hallway, her eyes sought the photograph of Corinne de Benoît standing in her garden. There was no mistaking what hid, thinly veiled, behind the cool smile. Arrogance, disdain, and cruelty.

•

The following day at Nanterre, Milena witnessed a brawl on the way to one of her classes. The sight of students exchanging blows in the hallway was strangely and shockingly different from the confrontation with the police in which she had participated in January. At first she was unsure what was happening, but when shouts vowing to throw the "Bolshevik scum" out of French universities rang out, she knew that the fire-eaters of Occident had begun to make good on their threats of violence against the Left. As she watched the scuffle, stunned, she wondered what would happen if she ever got embroiled in a physical confrontation. She doubted that even right-wing thugs would actively attack women. As for her own self-restraint in the face of growing provocation, that was another question. Fortunately, the week concluded without her having to test her aptitude as a pugilist.

On Saturday evening, she sat in Louise's kitchen, eating a sort of pie that Louise called a Tarte à la Moutarde in spite of the fact that the main ingredients appeared to be eggs, cheese, and tomatoes. The food was delicious, but Milena ate mechanically, without savoring it. There had always been things of which she and Louise did not speak, questions Milena had not asked when she should have done so. But now, knowing what she did after her conversations with Gabbard, it was no longer a matter of accepting one version of the truth and closing her eyes to other, more troubling ones. She was standing on a fragile bridge, unable to ignore the abyss that yawned underneath no matter how much she might refuse to look down. She stabbed her fork into the pie in frustration. There had to be a way of getting across to the other side, to solid ground. A way to cast light onto the bottom of the pit, stare at it in all of its horror, and be done with it. But the choice was not hers alone to make.

"Have you heard any news of your father?" Milena asked.

Louise shook her head. "Why would I?"

"Your uncle is in contact with your mother. She writes him, doesn't she?"

"That's their business," Louise said. "Not mine."

"I'd think you might at least want to know if your father was dead or not."

"I read that your friend Dany was arrested today," Louise said. "If you want to talk about something that interests me."

"I didn't know it did. You've been following the news, then?"

"I read my uncle's Figaro now and then."

"God, is that what he reads? Please try L'Humanité instead. Or at least Le Monde. If you want something resembling the facts, instead of opinion."

"Sometimes I have the radio on at the gallery."

"Don't simply believe everything they say, either. The ORTF is government controlled."

"I know that," Louise said. "In any event, they say your friend attacked another student."

"And did they mention that it was someone from a right-wing organization?"

"They said the other person belonged to a group called Occident."

"That's them," Milena said. "I've seen these thugs start one fight after another this week. There's no doubt in my mind that Dany was only defending himself."

"So much violence." Louise put down her fork next to her empty plate. Her appetite had been improving in recent weeks, but only gradually. "What is it about these reforms that has everybody so on edge?"

Milena was taken aback by the question—was it possible, not to know these things? But Louise, unlike most people, inspired nothing but patience in her. "You have your baccalauréat, I assume?"

Louise lowered her eyes. "I left Tours very suddenly."

"Without taking the bac?" Milena knew from her conversation with Gabbard that Louise's departure from her hometown had been sudden. But with all the tragedy and drama surrounding that decision, she hadn't given thought to its implications for Louise's education.

Louise shrugged. "I can still do it in the future, can't I?"

"Definitely." Milena took another slice of pie. "You should look into it." At any other time, she would have been eager to explain all the ins and outs of the Fouchet reforms and their impact on French education to Louise. But the concerns of the outside world seemed distant tonight, nearly unreal. The past loomed larger, closer, even if it remained unapproachable.

"Well, what about the bac? What does it have to do with those reforms?"

"Once you do get your bac, you're basically entitled to free admission to a university, or other forms of higher training."

"I would love to study art," Louise said. "Like my aunt."

"That sounds like a good choice for you. But if the reforms proposed by Monsieur Fouchet pass, admission may no longer be free. It may not necessarily pose a problem to you, but students from underprivileged families might no longer be able to pursue their educational goals."

"But that would be unfair," Louise said. "If they pass the bac, haven't they earned that opportunity?"

"Of course they have. But restrictions on admissions is not all the reforms are about. You see, de Gaulle's government believes that the purpose of the university should be to serve the interests of the new French economy, which has more use for scientists and administrators than for, say, art historians. And they want the universities to produce them quickly and efficiently."

"That's not necessarily a bad thing."

"Not in itself, no," Milena said. "But think about it. You say now you would like to study art. So you enroll in a few classes and begin studying. What if you suddenly realize that art doesn't suit you, and that you would rather do something different?"

"I suppose I would go ahead and change my course of studies," Louise said. "What else?"

"What else, indeed. But if the Fouchet reforms pass, you would have to choose your path early on, and adhere to it rigorously, fulfilling very specific requirements in a limited period of time. The university system would no longer allow for experimentation, for time to find out who you are and what you want to do with your life, and to change your mind if you felt you didn't make the right choice right at the beginning. You'd have to stick with it."

"I can't imagine wanting to study anything but art," Louise said. "But I had a lot of guidance from my aunt. I suppose without that, I would need more time to decide what suited me."

"Exactly. And the government wants to take away your freedom to find yourself. They want to turn the university into a factory that churns out trained stuffed geese, as someone put it, ready-made servants of the state, of a society stripped of its humanity. I've seen enough of that in my own country."

"I'm beginning to understand why de Gaulle is your archenemy," Louise said.

Milena frowned at the piece of pie crust skewered on her fork. "I don't know if I would put it that way."

"Really? Doesn't he stand for everything you oppose, all the policies and philosophies you detest?"

"It's never quite so simple," Milena said. "No one person embodies all that is wrong with a way of thinking, a way of looking at the world. Not de Gaulle, not Johnson, not Brezhnev. Not even someone like Stalin."

"You don't believe evil can be present in a person?"

"And how does such a judgment help us?" Milena shook her head. "What is important is to understand what makes people do the things they do. The circumstances that produce them. That is where lessons can be learned."

"I don't think people like Hitler or Stalin deserve our understanding," Louise said. "No matter what made them commit their crimes."

"They may not deserve it, Louise. But we owe it to ourselves to understand them. Because if we don't, they will never stop haunting us."

Louise made no response. For a moment, Milena was afraid that the all-too obvious allusion had irritated her. But she merely got up, took her plate to the sink, and began to wash the dishes. "I don't like the idea of these scuffles that are happening in your school," she said after a while. "What if you have to defend yourself against any of these thugs?"

"So far it hasn't happened," Milena said. "But I'm ready for it."

Louise made a face.

Milena brought her own plate to the sink and stood next to Louise. "What's the matter?"

"I don't want to have to worry about you."

"Ježíše Marie." Milena kissed her on the cheek. "There's no need."

"I don't know," Louise said. "I have a feeling what happened this week was only the beginning."

"I doubt things will get much worse," Milena said. But she wasn't sure of that at all.

•

Milena was alone in the apartment in Levallois, about to retreat to her room with a cup of tea and a book, when Gabbard called the following evening.

"I spoke to Louise's mother," he said. "Francois is not taking any calls, nor receiving visitors. Or perhaps just not mine."

"And? Any success?"

"I tried to bring up the matter of his letter with Louise's mother. She was indignant at being asked about what she considers ancient history, especially at a time like this."

"Did you explain to her what is at stake?"

"She would barely let me speak after I told her what I was calling about," Gabbard said. "I wanted to tell her that Louise might be persuaded to see her father if we could show her whatever documents he had referred to, but she wouldn't hear of it. She thinks all I want is to find out whether my wife had something to hide from me."

"Ježiše Marie, doesn't her daughter's suffering mean anything to her?"

"I wish I could have explained to her about that," Gabbard said. "But you will have to admit that it would take much more time and willingness to listen than she accorded me. Still, the forcefulness of her refusal puzzled me. I have a feeling that Francois is behind this. He must wish to take this secret to his grave, after all."

"He seemed willing enough to spit it out when he wrote the letter to your wife."

"But he also said he was reluctant to hurt me and Louise," Gabbard said. "I think he never really meant to go through with it. Who knows, perhaps the revelation that would have been so inconvenient for Corinne would also have reflected poorly on him, or even the rest of the family."

"I don't really give a damn," Milena said. "If Louise's parents are unwilling to help us, this is the end of the line. Unless you can think of some other way of getting at those documents. If they even exist."

"Of that I am certain," Gabbard said. "Now more than ever."

•

Five days later, courses at Nanterre were suspended due to the unabated violence at the school. There was only one place to go. The next day, a Friday, Milena arrived in the courtyard of the Sorbonne, together with a group that included Pauline, Marcel, and Jeanne, but not Jacques. The crowd around them was considerable, but not particularly overwhelming. Speeches were held, points to be debated were declared. What was going to be done about the lock-out at Nanterre, and the arrest and threat of expulsion faced by Dany and seven more students accused of leading the so-called agitation?

Then there were the more visceral threats.

"Occident burned down the office of a student association yesterday morning," Marcel said. "They mean business."

"Are you sure it was them?" Milena asked.

"They left a big Celtic cross painted on the wall," Jeanne said. "I suppose they wanted to be sure no one had any doubts as to their involvement. And there's this." She handed Milena a crudely printed flyer.

Milena scanned the text. It contained the characteristic vows to oust the 'Red Terror' from French universities by whatever means necessary, as well as more specific plans to drag Daniel Cohn-Bendit to the French-German border and toss him out of the country. She handed the flyer back to Jeanne. "The usual brutish drivel."

"It's still not something we should dismiss," Marcel said. "We knew their main tactics are intimidation and violence. But arson? That's a whole other story."

Milena looked around the courtyard. She saw a number of mostly male students who had shown up wearing crash helmets and carrying various types of sticks or clubs. "I guess it is going to get worse."

By the late afternoon, trouble did arrive, but not in the form of thugs from Occident. Pauline, who had meant to walk to a tabac for cigarettes, returned within a minute.

"That was quick," Marcel said.

"The school's surrounded," Pauline said. "Police. Lots of them, in riot gear, truncheons ready. I think they have gas grenades, too. This is not looking good."

"What the hell?" Jeanne spat on the ground. The vulgar gesture was characteristically incongruous with her delicate stature and features. "We haven't done a thing."

"Some people broke a few tables earlier," Marcel said. "To make clubs out of the legs, I think."

"That hardly constitutes a riot."

"Whatever the reasons," Milena said. "Someone lost their nerve, probably Rector Roche, and now the flics are here. What do we do?"

The question soon occupied the entire assembly. A few people called for an all-out confrontation, but eventually the majority agreed that they should avoid a fight.

"That's for the best," Pauline said. "We're sitting in a trap here as it is."

The consensus on non-violence had barely emerged when the flics began to pour into the courtyard. Someone shouted that they had heard no one was to be arrested if the crowd dispersed peacefully. Milena glanced at the policemen pushing people toward the opposite exit with their truncheons. She had her doubts as to any guarantees.

"Let's go," Pauline said. "No point in risking arrest. We don't want to be the last ones the flics mop up."

Outside, another surprise awaited them. Instead of clear passage away from the Sorbonne, they faced a whole fleet of Black Marias. Everywhere, policemen where busy throwing students into the vehicles.

Milena cursed in Czech. "So much for letting us go peacefully."

"This way." Marcel grabbed her arm and dragged her to the left. Pauline and Jeanne were already ahead of them. They slipped along the outer walls of the Sorbonne. Milena's heart pounded. Fisticuffs, tear gas, these things she was prepared for, mentally at least. Arrest, however, could mean jail, and a conviction, deportation. In other words, separation from Louise, most likely for good. Not to mention the disruption of her academic career. She was reluctant to admit it to herself, but in her heart she knew perfectly well which one of these consequences frightened her the most.

Somehow, they made it into a side street. Milena spotted a few flics standing by a corner, but they made no move to pursue them. A large number of other fugitives—the term struck her as overly dramatic, but wasn't that what they were at the moment?—were already milling about in the street, some exchanging hushed remarks, others arguing forcefully, but all clearly undecided, for the time being, as to what to do next.

"Well," Pauline said. "The time for passing around petitions is definitely over." She cocked an eyebrow at the flics by the corner. Behind them, more policemen were running in the direction of the Sorbonne courtyard, truncheons in hand. "We can't just let this happen."

From the far end of the street, rhythmic shouts of a multitude of voices rang out again and again: "Free our comrades!"

"Let's do it," Milena said.

•

Pauline's closed eyelids fluttered slightly. It was the only sign of discomfort she showed. "You really are pretty good at this," she said.

Milena dropped the alcohol swab into the trash can. "I still think we should have gone to a hospital."

"It's just a laceration." Pauline groped around the kitchen table until she found her cigarettes. "Other people got much worse."

"Hold still," Milena said. "I'm putting the gauze on." The gash in Pauline's forehead probably looked more serious than it was. But it was still a harrowing sight. It ran from the outer edge of her right eyebrow upwards past her hairline and about two inches into the bright red strands. Her otherwise cream-colored scalp was swollen and purplish around the wound. "Jesus, Pauline. I'm going to have to run a bandage around your whole head to hold this in place."

"I can't wait to see Alain's face."

"Don't expect him to see any humor in this," Milena said.

A scratchy voice from the transistor radio on the table informed them that the confrontations between students and police were continuing past sunset.

"We should have stayed." Pauline lit her cigarette. In spite of her nonchalant demeanor, her hands were still shaking.

"Not the way you were bleeding," Milena said.

"The gloves are off, Milena. They have definitely come off today."

"You could say that." Milena fixed the bandage in place with a safety pin and took a step back to inspect her work. "This should hold. At least through the night."

The telephone rang in the hallway.

It was Jeanne. "They released Marcel. I thought you'd want to know."

"That's a relief," Milena said. "Although I'm not that surprised. What charges would they bring, after all?"

"You never know. How's Pauline's head?"

"I just finished patching her up. She's got a huge headache. But I think she'll be all right."

Milena hadn't walked more than two steps from the phone when it rang again. Louise, this time.

"I've been listening to the radio," she said. "You were there, weren't you? At the Sorbonne."

"Of course I was," Milena said. "But don't worry, I was neither hurt nor arrested." She decided not to mention Pauline's lacerated forehead.

"Oh, thank God. I heard that they arrested hundreds of people."

"They'll let them all go again, I'm sure. They have to. No one committed any crimes."

"How long is all this going to go on?"

"Until they release the students they arrested," Milena said. "And until they reopen the universities, and withdraw the police from our campuses. The government must realize that they won't silence or control us by using force."

"And if they don't realize it?"

"Then each act of violence that they perpetrate against us will cause their legitimacy to disintegrate a little more, until it finally and completely crumbles. In either case, we will have won."

"It won't do you a lot of good if they throw you out of the country," Louise said.

Milena forced a laugh. "Why on earth would they do that?"

"The Figaro writes that your friend Dany should be deported. If they convict him of a crime, or disturbance of the peace, whatever it may be, they could do it, because he's not a French citizen."

"You're well informed these days. Even if you get your information from that reactionary rag."

"I almost wish I wasn't," Louise said. "What if they arrest you? You're not a citizen, either."

"They're saying that about Dany because they consider him one of the ringleaders," Milena said. "I'm neither notorious nor important enough to merit that kind of attention."

"You're important to me."

"I'll be careful," Milena said. "I promise."

When she returned to the kitchen, Pauline was no longer there. A crushed cigarette in the ashtray, only half smoked, still sent a thin thread of smoke up into the kitchen lamp. Milena picked it up and extinguished it under the faucet, then she walked down the hallway to Pauline's room and knocked softly on the door.

"Come in."

The room was dark. In the swath of light admitted by the half-open door, Milena saw Pauline lying on her bed, still dressed, shielding her eyes with her arm.

"Are you all right?"

"I thought I'd give you some privacy," Pauline said.

"It wasn't that kind of call, Pauline."

"Okay, chéri. I'm also exhausted. My head feels like an anvil dropped on it."

"Of course. I'm sorry. Do you need anything?"

Pauline slowly shook her head. "Just for the aspirin to kick in."

In the dark, in her own bed, Milena relived scenes of the day that lay behind her: being chased by the flics, the fear of arrest, visions of jail; Pauline getting clubbed, the blood running down her face, and the frantic race home. Hours seemed to go by before her thoughts finally slowed down. Again and again, she returned to the memory of her phone conversation with Louise. Every word Louise had said, every word she had answered. Because it had been that kind of call, and Pauline knew it too.

•

The next day, in the evening, Milena was studying in her room when the phone rang in the hallway. She ignored it. Nothing dramatic had happened during the day, and a call from Louise was unlikely. She heard Pauline's footsteps approach from the kitchen where she was cooking dinner. A moment later, Pauline knocked on her door. "It's for you."

"Who is it?"

"He didn't say. He certainly has a very nice voice."

It was Gabbard.

"I just spoke to Louise's mother again," he said. "Francois has taken a turn for the worse."

"With all due respect, I don't see how that concerns me anymore."

"He's not long for this world, as the saying goes." He paused. "Which gave me an idea."

"You think you can still get him to tell you about the letter, after all?"

"Hardly. And I certainly do not intend to incur his wife's ire by raising the subject again. My relations with the de Benoît family are strained enough as it is."

"I don't see why you should care, at this point."

"I might still be able to mediate between Louise and her mother at some time in the future," Gabbard said. "But for the moment, my main concern is that I will be attending Francois's funeral. I would not wish to add strife to grief."

"I don't mean to be rude, Monsieur Gabbard, but I was in the middle of—"

"Please hear me out, Mademoiselle Beranovà. Like I said, I will make it quick." Another pause. Brevity was not Gabbard's forte; apparently he had to plan his sentences ahead when forced to be concise. "In the past, when I visited the family château with Corinne, I sometimes spent time with Francois in his study. It is the only room in the house where we could smoke, you see. Louise's mother is highly averse to tobacco odors."

Milena remained silent but made sure the receiver picked up her forceful exhalation.

"I know where he locks away his most important documents," Gabbard said. "There is a special compartment in his secretaire. And I still have Corinne's old key to the house."

"So you intend to burglarize them?"

"As I said, I will have to attend the funeral. Along with every member of the household, including the personnel. The château will be entirely empty for several hours."

"Pity. The perfect opportunity, but you'll have to miss it."

"Indeed, indeed." He cleared his throat. "Unless, that is, I should be able to prevail upon someone to assist me."

Milena peered around the corner toward the kitchen door. Luckily, Pauline was making a din banging various dishes and pots around. "You're crazy," she hissed into the phone. "You know what the consequences would be if I got caught?"

"That is extremely unlikely, Mademoiselle."

"What makes you think I would even consider this?"

"If Francois truly has information that casts Corinne as a liar, think about what that would mean to Louise," he said. "She might be willing to consider someone else's view of her past. A less painful one."

"And whose would that be? Her father will be dead by then. This whole insane plan of yours hinges on that fact, doesn't it?"

"Her mother could still speak to her. I am counting on the documents in Francois's secretaire to support what she says."

"Forget it," Milena said. "It's too dangerous. Ježiše Marie, I could get kicked out of the country!"

"I already explained to you—"

"What if someone returns from the funeral unexpectedly? Not that I am in the least considering going along with this scheme."

"I would keep an eye on everyone," Gabbard said. "If anyone leaves, I'll call the phone in Francois's study to warn you. There would be ample time for you to leave."

"Besides, what good does it do to get into the house? You just said yourself, he keeps his important documents locked away."

"It's not as much of an obstacle as you may think, Mademoiselle. I can teach you how to pick the lock on the secretaire."

Again Milena looked toward the kitchen. She lowered her voice. "What?"

"Mind you, I have never in my life been involved in anything remotely illegal." The matter-of-fact calm with which he explained his bizarre proposal was infuriating. "But in my business, now and then, you are faced with the need to access what has been barred. People pass away without providing their children the keys to collections locked away in particular rooms, cellars, or attics, objets d'art in ancient armoires, and so on. I learned a thing or two from a locksmith whose services I frequently employed."

Milena listened with a mix of bafflement and fascination. Was this quiet, elderly gentleman seriously suggesting that she break into Louise's parental home and rifle through her father's secretaire, after picking the lock on it? She would have laughed, had she been able to bring herself to believe that Gabbard was joking. "I'm sorry, Monsieur Gabbard. I don't know what your niece has told you about me. Perhaps I am something like an anarchist or a rebel in your eyes. But I'm certainly no burglar."

"I understand," he said. "An old bourgeois like me, contemplating such a murky scheme, I know just how ludicrous it must sound. But consider what is at stake here. We could change Louise's life."

"What makes you think I care enough to get involved in something like this?"

"You're Louise's friend, aren't you? Her only friend, in fact."

Milena closed her eyes. She shook her head, even though he couldn't see her. "I have work to do, Monsieur Gabbard."

"All I ask is that you think about it, Mademoiselle."

"Fine. But don't get your hopes up."

She hung up and walked slowly into the kitchen. Pauline was pouring pasta from a box into a pot of boiling water. She smiled when Milena entered. "Almost ready."

A saucepan full of tomato sauce bubbled on the back burner, splattering occasional red eruptions onto the white enamel of the stove. All Milena could think of was blood.

•

Pauline's forehead barely had two days to heal. Over the weekend, Dany was released from jail along with several other so-called 'ringleaders' and most of the almost six hundred students that had been arrested at the Sorbonne. But on Sunday, four of the demonstrators were given prison sentences. Both Nanterre and the Sorbonne remained closed, the latter under police occupation. Things were neither going well nor likely to calm down.

"We need to make the worst fear of the bourgeoisie come true," Jacques proclaimed during a meeting that had been organized at Oriflamme. "The student movement must join forces with the laborers. Alone, we're easily portrayed as elitists, as an isolated segment of the population, sitting in an ivory tower, and easily dismissed. But if the university strike is joined with that of the workers, I assure you that the forces of oppression will be shaking in their boots."

In a corner, sitting by herself with a glass of Chartreuse, Milena applauded, along with the entire assembly. But before the night was over, she found herself on her feet in the middle of the room, in a fierce argument with Jacques. It began in a civil enough fashion. "Why should we have to forge links with the unions before we act?" she asked him. "We don't have that time. Our comrades in jail don't have that time. I will welcome a joining of forces with the workers when it comes, but who says we cannot set off the detonation that needs to shake the establishment on our own? We are able to do it. In fact, we have an obligation to do it, to play our own part, without being adjunct to anyone."

The argument wasn't new. Many of the more traditional groups didn't agree with it, while most of the more radical ones did. Nevertheless, the point was, by and large, hardly divisive. But Jacques's response, addressed to her across the crowded cellar, sounded singularly personal. "I know your firmest beliefs are rooted in the notion that no one should need anyone," he said. "But this is not a time for hotheaded loners to storm in, paving stone in hand, and make a mess of things."

The debate went downhill from there until Milena and Jacques and the respective factions siding with each of them were bellowing at each other at the top of their voices. They refrained from actual insults, but there was no shortage of mutual accusations: complacency versus radicalism, waffling versus recklessness, bourgeois slickness versus ideological anarchy. In the end, during a lull in the general tumult, Milena was incensed enough to fire a single searing barb at him. Perhaps he deserved it.

"So this is what happens when a man can't deal with rejection," she snorted. "Do you always use political debates to vent your personal frustration, Jacques?"

Jacques stared at her, petrified. For a moment she was certain that he would launch himself at her with a scream of rage. But after an instant, his shoulders sagged. The silence in the room was unbearable, like some flexible thing stretched beyond its limits, ready to snap at any moment with a devastating noise. The breaking point never came. Jacques cleared his throat, turned around, and sat down without a word. The entire room collectively exhaled. Gradually, conversations resumed, in little clusters here and there. Milena saw Marcel leaning over and saying something to Jacques, but he made no response. He just sat there, staring into space.

Milena returned to the corner where she had sat most of the evening. Pauline came over, gauze bandage still around her head, with a fresh shot of Chartreuse. "I guess he needed that."

"Maybe." Milena accepted the glass. "But I didn't."

•

Milena closed her eyes and groaned. "Ježiše Marie," she hissed through clenched teeth. "Are you done yet?"

Louise shook her head. "It needs to be properly cleaned, or you'll get an infection."

"All right." The stinging in Milena's arm wore off a little. How did Louise stand it? How had Pauline managed to barely flinch?

"It's a deep cut," Louise said. "A little deeper, and you would have needed stitches." She screwed the cap back on a small bottle of iodine.

Milena inspected her arm. The cut ran from the base of her right thumb in a straight line across the inside of her forearm. It had stopped bleeding sometime during her walk—or jog, rather—from the Sorbonne across the Ile de la Cité to Louise's apartment. But in the center, it still glistened wetly. All along its length—some five inches, from end to end—it was rimmed with a rust-colored perimeter of dried iodine solution. The bite of the disinfectant had been ferocious, like a pack of minuscule wolves sinking their teeth into her flesh.

"You're lucky it didn't go further to the side," Louise said. "You could have severed a tendon, or one of the veins in your wrist."

"I suppose you know every bit of what's under the skin in these areas."

Louise shrugged. "It's common knowledge."

Milena didn't feel like challenging the point. As she watched Louise fluidly wrapping her arm in reams of gauze, she saw the edges of a bandage under Louise's own sleeve. The irony of the situation was not lost on her.

"I knew you wouldn't stay away from trouble," Louise said. "But what in the world possessed you to help flip over someone's car?"

"That was not what I set out to do today, I assure you. It was supposed to be a peaceful demonstration."

"What went wrong?"

"Do you have any idea what's going on out there? The police have blocked the Sorbonne off like a fortress."

"I've seen it on the news." Louise said. "They do look intimidating."

"And that's exactly what we can't allow them to do, intimidate us."

"So you decided to provoke them?"

"We did nothing except to call for the reopening of the campus, and for the withdrawal of the police. Suddenly, they charged. I couldn't believe it. There were people lying on the pavement right and left when the assault was over. The flics had simply clubbed them down."

"Put your thumb on this for a second." Louise fished two bandage clips out of a small container. "It sounds like a scene from a war."

"This is a war," Milena said. "The government wants nothing more than for the French people to think that what is happening is just a confrontation between a few rowdy students and the police. But it concerns society as a whole. It's not just about the universities."

"But all the destruction that happened," Louise said. "The cars, the pavement. Even trees were ripped down, I heard. How can you justify those things?"

"We were under attack, Louise. I'm not talking about flics wanting to simply grab people and pack them into the Black Marias. They chased us down like dogs. Everywhere people were being brutally beaten. I saw a young woman getting clubbed by four flics at once. We had no alternative but to fight back. But they were armed to the teeth, and we had no weapons, no shields. We had to improvise some means of slowing them down, of protecting ourselves."

"Jesus Christ," Louise murmured. "Why are they so ruthless?"

"They thought we'd be easily cowed," Milena said. "When they realized that we resisted, and successfully, they got mad. And believe me, the residents of the Quartier were on our side, in spite of the damage we caused defending ourselves. They encouraged us. People screamed at the flics to stop the beatings."

Louise looked at her. "Don't get me wrong when I ask about the things that were destroyed," she said. "I'm just thinking of those people looking for their cars, and finding them wrecked." She lowered her eyes and checked the bandage for proper fit. "Perhaps you think of me as materialistic. But I wouldn't hesitate to give up everything I own, if it helped protect you."

The throbbing in Milena's arm seemed suddenly far away. "I would do the same for you."

Louise took the medical supplies back to the bathroom. When she returned, she sat down next to Milena. "You must be hungry," she said.

"I have to leave soon. It's past eleven."

"You have to eat something. After the day you've had."

Milena reached out with her unhurt hand and removed one of Louise's hairpins. A few pale blond strands unfurled; Milena felt them between her fingers, caressed them, played with them. So soft to the touch. So smooth. Like silk. "What if I miss the last Métro?"

"Then you'll stay here."

"For the night?"

"It wouldn't be the first time."

"That was different," Milena said. "I was sick."

"And now you're injured. It's not so different."

"Yes, it is," Milena said. She kept caressing Louise's hair, her ear, the gentle curve of her jawbone. Heat pulsed in her fingertips, in her throat, her temples. Her mouth was dry. Perhaps Louise was right. What was this, if not some sort of fever? "I don't want to trouble you."

"It'll be no trouble at all," Louise said.

Milena kissed her softly on the corner of the mouth. "I'm not so sure about that," she whispered.

•

Jeanne planted her black banner between her feet, propping the pole against her shoulder, and struck a match inside cupped hands. In the 10 PM darkness, the small flame lit up her palms like a vigil light.

Milena yanked the flag away from the burning match. "No need to start a fire." The sudden motion sent a sting through her arm. Louise had changed the bandages in the morning, fastening them a little more tightly so they would last through the day.

Jeanne grinned as she puffed the cigarette to life. "Not yet, anyway." She studied Milena's face and cocked her head. "Something's different about you tonight."

"What are you talking about?"

"I'm not sure," Jeanne said. "You look as if you want to keep smiling, but are forcing yourself not to."

"I'm just excited to be here." Milena took in the crowd surrounding them. Their numbers had to be in the thousands. Even now, marchers kept pouring in from the Champs-Élysées to join the gathering around the Arc de Triomphe. Indifferent, the monument towered above them, illuminated by the spotlights as on any other night, crowds or no crowds. Milena had only visited the site once, during her early weeks in the city. Through the moving silhouettes, she caught glimpses of the memory flame on the Tomb of the Unknown Soldier, twitching in the shadows under the massive arches like a solemn reflection of Jeanne's match. "I wonder what he would have thought of all this."

"The guy who's buried there?" Jeanne shrugged. "He probably just wants some peace and quiet. Poor bastard. I'd take the Montparnasse cemetery over this spot any time."

"Let's hope we don't end up there, before this is over."

"I don't think there's reason to worry," Jeanne said. "Today's been pretty quiet, so far. Just a lot of marching. And no one's gotten killed yet, even on the worst days."

"Assuming we've already seen the worst days."

Jeanne extended her pack of cigarettes to Milena. Milena shook her head. "Thanks."

"You stopped smoking?"

"I cut down."

"I noticed." Jeanne put the cigarettes away. "Any particular reason?"

"I got sick a while ago. After that, it started hurting my lungs."

"I guess that's good, then. I'm afraid the only way for me to stop right now would be if I did it for someone else. Of course, Marcel smokes like a factory chimney, so no luck there."

"I just don't enjoy it anymore."

"Marcel told me you're seeing someone," Jeanne said. "He heard it from Jacques. Is that why you look so happy?"

"Jacques told him that?" So Pauline had gone ahead and dropped a remark, after all. Perhaps it was for the best, although Jacques's recent behavior at Oriflamme seemed to indicate the opposite.

"You know, for the longest time, I thought there was something going on between you and Jacques."

"Well, there isn't. And there never was."

"Talk about something I couldn't wrap my mind around," Jeanne said.

"What do you mean?"

"Come on. He's not good-looking enough for you. Don't quote me on it, but the idea of you with him, Jesus…"

"I suppose I should be flattered," Milena said.

"I know it's not all about looks, but still. I'm with Michel de Montaigne on this point: in my bed, beauty comes before virtue."

"That's a bit superficial, isn't it? Besides, who says we can't have both?"

"Oh, ideally, sure. If you want to get serious, maybe." Jeanne flashed another grin. It lent her face something undeniably winning, in spite or perhaps because of the brazenness behind it. "But that's the last thing on my mind, these days."

"Marcel will be happy to hear that."

"Are you kidding?" Jeanne snorted. "He's not exactly gearing up to settle down, let's put it that way."

"You two are a good match, then."

"For the time being. But tell me about this mystery man you're seeing." The grin again. "Beautiful, or virtuous? Or both?"

Milena sighed. What harm could there be in simply telling the truth—in part, anyway? "Both," she said.

"The luck," Jeanne said. "I suppose it's no one I know?"

"I wouldn't think so."

"And in bed?" Jeanne flicked the spent cigarette to the pavement, barely missing someone's leg. "Fireworks?"

Milena felt heat rush into her cheekbones. "You cant' ask me that."

"Why not? Unless of course you haven't slept together yet."

"I'm not going to respond to that, either."

"I never took you for such a prude," Jeanne said. "Unless of course, you're not talking because it's something very serious."

"What would you consider serious, anyway?"

"It depends. How long have you known each other?"

"About two months," Milena said. "A little over."

"Then it all comes down to one question." Jeanne assumed the air of a doctor listening to a patient describing the history and symptoms of a moderately serious illness. "Are you in love?"

"In love?"

"Yes. You can tell me that much, can't you?"

"It's not that simple, Jeanne."

"Mon Dieu." Jeanne laughed. "Of course it is. If there's one thing I know, it's that."

Suddenly, from the farther reaches of the crowd, a melody surged toward them. A thousand voices began to intone the Internationale. Within moments, the sound engulfed them. Jeanne elbowed Milena in the ribs. "Come on." She began waving her black banner and joined in the singing at the top of her voice.

Milena sang along in Czech, wondering if the lone soul interred underneath the Arc de Triomphe would be horrified or elated to hear the hymn of communists, socialists, and anarchists worldwide sweeping over his tomb. She turned to look at Jeanne next to her, belting out the words in French, brandishing the immense flag above their heads. The sight made her smile. There were times when Milena felt like throttling her, for her cockiness, for her lack of tact. But tonight was not one of them.

·

Milena shook out her umbrella in the staircase and stepped into the apartment. Her feet were wet from another long march, this time through never-ending drizzle. Aside from a tense passage through the Latin Quarter, during which the demonstrators were keenly aware that the slightest incident would end their fragile truce with the police force, it had been a quiet day. Too quiet, in Milena's opinion: when they arrived at the Jardin du Luxembourg, she was among the many who lingered and debated the possibility that the uprising was fizzling, its demands about to be buried in deals made, for the sake of peace and quiet, between parties and unions who still felt only a tenuous solidarity with the students.

She had stripped off her damp shoes and clothes when the phone rang. It was Louise.

"Uncle Claude just called me," she said. "My father died an hour ago."

"My God. I'm so sorry."

"He held on for three weeks. Can you believe that?"

Because he hoped that you might still change your mind, Milena thought. "Do you want me to come over?"

"If you like."

Milena listened for a change in Louise's voice, a sob, perhaps. But there was nothing. "Give me forty minutes."

She got dressed again in a hurry. Just as she finished putting on dry shoes, the phone rang again. Gabbard.

"I assume you have heard the news, Mademoiselle Beranovà."

"Louise just called." Milena hesitated. "I'm on my way to see her."

"I'm sure she will welcome the company," he said. "I won't take up much of your time, then. But I need to ask you what you have decided, with regard to my proposal."

"I figured as much," she said.

"This is an opportunity that will never come back. I hate to sound clichéd, but it is literally now or never."

"I understand. I'll do it."

There was a pause at the other end of the line. "I'm glad that your response is so decisive, Mademoiselle. And so swift."

"Does that surprise you?"

"Somewhat, yes. I know how, shall we say, peculiar you thought my plan was."

"I still think that," Milena said. "But then life is peculiar, most of the time."

"Indeed. Very good. There will be some preparations we need to make, and soon. The funeral is to be held on Friday morning."

"Friday? That's two days from now."

"I am aware that this leaves us little time," he said. "But on the bright side, we can be done with this venture

the sooner, and, God willing, see the results that much
sooner, as well."

"Hopefully."

"Are you available tomorrow afternoon,
Mademoiselle? Some time after four? I doubt it will take
more than a few hours, to teach you the basics."

"I should be free then," Milena said. She looked at
her bandaged arm and wiggled her fingers.

•

Milena found herself searching for signs of grief,
in Louise's face, in her voice. There was nothing. She felt
guilty for her disappointment. Would it have been so much
better to find Louise in tears, her porcelain face swollen,
her voice cracking at every word? More reassuring,
perhaps. But to whom? She stepped into the apartment.
Louise shut the door. It closed with its soft click, its
assurance of privacy.

Milena held her, standing by the kitchen window,
while they waited for tea water to boil.

"I'm so sorry," she whispered into the blond hair.

Louise touched her hand and nodded. The kettle
whistled, and they separated.

They sat down on the couch in the living room
with their cups, close to one another. Milena put an arm
around Louise's shoulders. There was nothing she could
say, nothing she needed to say, perhaps.

"I wish things could have been different," Louise
said eventually. With a quick, almost angry gesture, she
erased a first few tears from her face.

Milena thought about asking her, yet one more
time, to change her mind, to make the trip to Tours. But it

would be no use, she knew. She kissed Louise's temple. "Perhaps they can be, still."

Louise shook her head. "The past is what it is." She put down her teacup and settled more deeply into Milena's embrace. Outside, the last of the gray light faded into the silent drizzle.

•

Claude Gabbard poured a stream of black coffee into a china cup. "Milk or sugar?"

"Black is fine," Milena said.

"I understand there has been quite a gathering today on the Boulevard Saint-Michel."

"The campuses are still closed." Milena blew on the steaming coffee and took a sip. Hot, bitter, and strong. "We have to hold lectures somewhere."

Gabbard pursed his lips. "It wasn't exactly a lecture in the conventional sense, though, was it? Monsieur Cohn-Bendit was there to give a speech, I hear. My niece mentioned that you know him personally?"

"He is a student of Professor Lefebvre's, like me."

"I see. And Louis Aragon dropped by at the Boulevard?"

"He did speak, barely. People weren't terribly eager to hear a functionary of the Communist Party."

"Why is that? I would imagine your movement has much common ground with them?"

"We share common ground with the workers," Milena said. "But the Communist Party itself doesn't want us intruding on its turf, simply put. So they try to discredit us as a band of bourgeois brats dabbling in populist politics, lest we unite with their base. I believe that the

PFC is no more interested in upsetting the status quo than the Gaullists are."

"Then why did Monsieur Aragon come to your gathering?"

"Personally, I admire Aragon," Milena said. "He is another one of those people willing to question the orthodoxy, even though he has always been loyal to the party. I think it was very courageous of him to come today, considering we don't trust him and his party does not trust us."

"Placing himself between two chairs, as they say."

"Very much so. In spite of the mixed reception he got, he promised to devote an issue of his journal to the student movement."

"Even so, I imagine today must have been rather uneventful for you," Gabbard said. "Compared to other recent days."

"I have a feeling it's the lull before the storm."

"It could be. From what I've been hearing, the crucial issues are far from being resolved." He frowned suddenly. "What happened to your hand?"

Milena looked down. Her right sleeve had ridden up her wrist, revealing the long strip of adhesive bandage covering the cut in her forearm. "It's nothing," she said.

He exhaled audibly. "You will excuse the bluntness of my question, Mademoiselle. But my experiences with my niece…"

"Believe me, I have a very healthy relationship with pain," Milena said. "The only way I will ever end up injuring myself is by accident. I got this cut while we were improvising a barricade on Monday."

"A barricade? You mean, in the Latin Quarter, during the confrontations between the students and the police?"

"Does that surprise you? I thought you knew my politics."

"Why, yes," he said. "I suppose I just didn't imagine you would be so directly involved in the fighting."

"And why wouldn't I be?"

Gabbard glanced at the wall clock on the far side of the room. "I hate to cut our conversation short," he said. "But I'm afraid we need to start attending to the business at hand."

"Probably." Milena finished her coffee. She accepted the refill he promptly offered her.

Gabbard got up and disappeared into one of the other rooms. Milena heard him rummaging around for a while. He returned to the living room holding a rolled-up leather sheath, which he unfolded on the table. It contained a number of metal staves, each about six inches long, tapering out into a variety of hooks, rakes, and saw-like shapes. Her first impression was of a set of dentistry tools, or perhaps the implements used by a medieval torturer.

"This is a fairly standard array of lock picks," Gabbard said. "There are more intricate sets, but I am quite sure that, for our purposes, these will do perfectly."

Milena nodded, staring at the tools in front of her. "It looks complicated."

"It can be," Gabbard said. "If you needed to be prepared to open any number of different locks, the time we have would most certainly not suffice for you to learn enough. But I've seen the lock on Francois's secretaire. I assure you, it is not likely to be very difficult to open. You might even manage it simply by taking these and fiddling around for a bit. Nevertheless, we can shorten the time it will take you if you practice first."

"All right. So what do we do?"

"Very simple." Gabbard picked up the leather sheath and got up. "This is a skill that is best learned by doing."

•

Gabbard sat on a chair and watched Milena as she tried her luck on the doors of an ancient cherry wood armoire. "This was Louise's room," he said. "During the weeks she stayed with us."

The room was situated toward the back of the apartment, facing what Milena assumed to be the courtyard. The curtains in front of the single window made it difficult to see what lay in the darkness on the other side. A bed occupied the middle of the room, faced by a desk and chair on one side, by the window, a dresser and mirror opposite its foot end, and the massive armoire whose lock Milena was trying to pick on the other side. The walls were covered with paper bearing a floral design in pastel tones. A cheerful room for what had to have been, at the time, an utterly cheerless girl.

"I notice that you're having difficulty moving your left arm," Gabbard said. "Another injury incurred during the riots?"

Milena shook her head. "An old fracture."

"May I ask what happened?"

"I was at a Christmas party, in Prague, eight years ago." She inserted another one of the metal staves into the lock. She was beginning to get a feel for the components of the mechanism, or so she thought, but so far, whatever movement she was able to effect inside the lock did not cause it to open. "A friend gave me a ride home on his motorcycle. We'd had quite a bit to drink, and the streets were icy. At a turn in the road, he lost control of the bike, and we crashed into a lamp post. I woke up in the hospital with a shattered shoulder blade. My friend was luckier, he just had a few bruises."

"Your shoulder blade was shattered? You must have fallen in the most unfortunate fashion."

"Evidently."

"It's a very thick bone to break," Gabbard said. "It would take an impact of considerable force."

"You know your anatomy, I see."

"I studied painting, when I was young. For a while, I think I knew as much about the human skeleton and the muscles clinging to it as any doctor."

"I wouldn't stake much on what my doctors knew," Milena said. "As you can tell, the fracture didn't heal properly." She twisted the pick in the lock, gingerly poising it against what resistance she felt. With a gravelly crunch, the bolt moved, and the armoire's door swung open.

"Excellent." Gabbard checked his wristwatch. "Under ten minutes on your first try. I'm willing to say that makes you something of a natural, Mademoiselle Beranovà."

"Thank you." Milena wasn't sure if she should take pride in her new-found aptitude. Gabbard kept pointing out the countless legitimate uses of the skill, but it was hard to forget that lock picking was among the tools employed regularly by the State Security to spy on Czech citizens, making it the kind of talent you felt dirty to possess.

"Let's do it one more time," he said. "Just to make sure it wasn't a fluke, as the expression goes. Then we'll move on to something else."

"All right." Milena locked the armoire again and started over.

"Do you ever find yourself blaming him?"

"Blaming whom?"

"Your friend," Gabbard said. "The one who drove the motorcycle. It was his responsibility, after all, what happened."

"I was aware that he'd been drinking. I could have refused the ride."

"Perhaps. But even so. He put your life at risk, not you his."

"Laying blame doesn't change anything, does it?" Milena selected a second pick and inserted it into the lock. There could be no doubt that she felt more confident of what she was doing. For a second, the possibilities seemed dazzling—for someone considering a career as a burglar, or a state-licensed spy.

"Was he someone with whom you were romantically involved? If you'll forgive my inquisitiveness."

"Not exactly," Milena said.

"I see." Gabbard fell silent for a while. Milena hoped that he was done with his questions. Much as she had refined and retold her story, each telling brought with it the fear of getting caught in inconsistencies. Sometimes she wondered if her abhorrence of lies was really motivated by moral principles, or by a lacking flair for fiction.

"I hope you did not deem it expedient to incriminate the male population in general," Gabbard said. "Not all of us are so irredeemably reckless."

"Did I give you the impression that I hate men, Monsieur Gabbard?"

"Oh, no, certainly not. But my niece—" He laughed quietly. "She told me quite a bit about you, as you are undoubtedly aware. But she never mentioned any personal attachments."

"Between my studies and my political engagements, I have little time left for such things."

"I understand. It's none of my business, of course." There was another silence, punctuated by the clicks and scrapes Milena produced as she moved the picks around inside the lock. But she knew that he wasn't done with the subject. "My niece, you know, is much like you in this regard. For different reasons, evidently."

"In what regard, exactly?"

"In all the time that I've known her, she has never had male company, to the best of my knowledge."

"I have male company all the time. Not that it's always welcome."

"You know what I mean, Mademoiselle."

"Perhaps she's picky," Milena said. "Or perhaps you don't know as much about what goes on in her life as you think." She wasn't sure why, but she was beginning to take a sort of perverse pleasure in these veiled exchanges.

"That is possible, no doubt." Gabbard sighed. "We're no longer nearly as close as we used to be, during her early months in Paris. But what I really fear is that it is the past that stands between my niece and happiness."

"And you think it's the same with me?"

"I apologize if I gave the impression that I meant to make conjectures about your private life, and your past. But the injury you suffered—" He paused. "If the young man at fault had been close to you…"

"It was someone close to me." Milena put down the lock picks. "But I don't blame her."

"Her?"

"It was a girl." She turned to look at him. For a moment, she saw her father. She squared her jaw and started working on the lock again. "The reason why the whole thing happened."

"I'm not sure I understand, Mademoiselle."

"I don't blame her," Milena said. "Nor anyone else. Let's leave it at that."

"Of course. I'm sorry."

Milena gave the lock pick a twist while at the same time gently pushing it upwards. She felt the tumbler give. A dull click reverberated through the cherry wood as the bolt slid aside, and the door opened.

"Bravo," Gabbard said. "I suggest we try my silver cabinet next. It is quite a bit older than the armoire. I suppose it will present a suitable challenge."

Milena returned the lock picks to their leather sheath. "Are older locks more difficult to pick, in general?"

"In many ways, they are simpler, more fundamental, in their construction," Gabbard said. "But they are less willing to move, in a manner of speaking, and they offer more resistance." He smiled. "Even with the proper key, they can be hard to open."

"I see," Milena said. "Let's give it a try."

•

They stood in the attic again, under the window. It was still raining. The sound of the drops hitting the grimy pane above their heads was less subtle than the whispering snowfalls in February, perhaps, but Milena found it just as magical. More pronounced, and clearer. The way many other things had become. The attic wasn't as cold as it had been in winter, either. They still had to wear coats, but it was easier to stay warm; they had gotten used to standing closely together, with their arms around each other. Every so often, the wind turned and blew a thin spray of rain into their faces.

Someone had hung laundry earlier; on the clotheslines behind them, white sheets billowed in the cool air. They never encountered anyone in the attic: Louise seemed to have a knack for choosing those times to come up here when no one else did. Outside the narrow window, the surrounding roofs stretched into the night, all the way toward the looming outline of Notre Dame, a massive but somehow still insubstantial shadow, its outlines blurred by darkness and rain. Milena felt Louise's hand slip under her jacket, caressing the spot under her left shoulder where she knew the scars to be. She had taken to doing this since Milena had told her the story. It felt good, it felt sweet, it made Milena want to turn and kiss her, even on the chance that, improbably, someone else was watching them from another attic window, another roof somewhere. Perhaps one day they would get to a point where none of that mattered any longer. But for now, admitting the desire to herself represented the pinnacle of Milena's courage. She watched Louise's face in the near darkness. Her eyeliner had begun to run because of the repeated gusts of rain. Here came another one. She blinked. Tiny black specks of mascara dotted her lids. She looked less ethereal, less rigid now than during the first days of their acquaintance. Still pale, but warm; fragile, but not in such a way that one might think she could shatter, irreparably, like a vase made of bone china. Milena brushed Louise's forehead with her lips. Watch them whoever might care to.

"I'm going to be out of town tomorrow," she said. "But I should be back in the evening."

"Okay." No question as to where Milena was going, what she was doing. It wasn't surprising, of course. Entire days, sometimes several in a row, regularly went by without them seeing each other, without any explanations being offered or requested or, for that matter, needed. There was the university, work, the demonstrations. But tomorrow wasn't going to be a day like any other. They both knew it.

"Uncle Claude won't be in Paris, either," Louise said. "He's going to Tours."

Milena nodded. "To the funeral, I presume."

The hand on her shoulder intensified its caresses. "Can you forgive me? For not going myself?"

"It's not for me to forgive you," Milena said. "I'm just afraid you won't be able to forgive yourself, in the end. More than ever."

"Why do you say that?"

"I don't know. I keep thinking, what if?"

The hand stopped. One finger rested, lightly, in the deepest of the dimples, the most severe scar. "What if what?"

"I don't know," Milena repeated.

"You don't despise me, for the kind of person I am? The kind of person who would do what I am doing, or not doing?"

Milena shook her head. "If I knew what you know…" She reminded herself that she couldn't mention any of what she had learned from Gabbard.

"It's too late now, anyway," Louise said. "He's dead. There are no more what ifs. The dead don't change."

"I'm concerned with the living, Louise."

Louise shrugged. "Sometimes we're no different."

A sudden gust of wind rattled the window, drenching their faces with a cold mist. Milena shuddered, felt Louise shivering next to her. They drew closer to each other. It was time to head downstairs, to the warm, well-lit apartment. But neither of them suggested it.

•

Gabbard brought his Mercedes to a halt under a large elm tree. The road, only a few meters behind them, was invisible through the bushes and ferns that lined the edge of what seemed to be a small forest. It would have been easy to imagine that they were far from civilization, deep in the woods God only knew where, as opposed to just across the Loire from the small but busy town of

Tours. Milena felt lightheaded with the surreal quality of the situation.

"I will meet them at the house," Gabbard said. "It is about a quarter hour's walk from here, if you follow the avenue." He pointed ahead of them at what Milena had taken for a trail of some sort. She now noticed that it was paved, and lined with small moss-covered road markers.

"A footpath forks off to your right just before the property," he went on. "It will take you up a small incline. There's a bench there, under some fir trees. A beautiful spot, really. It overlooks the château. Wait there until everyone has left."

"What if anyone sees me sitting there?"

"The footpath is not part of the property, Mademoiselle. People often walk there. It is half concealed by the boughs of the trees, and aside from me, no one has any idea who you are. If anyone should see you, you'll be merely another stroller resting during her walk."

"I still can't believe I agreed to do this," Milena said.

"Frankly, Mademoiselle, neither can I." Gabbard reached into his pocket. "Here's the key to the front door."

"What about the lock picks?"

"Right." He handed her the now-familiar sheath of metal staves. "Remember what I told you, Mademoiselle. It is, to some extent, a matter of chance, or luck. If you don't manage on the first or even the second or third attempt—"

"We've gone over this often enough," Milena said. "Either I'll get it open, or I won't."

"And one more thing, Mademoiselle. Do not smoke, even before you enter the villa. Louise's mother is vehemently opposed to the habit, and cultivates a keen sense of smell in this regard. She would notice any lingering tobacco odors long after your departure."

"I haven't managed to finish a cigarette in weeks," Milena said. "I might quit altogether, as it is."

"Good. Very good, indeed."

"Do you have any idea at all what I am looking for?"

"Documents. Letters." Gabbard thought for a moment. "I imagine it will be evident when you find what we are seeking. It will be something that constitutes a threat to Corinne's reputation."

"And your marriage."

He nodded. "And that."

"There is just one thing I don't understand," Milena said. "If these documents are so dangerous to your wife's credibility, how come Louise's parents never tried to show them to their daughter?"

"Who is to say they didn't? But after their disastrous visit to the gallery, it was practically impossible for them to get anywhere near her."

"They could have sent them to you. After all, they intended to reveal them to you and your wife, anyway."

"While she was alive, yes," Gabbard said. "We've been over this, Mademoiselle. Francois did not wish to smear his dead sister's reputation, regardless of their differences in life."

"Or these documents have no relevance to Louise at all," Milena said. "Only to your wife. And you."

"I pray that is not the case, Mademoiselle. But we have to get moving. They are expecting me."

"All right."

"You will have three hours, at the least," he said. "As soon as anyone leaves the ceremony, I will make some excuse and call the telephone in Francois's study to warn you."

"How will I know it's you? It could get awkward, if someone else happens to call."

"I'll ring twice, as a sign, hang up, and then dial again. When you pick up, wait until you hear my voice, otherwise hang up."

"That should work." Milena stepped out of the car. The air was fresh and rich with the fragrances of wood and earth. It was still cool, but she could feel the warmth of the sun filtering down through the branches of the trees. She looked up and, for a moment, lost herself in the leaves swaying in the breeze, luminous with late morning sunshine. In the distance, beyond where the château of the de Benoîts had to be, a dark wall of clouds loomed in the sky like a tidal wave cresting in slow motion. If the wind didn't change, there would be a downpour, perhaps even a thunderstorm, in an hour, give or take.

Under other circumstances, it would have been a perfect day for a brisk walk in the woods.

"Good luck," Gabbard said. The Benz began to roll. Pebbles and gravel crackled under the tires as it moved away.

Milena waited for the car to pick up speed and grow smaller between the trees, then she started walking.

•

It occurred to her, as she walked up the incline Gabbard had described, that she had never asked him whether the de Benoîts kept dogs. Louise had never mentioned any, but then there were many things regarding her parental home of which she never spoke. Surely, if there was a danger of Milena being accosted by ferocious Dobermans or the like, Gabbard would have brought it up?

She reached the bench under the fir boughs. It was an idyllic spot, just as he had said. She sat down and inhaled the scent of resin warming up in the rising sun.

The clouds hadn't changed direction; if anything, they loomed larger and darker than before. Milena wondered how much shelter the fir trees would offer were she to get caught in the downpour in this spot. But of course she would no longer be sitting on the bench, when the deluge came. She would be inside the villa, doing a burglar's work. Or that of a Czech State Security officer.

She rested her elbows on her knees and took in the château. She counted ten windows on the side she could see, plus three more under the mansard roof. It was hard not to wonder which one opened into Louise's bedroom; harder still not to picture the scene that had played out there so many years before—if her aunt was to be believed. Milena made a conscious effort to focus on more immediate questions, such as the challenge of finding her way around the château, to the secretaire, and then back out again. Gabbard had provided her with what appeared, in theory, foolproof directions, but what if the furniture as he remembered it had been moved around to other rooms or even discarded altogether? It had been years since his last visit, after all. Finding her way back out would be easier, at least.

On the other side of the house, where a gravel road led to what had to be the front entrance, a lush lawn stretched for about thirty yards to the bank of the Loire. Milena saw no trace of where the pier might once have stood. No remaining pavement or flagstones, not even a rotting old pole. Three weeping willows lined the water's edge, at an even distance from each other, dipping their branches into the river. Sunlight danced on the waves beyond the trees, turning the stream into a constantly shifting and at the same time changeless band of gold. For a very short while, Milena managed not to think of anything at all.

As she looked on, the storm clouds passed in front of the sun. The light changed. Within seconds, the waves on the river went dull and turned to lead. The château took on a gloomy and forbidding aspect. Milena heard the distant sound of a car engine rumbling to life. From where she sat, it was impossible to see the front of the château, but soon a black Benz—Gabbard's or one just like it— emerged from behind the building and moved along the forest road leading away from the property. A moment later another Benz followed, also black. Then a third, smaller car of a model and make Milena didn't recognize. She waited until she could no longer hear the engines. She glanced at her wrist watch and let another five minutes go by.

No more cars appeared. The château was empty.

·

She walked briskly through the belt of birch trees that marked the border of the de Benoît property. What a ridiculous caper, she thought. She immediately felt ashamed. Risky, yes. Crazy? In all likelihood. But not ridiculous. If there was the slightest possibility that she might discover what Gabbard sought—what she sought, as well—then it was worth it. Not that Milena thought much of the chances. But why on earth not try? It was the sort of irrational resolve she would, a few months ago, have refused to consider herself capable of.

A sudden crunch under her feet underscored her emergence into the open, onto the beige gravel road that led to the château. The time for contemplation was over.

Milena's heart began to hammer. She touched a temple and massaged the vein that had begun to swell there.

Ježiše Marie, she thought. I'm too young to have a stroke.

Step after noisy step she approached the front door. There was no need to be so nervous—not yet. All she had to do was ring the bell and wait for someone to open. If they did, she would simply babble something about having the wrong address. If not...

She paused at the door and peered through the tinted glass panes. She saw a blurry chest of drawers, house plants, a coat rack. Stairs leading to the second floor. Toward the back, beyond what appeared to be a large foyer, another window that would look out on the pine trees under which she had been sitting minutes earlier. Even on that side of the house, there was no more sunlight. The storm had arrived.

She rang the bell. A brassy chime shrilled through the hallway. When nothing stirred inside the house, she rang again. And again. And one more time to be sure. In between, she rapped on the door for good measure.

Still nothing.

She reached into her pocket and pulled out the key Gabbard had given her. Surprisingly, her hands did not shake. In fact, she felt suddenly every calm. Perhaps the unanswered doorbell had reassured her, perhaps she was resigned to whatever disasters might ensue. She inserted the key: the point of no return. She looked over her shoulder. If anyone were to arrive now, from within or without the château, it would mean catastrophe.

With a swift motion, she turned the door handle, retrieved the key, and slipped into the house. She told herself that there was no need to be quiet now—only a deaf person would have failed to hear the repeated ringing of the bell—but all the same, she closed the door behind her without making any noise. She cast one last glance through the door, at the gravel road outside, then she looked at the stairs, mentally reciting Gabbard's instructions. Up to the second floor, then turn right into the hallway, and head for the last room on the left. She set a foot on the first step and shifted her weight. The wood emitted an alarmingly loud creak. She listened for some sort of response from within the house.

"Nonsense," she said. She'd meant to speak at her normal voice to bolster her courage, but the word came out as little more than a hoarse whisper. She cleared her throat, noisily, and climbed the stairs.

•

Milena reached the top of the stairs and, leaning forward with her feet in place, one hand on the banister, peered into the hallway to her right. She glanced at her watch. Twenty minutes since the cars had left for the funeral. There was still plenty of time, according to Gabbard, but who knew how long it would take to work the secretaire open, and how many documents she would have to read. With resolute steps, she marched down the hallway and stopped in front of the door in question. She looked back toward the stairs. Illuminated only by the sulfurous daylight coming from the windows near the landing, the hallway seemed to extend back through miles of gloom.

As an escape route, it was terribly long.

She came close to knocking before she turned the doorknob. What would be more terrifying—if someone answered from inside the room, or if she simply walked in, and surprised someone sitting at the desk? She muttered a curse. The mind groped for just about any absurd thought to provide food for fear and doubt. She swung the door open.

The room was unoccupied, of course. She noted with relief that it was brighter than the hallway, as there were two windows. Two of the walls were occupied by massive oak bookshelves. One of them contained the telephone Gabbard had mentioned. Hopefully, there was going to be no need for him to call. On the third wall hung a painting of a red-haired woman wearing a lavish dress in the style of the eighteenth or perhaps seventeenth century, seated at an ornately carved desk covered with books and letters. Around her neck, she wore a crucifix on a chain interlaced with small red beads—jasper, perhaps, or garnet. Could she be an ancestress? It was hard to tell. Milena was unable to discern any resemblance to Louise or her aunt. The woman gazed off into the shadows to her left, at something beyond the frame of the painting.

Good, Milena thought. At least she wouldn't feel watched.

At the fourth wall, between the two windows, was the secretaire. Gabbard had described it in detail, from the wood it was made of—mahogany, to the best of his knowledge—to the various surfaces and compartments. The antique banker's lamp with its brass base and green glass screen, the inkwell accompanied by the exquisite Montblanc fountain pen, everything was precisely where he had predicted it would be.

The only detail he had left out was a small framed photograph of Louise next to the lamp.

Milena's chest constricted at the sight. Here was the woman she knew, but at the same time, a stranger. Louise was very young in the photograph, a girl, nearly. She wore her hair shorter. But the sadness in her eyes was the same. She looked as if someone had urged her to smile before taking the picture but then realized the futility of the demand.

Was it possible, for a father to have done what Francois de Benoît was accused of, and then to keep this photograph near him, only memory of a child who would never again speak to him until the day of his death?

Entirely possible, Milena told herself. What rapist did not delude himself into feeling some twisted perversion of affection, unrecognizable to anyone but him?

She sat down at the secretaire and took out the lock picks. Contrary to Gabbard's expectations, the secretaire's hinged writing surface was not folded up and locked. One less obstacle to overcome. She glanced briefly at the various letters that had been meticulously arranged on it. She saw nothing remarkable, nothing postmarked more than a week or two ago. She tried to memorize the position of every object, including the inkwell and the Montblanc fountain pen. Other than the writing surface itself, the only enclosure she could see that was equipped with a lock was a small wooden compartment flanked on each side by four slots designed to hold papers and mail. Underneath this assembly was a total of four small drawers, all of them without locks, and too small to hold any documents. Milena pulled out one after the other: a stapler in one, paper clips and an inkpad in another, and so forth. She checked underneath the secretaire for more drawers. Nothing there. Simple elegance, indeed. The small compartment in the middle was it, then. Carefully, she unfolded the sheath holding the lock picks and tried the brass knob on the small door. Locked. Here was her chance to prove herself, then. She didn't particularly welcome it.

Fortunately, the mechanism didn't pose more of a challenge than the locks she had practiced on. Three, maybe four minutes, and she heard the tell-tale click. The wooden door opened, and she peered into the enclosure. She saw two envelopes, one large, one small. Underneath them, barely visible in the shadows, a necklace.

•

She retrieved the necklace first. It was a fine silver chain, long in need of being polished, interlaced with red beads. Suspended from it was an equally tarnished but beautifully worked crucifix. The necklace from the painting. Milena looked up at the silent woman with the red hair, then at the necklace again. An heirloom of some sort, apparently. Other than that she had no way of telling what its significance might be. She returned it to its place in the compartment and pulled out the large envelope. There was no address or any other writing on it, and it wasn't sealed. She shook it, and two pieces of paper slid into her hand. One of the papers was folded in half; the other was somewhat smaller. Both of them were yellowed with age. Milena examined the smaller document. At the top were three words in boldface:

Acte de Naissance.

A birth certificate. The fields on the form were filled out in jagged handwriting. The date was printed clearly enough—February 22, 1935—but the scrawl that identified the place of birth was next to illegible. What Milena could make out resembled the name of no French town or city she knew. The next line was easier to read, because it contained a familiar name: Frédéric Baptiste de Benoît.

Milena glanced at the other sheet, lying next to the envelope, still folded. Two children, two birth certificates. It only made sense for their father to keep them both in the same place. She was overcome with a sinking feeling, a sense of defeat. Aside from Louise and her brother's middle names, there would be nothing new to be learned from these documents, certainly nothing useful. She was about to put the form away when she noticed something odd.

The field intended for the name of the father only contained one word.

Inconnu.

Unknown. How was that possible? She jumped to the next line. The mother's name had been recorded. Middle name and all.

Milena's mouth ran dry. She scanned the scratchy ink strokes again and again. But there could be no doubt. Letter by spidery letter, they spelled out the name Corinne Marie de Benoît.

•

The last of the sunlight faded from the room. In the near darkness, the characters on the paper seemed to crawl under Milena's eyes. But whichever way they squirmed, they always ended up in the same immutable configuration.

A flash of lightning sent the shadows in the room twitching. Milena started and dropped the sheet of paper. Seconds later, a peal of thunder crashed through the air. The entire château was seized by a tremor. She let out a small gasp. She hadn't been scared by a thunderstorm in years. But sitting here, alone in this strange house in which heartbreak and grief hung in the air like the smell of smoke clinging to burnt rafters, she had difficulty maintaining her adult calm. She was reluctant to switch on the light—what if some lone walker saw it from outside?—but when the next bolt of lightning snaked across the sky, she quickly pulled the string of the lamp on the secretaire. The warm yellow light, filtered above through the screen of green glass, reassured her somewhat. She was less shaken by the second thunderclap.

The rain began to fall. It started as a light rustle in the trees outside, nearly indistinguishable from the wind stirring in the leaves, but within seconds, the drops swelled to a deluge that rattled the window panes.

How on earth had Frédéric's birth certificate ended up in the possession of Louise's father? Shouldn't it have been among Corinne's files?

Milena forced herself to keep the throng of questions in her mind at bay. There'd be plenty of time to think about them once she was done here. No doubt Gabbard would be able to come up with the necessary explanations.

She put down the first sheet and unfolded the second document. The paper was covered with several paragraphs of densely spaced typeface. It bore the formal letterhead of the municipal office of another town whose name Milena had never before heard, and at the bottom, next to an official seal, the scrawled signature of whatever administrator had borne testimony to its contents. But no neat heading in boldface identified the document's purpose or nature.

Milena had a hard time focusing on the closely spaced text. After a few lines, she began to realize what she was looking at. The document attested to the adoption of one Frédéric Baptiste, family unknown, by a Francois Matthieu de Benoît and his wife, Eugénie Justine de Benoît. It was the first time Milena saw Louise's mother referred to by name.

She looked at the date next to the seal and signature at the bottom.

Monday, March 4, 1935.

In the ten days following his birth, Frédéric had somehow been stripped of his name, only for it to be subsequently restored to him by his adoptive parents.

Milena let the sheet slip out of her hand, onto the dark wood surface of the secretaire. Outside, the rain kept rushing down, hammering on the window panes with furious force.

Supposedly, Francois had possessed the connections and influence needed to make it all happen. Who knew.

But why make it happen at all?

Milena felt too exhausted to attempt to form conjectures. Let Gabbard explain this bizarre story, or try to. She retrieved the smaller envelope and inspected it. Unlike the larger one, it had once been sealed, and subsequently sliced open along the top. It was addressed to Louise's father. The sender's name and address was stamped in a corner: Cabinet d'Avocats Perraudin & Associés, Paris. A law firm. She looked at the postmark. March 1962. The year Corinne had died.

Inside were two letters in crisp typeface, accompanied by a document the nature of which wasn't immediately apparent. Milena read the first letter. It informed Francois that due to the fact that his sister had not left behind a will, the property originally transferred to her in 1934 by their father, Raymond Marcellin de Benoît, was reverting to him as the oldest surviving member of the family.

Milena skimmed the attached document. Not surprisingly, it was the deed to a house. Her eyes raced over the paper in search of the address. There it was. Montmorency.

Contrary to what Gabbard believed, Corinne had never sold the house. It had been in her possession until her sudden death. Why had she kept this fact from him?

The second letter was from the same law firm, composed almost a year later, in 1963. It contained a simple statement confirming that Perraudin & Associates had handled the payment of all applicable taxes for the Montmorency property, drawing the funds from one of Francois's bank accounts as per his instructions, and would continue to do so annually until he decided to dispose of the property by selling it. That was all.

The whole business was clearly unrelated to the papers concerning Frédéric. Whether it meant anything, if it figured at all in her quest to help Louise, was another question that could be answered later. Milena shuffled through the documents spread out on the secretaire. She had read everything the locked compartment had contained. It was time to leave, rain or no rain.

She hesitated before returning the two envelopes to the compartment.

Gabbard might be willing to accept the information she had found without seeing solid evidence— and if not, Milena was hardly in a mood to give a damn— but what about Louise? The whole plan was supposed to have been about her, after all. Whatever the knowledge of Frédéric's origins might mean to her, she would have to see proof of it.

Milena slipped the birth certificate and the adoption document into her pocket and replaced them with two randomly selected sheets from the mail slots. With luck, whoever inspected the envelope next—Louise's mother, most likely—would simply assume that Francois had misplaced or destroyed the original contents.

As for the letters from the law firm, she was hesitant to take them. Removing the deed to the property itself was out of the question, naturally. Besides, if the business with the house turned out to be of any importance, it would be easy enough to contact Perraudin & Associates and inquire about it. Milena jotted down the firm's address along with that of the house in Montmorency on a piece of notepaper and slipped it in her pocket as well. Then she put the envelope back inside the compartment.

She checked her watch again. Plenty of time left. But she couldn't bear the thought of sitting in this room any longer. She got up, moved the chair into its original position, and carefully examined the secretaire. Everything was as she had found it.

She took a last look at the photograph of Louise.

Strange, now that she thought about it, that there was no picture of Frédéric. Granted that he was not truly Francois's son, but if he had taken the boy into his home and raised him as his own, would he not have wanted to remember him, as well?

She turned off the banker's lamp. The half-light of the storm reclaimed the silent room. As she slipped out the door, she glanced at the windows.

The rain was still coming down.

•

Milena paced back and forth on the side of the intersection where Gabbard was supposed to pick her up. She was drenched to her underwear, and although she had kept moving since she left the château, she couldn't manage to stay warm. She blamed him for her miserable predicament. He knew Tours and its surroundings; there had to be places he could have picked that offered more shelter in a downpour than a spot by a country road lined with birch trees. There was a bench, at least he had thought of that. Not that she felt like sitting down. The young birch leaves offered about as much protection from the rain as a fishing net. On top of it all, her shoulder had started to hurt severely.

After an eternity of shivering and pacing and massaging her aching bones, she heard the sound of a car approaching. Gabbard's Benz turned a corner. He pulled up slowly through the mud and puddles lining the road. Milena slipped into the car and shut the door with a resounding slam.

"I am so sorry." He steered the Benz away from the intersection. "I really should have considered the weather."

Milena leaned back into the leather seat. She felt suddenly too exhausted to berate him for his poor planning. "It doesn't matter now."

Gabbard turned the car heater to its highest setting. A stream of warm air washed over Milena's face. "Please put on my trench coat, Mademoiselle. It is on the back seat, and quite dry. My sister-in-law was thoughtful enough to bring along an umbrella for me."

"Lucky you." Milena squirmed out of her soggy duffle jacket and wrapped his coat around herself. It didn't make her feel much drier, but along with the warmth coming from the heater, it helped her stop shivering.

He reached into his jacket and pulled out a snow-white handkerchief. "Your hair. It's entirely wet."

Milena accepted the handkerchief and patted her hair with it. "How was the funeral?"

"How such things usually are, Mademoiselle. Not particularly cheerful. But one gets through them, somehow."

Milena nodded. "I have some things to tell you that may not be easy to accept."

There was a pause. He cleared his throat. "I suppose I will get through that, as well."

Milena pulled her coat off the back seat and extracted the two documents from the pocket. They were damp in places but otherwise intact. She handed them to Gabbard. "You may want to pull over before you read these."

He frowned. "What are they?"

"Some things are easier to believe if you see them black on white."

He steered the Benz to a spot beside the road and let the engine idle. Milena watched him unfold the documents. The birth certificate was on top; at least the chronology would be easy to grasp. She closed her eyes and settled more deeply into her seat while he read.

For a long time, she heard only the rain, the intermittent sighs of the windshield wipers, and the hum of the engine, sounds so regular they nearly amounted to silence. Once, a distant peal of thunder intruded on the steady harmony. Warm air from the heater continued to stream over her face.

A rustling of paper told her that he was done. She opened her eyes. He was looking directly at her, the two documents still in his hand. His expression was hard to read, his gaze, though fixed on her, turned inwards. "You found these in Francois's secretaire?" His voice sounded flat.

She nodded.

"You were right to take them," he said. "I'm unsure if I could have brought myself to believe this, without seeing the evidence with my own eyes."

"You seem awfully composed about it," Milena said.

"What were you expecting, Mademoiselle?"

"I don't know." She shrugged. "A little more emotion, perhaps." She couldn't say when the suspicion had taken hold in her mind. Perhaps it was the strain of the whole crazy ordeal she had undergone. But the more she thought about it, the more everything made sense. In a bad way. "Somehow I get the impression that you're not all that surprised."

"Mademoiselle, I assure you, just because you don't see me burst into tears, or launch into a fit of rage—"

"Your wife must have said something to you," Milena said. "She knew her brother was about to destroy her marriage. She must have tried to explain her side of things to you, before he did."

"But think about what you are saying, Mademoiselle. If Corinne had already told me about Frédéric, why would I be seeking further proof?"

"Francois, then." His calm was infuriating. All the more so because he was making sense. "He hinted at something, at some point. And it's been eating at you ever since."

"We've already discussed this, Mademoiselle. I knew nothing of Francois's threats while Corinne was still alive, and he never told me anything after she died."

"So you say."

Gabbard sighed. "I am aware that you have been under tremendous strain over the past hours," he said. "But you cannot allow yourself to be so unreasonable. Your suspicions are absolutely unfounded."

"Don't patronize me," Milena burst out. "I think you knew exactly what was in that secretaire. And you sent me in there to get it for you like a trained monkey up a palm tree."

"Mademoiselle, I assure you—"

"You lied to me, God damn you. You lied to me and you used me and none of this has anything to do with helping Louise."

"Mademoiselle, I must ask you to mind your language. Don't raise your voice. Helping Louise is the one thing I meant to accomplish by all this."

"Bullshit," Milena snarled. She felt something rising violently inside her chest. She knew she was going to cry. A matter of seconds. "All you wanted was to pry into your wife's past, because you never trusted her."

"My wife's past is part of this, naturally," Gabbard said. "But it was not my paramount interest."

"Let me out of the car."

"It is raining, Mademoiselle. And we're still nearly two hours away from Paris."

"I don't care." Milena fumbled with the door lock. She heard him mutter something under his breath.

"Mademoiselle, please."

She opened the door and hurled herself into the driving rain, blind with tears. Something cold and wet touched her ankles. She looked down and realized that she was staggering through a field. With each step, her feet sank into mud. Ahead of her, some twenty feet away, she saw a fence. Behind it, several cows stood motionless, chewing their cuds, backs soggy with rain, watching her with calm curiosity. She reached the fence, leaned on a post, and stared at them. A few of the animals began to slowly move away.

That's right, she thought, be careful. You never know with human beings.

She heard footsteps approaching behind her. The sound of a plunger slowly being moved up and down in thick muck. Gabbard, no doubt, ruining his elegant leather shoes in the muddy field, and getting drenched himself. His trench coat was still wrapped around her. It kept her dry if not warm, but her hair was dripping wet again.

She felt a hand on her shoulder and cringed. With her feet stuck in the mud, she lost her balance and instinctively grabbed the wire in front of her. One of the barbs buried itself in her palm. "Don't touch me."

The hand withdrew. She regretted her words. The touch of his hand had felt comforting, paternal. Ježíše Marie, how she missed that touch! The sobs came again, with even greater intensity. "I didn't mean that," she stammered. But the hand did not return. He stood at a step's distance from her, waiting, a tear-blurred figure in a black suit.

"Please, Milena." It was the first time that he had addressed her by her name. "We should return to the car."

Milena sucked on her palm.

"Are you all right? I have a first aid kit in the trunk, if you need it."

She shook her head. "It's nothing." The offer of the first aid kit made her laugh, in spite of everything. That's how it had all begun, hadn't it? God, it already seemed like years. When would her life stop revolving around injuries?

•

They sat in the Benz for a while, both in their shoes covered with an inch-thick layer of dirt. Gabbard's blazer was soaked. His gray hair clung to his skull in wet curls. The rain, unrelenting, drummed on the roof of the car, its percussions underscored by the rumble of the idling engine. In regular intervals, the squeak of the wipers passing over the windshield cut through the soporific hum. Occasionally, a pair of headlights emerged out of the downpour and slipped past them with a hiss.

Milena felt nothing now, except for a profound weariness. "I'm sorry for what I said," she murmured. In her hand, she held a second handkerchief he had produced from somewhere. It was stained with her blood.

"Let's forget it happened," Gabbard said. "It's the strain of what you have been through. I should never have suggested any of this. It was nothing but a foolish hope."

"You really had no idea?"

He slowly shook his head.

"It must come as a shock," Milena said. She was convinced now that she had misjudged him, that he truly hadn't known. "I'm sorry."

"Don't be," he said. "What have I learned, after all? That my wife made a misstep in her youth? It's not so hard to forgive. God knows I made a few, and was spared the consequences only through the kindness of fate, and chance."

"It doesn't bother you, that she kept such a secret from you?"

"The poor boy died years before I met Corinne," Gabbard said. "Can I blame her, for wanting to leave behind such a dismal past? The only thing that saddens me is what she must have gone through, for fear of the judgment of others. Even mine. I wish she had known that she could tell me the truth."

"I don't think many men would look at the situation this way. And I can certainly see now why your brother-in-law was ultimately so unwilling to disclose any of this."

"Oh, yes." Gabbard smiled sadly. "For my part, I only hope I would have been as forgiving had I learned of this while she was still alive."

"I just don't understand any of it," Milena said. "Why would Francois adopt his own sister's son and pass him off as his own?"

"I can only imagine. Perhaps to avoid a scandal. For Corinne to have given birth to an illegitimate child would have brought disgrace to the family name."

"That makes no sense," Milena said. "If your wife was willing to give the child up, why not let complete strangers adopt it and be done with all these troubles?"

"What if she wasn't willing to give it up?"

"Then she would obviously have kept it." Milena sighed in frustration. "We're moving in circles."

"But didn't she keep it, in a way? By letting Francois take the child in, Corinne would have been able to continue to see it."

Milena frowned. "Is that the bargain you think your wife and her brother struck?"

"I don't know." Gabbard rubbed his forehead with his hands. "It's the only way I can see to account for what you found out."

"I guess it would have been a very good deal for your wife," Milena said. "She retained the freedom to pursue her career unfettered, without being saddled with a child. At the same time, she could still see her son. Not to mention other benefits, I'm sure."

"What do you mean?"

"From what I know about the stuck-up clan she belonged to, she would probably have risked her inheritance by openly acknowledging her son."

Gabbard pursed his lips. "It is very likely that the old de Benoît would have disowned Corinne, had he learned of her condition, that is true. Still, I doubt it was as callous a calculation on her part as you imply, Mademoiselle. Consider the alternatives she would have faced. Giving up her son forever, or being subjected to the prejudice an unmarried mother would have been exposed to in those days."

"And Francois was willing to assume the responsibility of raising someone else's child while his sister got all the perks, just like that?"

"Francois always thought of himself as a steward of the family reputation," Gabbard said. "That alone would have been worth the effort to him. And he certainly had the means at his disposal. It doesn't seem so implausible to me."

"Ježíše Marie." Milena exhaled heavily. "I really don't care one way or another, in the end. All this hypocrisy just sickens me."

"It is a complicated story, without a doubt." Gabbard shifted the engine into gear. The Benz rolled onto the road and began to accelerate. "But what is important is what this will mean to Louise."

"And what is that, exactly?"

"If I am right, we can show her that Francois went to great lengths to help Corinne in the most difficult situation of her life."

"It's just as easy to argue that he wanted to force his sister to give up her child to preserve an antiquated and duplicitous ideal of propriety, and that he struck a compromise only for fear that his plan would backfire, if she refused to play along."

"Or we can argue that he was capable of doing good, after all."

"Don't forget what else Louise believes he was capable of." Milena rested her forehead against the cool window pane. "Have we found anything to disprove that?"

Gabbard remained silent.

"We have nothing," Milena murmured. "Nothing at all." A few minutes later, her eyes fell shut, and there was only the humming of the Benz as it plunged through an endless expanse of gray.

•

Milena lay on her bed, the mud-encrusted shoes still on her feet, and stared at the ceiling. The curtains were drawn against the pale afternoon light. The house was absolutely quiet. Pauline was out, gone to the university, perhaps, or to some gathering somewhere. Things Milena would have done as well, on a normal day. She wondered if there were ever going to be any of those again.

She could not manage to fall asleep. Her thoughts kept chasing one another, connecting and disconnecting in random patterns but refusing to carry her over into the restful haze of dreams.

Something snarled inside her stomach. It might have been better to eat something, anything, before lying down. Gabbard had offered to take her to a restaurant before dropping her off outside her building, but she had refused. A shower and some sleep was all she wanted. That, and to see Louise. Only she couldn't bring herself to pick up the phone. What was she going to tell her? Nothing, perhaps. Since she felt it made no difference. Frédéric had not really been her brother, but her cousin. So what? Still, it was the kind of thing you shouldn't keep from a person.

Sleep on it, Gabbard had recommended. We can decide how to break the news to her tomorrow, in the morning.

If at all, Milena thought, for the thousandth time.

She knew what bothered her was not simply the disappointment of having found nothing in the secretaire that would have exonerated Louise's father, or incriminated her aunt. Not simply a general sense of defeat, but the feeling of having been defeated by Corinne de Benoît. Milena realized that it was a ridiculous sentiment. But it wasn't going away. She was convinced that Corinne was rotten. That she had lied, and done exactly what her brother had accused her of, in the letter Gabbard had shown her: poisoned Louise's mind. Poisoned her life, turning it into a slow ebb and tide of silence and torture, where peace was bought only, and intermittently, at the cost of severed flesh and spilled blood.

When Milena closed her eyes, she saw Corinne's face in front of her, the smile thinly veiling arrogance, contempt, triumph. She could almost hear her laughing. Corinne had given them all the slip, leaving the only member of the de Benoît clan worth saving broken and suffering in her wake. She had used everyone, including her brother. It was easy to argue, as Gabbard wanted to, that Francois had helped her in a desperate situation when her only choice was between familial disgrace and giving up her child. It was just as easy to argue that he had forced her into their bizarre arrangement with no other goal but to preserve the family's good name. Undoubtedly, Louise would interpret things that way. In each scenario, Corinne was cast as the victim, the helpless young woman at the mercy of her phallocratic clan. But Milena was convinced that somehow, Corinne de Benoît had been in complete control over her own destiny. And she had gotten everything she wanted: her son, the freedom to pursue her career, her inheritance, the house in Montmorency.

Milena sat up with a start.

The house that she had never sold.

That fact in itself didn't interest Milena. Nor did she give a damn about Corinne's reasons for lying to her husband about keeping the property. It was just another example of the tawdry deceits and secrets in which the de Benoîts dealt, without relevance to the task of helping Louise.

But what had Francois done with the house, after it reverted to him?

Perraudin & Associates, in their second letter, had confirmed that they were going to handle the payment of the property taxes, year after year, until he decided to sell it. Which had never happened. Instead, Francois had locked away the deed to the house in his secretaire, along with all other documents linked to Corinne and Frédéric.

Let the dead rest.

Gabbard had made it clear enough that after Corinne's death, all Francois wanted was to forget her, along with the man who had been married to her.

Had he wanted to forget the house as well? It would have been full of memories, full of things Francois wanted never to be reminded of again. Things, perhaps, that Corinne herself would not have wanted anyone to see or know.

Milena's mouth ran dry. She could feel her pulse pounding in her head, beating against her eardrums like boiling surf. Six years since Corinne had died. It was not an impossibly long time for a piece of property to remain untouched. The city of Montmorency wouldn't care, as long as the requisite taxes were paid.

She came close to going through the pockets of Pauline's various coats hanging in the hallway in a desperate search for a cigarette.

Now that Francois de Benoît was dead in the ground, who knew how long it would be until someone decided to finally have a look at the house?

Ježiše Marie, it could happen tomorrow.

She stood in the hallway and stared at the paper on which she had written down the address in Montmorency. She shoved the note back into her chest pocket and glanced at the phone. Should she call Gabbard? He had a right to know that Corinne had lied to him, after all. He might even come up with another one of his theories, to account for the fact that his wife had kept her continued possession of the property from him. Milena didn't particularly care.

Somewhere in Montmorency, Corinne's house still stood, silent and, with luck, unvisited in six years, perhaps longer. Silent, but not empty.

She would make Corinne de Benoît stumble yet. Gabbard's explanations could wait.

·

Milena looked up at the streetlamp casting its yellow glow through the branches of a beech tree, one of many lining the street. The lights had come on some ten minutes ago. Dusk was settling over Montmorency. In front of her, a long hedge of arborvitae concealed the house she sought, like a troop of solemn guards closing rank to bar her way.

She heard the door of the cab opening. For a moment, music streamed from the car radio. The sound seemed out of place on this silent tree-lined street, in the dimming light. The door fell shut, muffling the music again. Milena turned around. The driver leaned on the roof of his cab, a fresh cigarette between his lips. "So do you want me to wait?"

She nodded. "I'd like to make sure I have the right place."

"This is the address you gave me." The driver shrugged and lit his cigarette. "But take your time."

Milena walked along the row of arborvitae. The trees had grown into each other, making it impossible to see what lay behind them. She came to an iron gate tucked so deeply into the hedge as to be nearly invisible until one stood right in front of it. Approaching the gate was like stepping into a green tunnel, shut off at its end by a metal trellis. Peering through the steel bars, she got her first view of the property. The garden was a mess. In patches, the lawn was knee high, in others, yellow and dry, with dark earth showing through like floorboards under a tattered carpet. Several rhododendron shrubs close to the house had grown so tall they seemed to be trying to devour it. Two chestnut trees stood on either side of a stone stairway leading to the front door. Everywhere near the trunks, the ground was littered with debris and chestnuts from bygone summers.

The walls of the house itself, originally painted some bright color—perhaps even white—were an indistinguishable grey in the fading light, with large stains of moss or runoff underneath the rusted gutters. Milena spotted several broken pantiles on the roof. On the second floor, a window pane had been patched over with a sheet of cardboard.

All in all, the sight made her hopeful. Everything she saw was in keeping with what one would expect from a house unoccupied and untended for years. The question was what to do next. Or rather, whether to do it at all.

She tried the gate. Locked. A wire mesh welded to the bars prevented anyone from reaching through and opening the gate from the inside. There was a ringer next to the gate, with a nameplate holding a piece of warped paper, spotty with mould. If it had ever borne any letters to begin with, they had long faded. She pressed the button. Nothing happened, of course. She would have to consider more practical means of entering the house. She inspected the edges of the gate and found that it was part of a steel fence that ran the length of the property behind the arborvitae. About seven foot tall and crowned with nasty looking spikes. Halfway up each pole, leaf-shaped ornaments provided potential footholds.

She walked back to the cab.

The driver watched her approach, dragging leisurely on his cigarette. "No one home?"

Milena shook her head. "This isn't the place."

"Really? But the address—"

"My grandparents had a house around here," she said. "A long time ago. I'm trying to find it. This was just one of several possibilities."

"Okay." The driver dropped his cigarette and stepped it out. "In that case, where to next?"

"I think I'll try my luck on foot for a while." Milena reached for her wallet. "How much do I owe you?"

•

Milena watched the cab disappear around a street corner. She wasn't particularly happy to have to send the man away. It was getting dark, and she had no idea exactly where she was. She couldn't remember seeing any phone booths or shops where she might call another taxi to take her home.

On the other hand, she could hardly let him watch what she was about to do.

She walked back toward the elm tree by the street lamp, where she had first stepped out of the cab. But she continued along the hedge until she reached a spot where the lamplight didn't reach. She looked left and right—no one to be seen—and squeezed through the arborvitae. Something soft brushed against her face, and she recoiled. A spider rappelled down onto her shoulder and headed for the collar of her duffle coat. It was enough to make her want to dash back to the sidewalk, to sanity. She grabbed her lapel and shook it frantically. The spider tumbled out, landed on her boot, and scurried away into the grass. Milena picked the remainders of the web off her face and sized up the fence. Getting over the spikes on top would require some care. She grabbed two of them, put a foot on one of the metal leaves halfway up and made sure her sole wouldn't slip off. A moment later, she was teetering on the fence. She almost fell backwards, but she regained her balance long enough to jump off on the other side. She slipped on the grass as she landed and tumbled forward, bracing herself on her hands. She was instantly aware of a dark shape in front of her. Had it been any darker, she would have backed into the steel fence in panic. But there was still enough light to see clearly what she was looking at. She had landed in a patch of foxglove that had long grown wild. About three feet away from her, half concealed by the plants, stood a garden urn on a weatherworn pedestal. Clinging to the side of it, its blind stone face snarling at her, was the faun from the photograph.

She got up and brushed soil and dead leaves off her knees. Slowly, so as to make a minimum of noise, she walked toward the faun. Once, she turned around to look at the towering hedge of arborvitae. The sight gave her an oppressive sense of being cut off from the outside world.

She reached the garden urn and touched the faun in the spot where Corinne's hand had rested in Gabbard's photograph. The stone was covered with a thin layer of moss. It felt soft, almost velvety, but utterly cold. Like clammy skin. Milena wiped her fingers on her pants leg and immediately felt foolish. The sole purpose of her presence in this place, after all, was to get her hands on things that had once belonged to, had been touched by, Corinne de Benoît. Climbing the garden fence and facing the faun had been trifles. She needed to get inside the house.

Milena looked ahead to size up her objective. Daylight was fading fast. With every moment, the house became more of a shadow, a dark and featureless bulk in the dusk, as if even now, it was trying to make itself disappear, to slip away from her inquiry. She pictured the inside of the place, the gloomy rooms, with dust thick on everything. Would the lights even be working? She cursed herself for not remembering to grab the flashlight Pauline kept in the kitchen closet in case of blown fuses. She reached into her pocket. No cigarette lighter, either. More than ever, she regretted quitting. But suppose the lights were working. Wouldn't switching them on attract attention? She looked back toward the dark wall of the hedge. No more than a flicker of light from the streetlamps filtered through near the treetops. No, the house was invisible from the street, and further concealed by the two chestnut trees and the rampant rhododendron shrubs. One had to walk right up to the garden gate nestled in its hollow deep inside the hedge to even see it.

A tingling sensation crept up Milena's nape. Again, the idea that the property was so secluded, so isolated, filled her with dread. Unless the lights did work, she was about to enter the dark core of an already lightless and forsaken place.

She began picking her way through the foxglove and tall grass, toward the shadow looming in front of her. Why be scared, she told herself. It was just a deserted old house, with no one inside. When she had entered the château in Tours, she hadn't been so sure of that, in spite of Gabbard's assertions. Ježiše Marie. Had it really only been that morning? It seemed like ages ago that she had slunk into Francois de Benoît's study. But here it was, her second count of burglary in one day. At least in Tours she'd had a key; it had made her entry into the château feel nearly legitimate. Here, she would need to find some other means.

She reached the house and crouched underneath a window. What was next? In the movies, they made these things look pretty easy: smash a window, reach inside and unlock it, voilà. Perhaps it really was that simple. She stood up and peered through the grimy pane. All she saw was the fabric of a drape, its color indiscernible in the darkness. She walked around the back of the house. It was the same with all of the ground floor windows. Heavy drapes, no way of seeing inside. Milena sighed and spat a curse. So much for being able to decide beforehand whether breaking in was even worth the trouble.

She was casting about for a rock or some other object to smash a window with when she remembered the front door. She was certain that she'd seen glass panes. Perhaps she would be able to get a look into the hallway.

For a moment, she stood still in the near blackness underneath one of the chestnut trees. A few yards off in the decrepit garden, bone-pale in the dusk, the faun on the urn snarled his mute hatred at her.

The entire place felt hostile. Perhaps that was to be expected, when you were an interloper where you didn't belong. Before she walked up to the front door, she glanced at the garden gate. Should she try whether it was locked from the inside? But that would mean giving in to paranoia. If the gate was locked, she'd have to climb out over the fence, the way she'd come in. Simple. As long as she didn't manage to impale herself on the steel spikes.

The front door was a disappointment. There were no drapes, but a canvas sheet had been hung over the panes from the inside. It was light brown, with stains in places.

"I'll be damned," she murmured. She felt frustrated enough to smash the glass with her bare fist. But cutting herself wouldn't help anything. She noticed a crack running diagonally across one of the glass panes closer to the door handle. Perhaps she could push it in with her elbow. She inspected the putty holding the glass in place. It looked brittle; in places it had already crumbled and fallen off. She picked at it with her fingernail. The more of it she removed, the more easily the glass should give. But the stuff didn't come away quite as quickly as she had hoped. She scanned the stairs in front of the door for a stick to scrape the putty off. She remembered her keys. Of course. That would work just fine. She turned around to resume working on the glass pane.

A hand disappeared behind the stained canvas.

With a gasp, Milena sprang back from the door. Her entire body ran cold.

Someone was inside the house. On the other side of the door, watching her. A man. It had been a man's hand. No doubt about that.

Her knees began to shake. She'd never believed that actually happened to people. She stumbled backwards on numb legs, nearly tripped and fell on the stairs. The ratty shrubs of the garden seemed to take a jump toward her, crowding her, trying to bar her retreat.

Why didn't he open the door to ask her what she was doing here?

She thought of the cardboard covering the second-floor window. Ježiše Marie, it made sense now. No representative of the de Benoît family would resort to such makeshift repairs. There was some vagrant on the other side of that door. Perhaps worse. A criminal, a deranged drifter. Hiding out. Making up his mind what to do about her. Or with her.

It was nearly dark and not a soul in the world knew that she was here. What was there to think about?

She flew toward the garden gate.

God, don't let it be locked!

She pressed the handle. The hammering of her pulse against her eardrums muffled the creak of the gate swinging open. Delirious with fear, she plunged through the tunnel of the hedge, and into the street.

•

She had no idea how long she had been running through the tree-lined streets when she stopped. Not that she didn't want to keep running. But her lungs were filled with fire and no amount of straining could get them to deliver any more oxygen to her legs. She leaned against the trunk of a tree and tried to catch her breath. Her shoulder locked up in an excruciating cramp. Groaning, she massaged the knotted muscles.

She looked down the street along which she had run. No one in sight. As she regained her capacity to think rationally, the idea of the man inside the house chasing her through the streets of Montmorency for several blocks appeared more and more absurd. God only knew why he was holed up in that rotting old house, but he was probably as glad to see her leave as she was to get away, and that was that.

She forced herself to focus on more practical concerns, like the need to get back to Paris, to find out about the developments of the day from Pauline, to get in touch with Louise.

Her lungs stopped burning and the cramp in her shoulder dissolved. She was drenched in sweat and now that her pulse was returning to normal, she felt a chill. Best to start walking. After a few blocks she came to an intersection that was lit up by a café, a small supermarket, and a gas station. She felt ridiculously relieved at these sights, like an adventurer stumbling out of the jungle and back into civilization.

At the gas station, she called Louise's apartment. No one picked up. She glanced at her watch. Seven thirty. Perhaps she was working late. With her uncle gone for the day, more work than usual had probably piled up. She dialed the gallery's number. Nothing. She pressed down on the cradle and called the apartment in Levallois. Again, no one answered.

"Good God," she muttered. "Where is everybody?"

After that, she called a taxi. She asked the driver to turn on the radio and find the news station. The strident voice of the announcer informed them that there had been renewed demonstrations in the area around the Sorbonne, but instead of dispersing in the Jardin du Luxembourg after their march like the day before, the students had dug in along the Rue Gay-Lussac, across from the Gardens. Barricades were going up again, under the watchful eyes of a formidable police force.

The driver refrained from commenting on the report. Either he was listening intently, or he didn't give a damn. Milena was grateful. Normally, she welcomed discussions with strangers, particularly if they weren't students, and if their views differed from her own; there was always the potential opportunity to change a mind. But she didn't have the energy left.

Only once, when the announcer mentioned that some of the demonstrators had broken into a construction site and were using an air hammer to rip paving stones from the street, the driver muttered something to himself. "Unbelievable," he said, shaking his head. Milena didn't respond, and he remained silent after that.

She debated whether she should to tell him to take her straight to the Rue Gay-Lussac, or as near there as was possible with the police and the CRS in the area. Pauline would be there, with the others. But she knew she had to rest. So far, the police had held off, in spite of the fact that the demonstrators were tearing up the street right under their noses. No doubt they were waiting for their superiors to make their decisions and statements, whichever came first. It would take a while. She could probably afford to catch a couple of hours of sleep before heading over there. A nap, if nothing more. In her present condition, she wasn't going to be of use to anyone in a street battle, if it came to that.

She glanced at the driver. In the rearview mirror, she saw a pair of bright blue eyes underneath the rim of a worn leather cap. He looked at the mirror as well, and Milena averted her gaze. But he wasn't looking at her.

She sat up and squinted out the rear window. A single headlight was turning the corner they had just rounded.

"Guess he's heading into the city, too," the driver said. "Been behind us for a while."

"The same one?"

"I thought it was. Hard to say for sure, of course."

Milena shook her head and sank back into the upholstery with a sigh. "There's got to be hundreds of those things on the streets."

The driver chuckled. "Thousands, more like."

When they got to Levallois, Milena told him to drop her off a block away from her apartment. She looked up and down the street before she walked home.

You never knew.

•

It took her several seconds to realize that the ringing of the phone was real and not a dream.

She swung her legs over the edge of her bed and noticed that she was still wearing her boots. Her eyes felt swollen. She'd slept at last. No idea how long, only that it hadn't been enough.

It was Pauline on the phone. "Mon Dieu, where have you been? I called a couple of hours ago and then a couple more before that."

"I was asleep. What time is it?"

"Almost eleven."

"Jesus," Milena said. "Three hours."

"What?"

"I slept three hours. I got home around eight, I think. I was out."

"Evidently," Pauline said. "Listen, chéri, I don't have a lot of time. We're at Gay-Lussac, as you may know."

"I heard the news, yes. What's going on?"

"What's going on?" Pauline chuckled. "We had a statement from Roche earlier offering to discuss the reopening of the Sorbonne. Nothing about the release of the guys sitting in jail. Well, so we asked. The deputy rector promised to get an answer on that from the minister of education in ten minutes. That was an hour ago. Then he comes on the air and rereads Roche's statement. Rereads it! That's the state of affairs here. Huge progress is being made, as you can see."

"And the CRS?"

"Watching us," Pauline said. "A lot of people think this night will fizzle, like yesterday. But I have a feeling it won't. People are piling up paving stones as ammunition. There's a huge number of flics here. It'll be a mess and a half if this blows up."

"I'll get there as soon as I can."

"Head to the little square, where Gay-Lussac meets the Boul' Mich. That's where we are."

Milena called another taxi. That made three in one day. She couldn't really afford it, but she felt such an urgency to join Pauline and the others, to return to the real world where what you had to do or not was dictated by solid exigencies like your convictions or the actions of a bunch of rabid policemen. It didn't always make a lot more sense than her afternoon in Montmorency, but at least you could be sure it wasn't all just in your head when several thousand others experienced it with you.

Or one, she thought.

While she waited for the taxi, she called Louise's number again, then the gallery. No answer. She decided to call Gabbard. It was late, but after what he had put her through, she'd be damned if she didn't have the right to ring him out of bed.

He picked up almost immediately. Unable to sleep, probably. Not surprising.

"I have no idea where my niece is," he said. "Did you try the gallery?"

"Twice."

"I suppose it's possible that she may be sleeping. She was alone at the gallery today, obviously. She had quite a bit of work to do."

"It's not off the hook," Milena said. "She's not answering."

"Or perhaps she went out."

"She never goes out this late," Milena said. "To my knowledge."

"I'm sure it's nothing, Mademoiselle. Perhaps you are a bit overwrought. Today has been—"

"That's exactly it. Today hasn't been a day like any other. Not for any of us."

"That is certainly true." He paused. She could hear him breathing. "Very well. I can go to her apartment and see if she is all right. I still have a key."

"I'd be grateful if you did, Monsieur Gabbard."

"Of course. Call me at Louise's number in about half an hour."

"I'll do that." Milena felt a brief urge to tell him about her trip to Montmorency. Just to share it with someone, to get the weight of it off her mind if nothing more. But he would have questions, naturally, and there was no time. Tomorrow. Maybe. "Thank you again."

She hurried into the kitchen. There was some cold coffee left in the pot. She gulped down a cupful, tore a piece off a stale baguette and headed down the stairs, chewing the bread. In the dark street, the sense of being watched returned. She regretted instructing the taxi dispatcher to send the car directly to her door.

The taxi arrived five minutes later. She told the driver to take her to the Val-de-Grâce hospital, a short walk from the Rue Gay-Lussac. As he put the car into gear, Milena heard an engine starting. A headlight came to life and moved out of a parking spot behind them. A motorcycle. Or a scooter. She reminded herself of what the driver had said, on the way over from Montmorency: there had to be thousands of the things on the streets.

Nevertheless, she sighed with relief when the bike only followed them to the corner of her street, where it turned and headed into another direction.

•

Milena entered the Rue Gay-Lussac from the south and walked north, toward the Jardin du Luxembourg. Even after her previous experiences fighting the flics and erecting barricades, the sight that greeted her was stunning.

The street had been readied for a massive assault. In intervals, the demonstrators had turned over cars and used them as foundations for barricades, with other objects piled on top, often several feet high. Heaps of paving stones had been gathered near these obstacles. That the CRS should have stood by and allowed this sort of preparation to proceed was nearly unbelievable. Milena wondered just how full of pent-up rage the flics were by now.

Halfway up the street, she found a public phone. She called Louise's number. Gabbard picked up.

"She's not here. I'm at a loss."

"I'm worried," Milena said. "What could have happened?"

"I can't imagine. Perhaps it has something to do with her father's funeral. She acts as if his death does not affect her…"

"I know. But it does."

"I'm sure there is a perfectly reasonable explanation." He laughed unconvincingly. "Who knows, maybe my niece has a secret lover somewhere, after all."

"Nothing's impossible."

"We'll know more by tomorrow, Mademoiselle. I suggest you get some sleep. It has been a difficult day."

Milena looked at the torn-up street behind her. "It might not be over yet."

There was a pause. He was listening to the background noises, no doubt. "You're with your friends, aren't you? Your comrades? On the street?"

"Of course."

"Good God. How did you find the strength, Mademoiselle?"

"I didn't," she said. "But I came anyway."

"Please be careful. I would hate for anything to happen to you."

Milena frowned. "Why is that?"

"For my part, I've come to think of you as something like a friend," he said. "And there's my niece. She has so much affection for you."

"Too much?"

Silence. Ježiše Marie, what had possessed her to say that?

"I don't believe there can be such a thing," he finally said. "But it is late, Mademoiselle. I, at least, have to return home and recoup my strength."

"Of course. Good night."

"Good night."

She found Pauline and Jeanne behind a barricade toward the north end of the street, just as Pauline had said. Across the small square facing the Jardin du Luxembourg she could see rows of CRS forces with their riot helmets and shields. The sight made the hairs on her neck stand up, partially with fear, partially with anger. But the troopers remained in place. For the time being.

Pauline frowned when she saw her. "You look tired." She gestured to Jeanne, who pulled a thermos out of her backpack and filled the lid with the black liquid inside. Steam rose into the cool air. She handed the cup to Milena.

"Perfect." Milena took a sip. The heat and aroma of the coffee was as close to bliss as she'd been in a while. "Any news?"

"Nothing much has changed here since I called you," Pauline said. "The atmosphere remains a little tense."

"I can see that."

"Dany went with a delegation of students and professors to talk to Roche," Jeanne said. "No idea what will come of that." She spat on the ground behind her. "I don't expect much, I can tell you that."

"Let's hope you're wrong." Pauline nodded toward the armored troopers across the square. "Those guys are primed to explode in our faces. Once the pin comes out, there'll be no putting it back in."

Milena looked around. She spotted Marcel a few yards away across the street, leaning against a white Citroën Bijou turned on its side. The car's windows had cracked and broken glass was scattered on the ground. He was smoking a cigarette and chatting with a young man and woman Milena didn't recognize. When he saw her, he smiled and waved. She waved back and turned to Pauline. "And where is Jacques?"

"He left to get something to eat. About ten minutes before you got here."

"He might as well have stayed," Milena murmured. Here and there along the ravaged street, residents had come down from their apartments and were handing sandwiches and drinks to the demonstrators. "Amazing. We rip apart the place where they live, and they still offer us support."

"That goes to show," Jeanne said. "Our cause is just." For once, there was no sarcasm in her tone.

Milena nodded and extended the empty plastic up. "Is there any more?"

.

By two in the morning, little had changed. Jeanne's thermos was empty. She herself was sitting on a tire, leaning against their barricade, eyes closed. Milena kept pacing back and forth between the barricades at the front to keep warm. The CRS troopers were still in position across the small square. It was hard to tell at a distance, looking into the stony faces under the helmets, but they seemed fidgety to her.

Jacques had returned, briefly, around one. A terse hello, how are you, an abortive smile, then he wandered off down the street, stopping here and there to talk to people. Soon after, Milena lost sight of him, and he did not come back. Pauline shrugged, as if to say: what can you do, give it time. But Milena wondered if their friendship would ever mend. If, in the ultimate analysis, it had even been one.

"I need to go make a phone call," she told Pauline. One last attempt. "I'll be right back."

She made her way down the street to the payphone and dialed Louise's number. She let it ring at least a dozen times, without expecting an answer, and there was none. Nothing to do now but wait till morning, as Gabbard had said.

When she turned away from the phone, something felt different. The atmosphere had changed. People were singing. Chants of "Libérez nos camarades" echoed between the tall buildings, accompanied by a multitude of footfalls. A movement rippled through the street, as if a giant muscle was bracing itself for some imminent exertion. A young man hurried past her. "What's going on?" she shouted at him.

"The troopers have cleared the barricades in the square," the runner said. "They're on the move. We have to defend." Then he was gone.

Milena muttered a curse. The son of a bitch Fouchet had given the word.

A deafening noise silenced the chanting. It took her a moment to realize that it had been an explosion. She began making her way back north, to Pauline and Jeanne.

She heard a series of hissing sounds. A brief silence followed. Then another explosion, and another. Somewhere, flames leaped up and cast a flickering light on a facade. Ahead of her, people screamed. She felt the sting of CS gas in her eyes and lungs. By the time she reached the barricades near where the Rue Gay-Lussac crossed the Rue Le Goff, a block south of where Pauline and Jeanne had been, her head felt numb from the explosions. She could barely breathe. Tears streamed down her face. Ghostly figures with handkerchiefs tied in front of their faces were hurling missiles at the advancing police. One of them suddenly moved toward her, waving. "Get back!" It was Marcel. "Here, cover your face." He gave her a handkerchief and a paper pouch. She hesitated. "Baking soda?" He nodded. "Absorbs the gas. Throw it on your face, quick!" The gas overwhelmed her before she could get the handkerchief in place. She couldn't stop coughing. There were more explosions, screams, and shouts accusing de Gaulle as a murderer, announcing that the final battle had come. Further back, some still found the air in their lungs to sing the Internationale. Marcel dragged her into a doorway. "Where are Pauline and Jeanne?" she asked.

"I don't know!" He had to shout to be audible over the din. "Hopefully they fell back. This is turning into a massacre. Stay here until you catch your breath."

Before she could make a reply, he turned and disappeared into the crowd and the smoke. For a brief time, the wind turned. There was cheering as the tear gas was blown back at the advancing police, forcing them to retreat. But almost immediately, they renewed their attack with doubled ferocity. The air was thick with yellow fumes. More fires sprang up. The foremost barricade was breached. Milena heard more footsteps and shouting: the troopers were trying to enter the side street, to cut off their retreat. She stepped out of the doorway and made her way south. As she emerged into the street, she was hit by a splash of cold water. She looked up in shock and saw someone at a window holding an empty bucket.

"What the hell?" she spat. More bucketfuls came from other windows. Were the residents turning on the students, after all? But her eyes stung a little less. She realized that the pelting was well-meant: people where throwing the water in an attempt to clear the gas-choked air. She heard a sound of glass shattering further up the street, followed by screaming. Something whistled through the air above her and she saw a window explode into a shower of shards. The window flew open and several figures leaned out, yelling and coughing. Thick yellow vapor streamed out of the room behind them. The police had started counting the residents as combatants.

She shook the water out of her hair. The handkerchief Marcel had given her was soaked. She was about to tie it in front of her face when a concussion grenade went off close to her. The ringing in her ears extinguished all other sound.

A group of people ran toward her, carrying injured comrades away from the most dangerous area at the front of the street. She quickly stepped out of the way. When they had passed, Milena noticed a figure on the other side of the street, standing still amid the surrounding chaos. She felt certain that the person was a man, and that he was looking at her, but she couldn't make out his features; her eyes still swam from the tear gas. There was something familiar about his frame, but she couldn't place it. If he was one of her friends, why was he standing there like that, watching her? Suddenly, he bent down. He was picking something up from the ground. He came back up, raised his arm, and swung. Instinctively, she glanced around for advancing troopers. None in sight. Who was he aiming at?

His hand flew out toward her.

She frowned in disbelief. It cost her only a fraction of a second. But that was all it took.

The impact knocked her head back. Her shoulders crashed into the wall behind her. She was astonished, in a detached manner, by the briefness of the pain. For an instant, she wondered if anything had happened at all. She saw a pavement stone lying at her feet. Could it be? The ringing in her ears turned to white noise and faded. She had a sudden sense of weightlessness. The pavement flipped under her feet, became a wall, rushed at her, hit her like a runaway bus. Everything went dark. The last thing she felt was wet stone pressing against her cheek. Then she was gone.

3 BLOODLINES

Paris, May 11, 1968.

Louise watched the blood flow.

A dark red line inched slowly toward her wrist. She held her breath in anticipation of the relief, of the filth inside drawing out of her skin, like purulence.

It wasn't enough.

She hadn't been this close to him in six years. The fact that he was dead, in the ground, under the freshly turned earth on which she had spat and then wept, made only so much of a difference.

She placed the white shard on her forearm again, a little higher, on the fleshiest part. Before she pressed down, she glanced at Saint Geneviève in her golden frame.

Would you approve? You never had to open up your body like a boil. But you would have understood.

She pushed the glass downward and her skin came apart as if along an invisible seam. It would have to be deeper, longer, than any of the scars around it.

A spurt of blood shot up. In seconds, it enveloped her arm and dripped onto her thigh. It was going to be a mess but it had to be.

She dropped the shard on the night table, next to its lacquer case, where she had laid out a red napkin for the purpose. Something inside her melted away as she watched the blood pulse out of her skin. Part of her, part of him. She exhaled so deeply that her breath sounded like a hum, a distant chant that seemed to come from a throat other than her own. Someone else was humming, far away, deep inside of her.

I'm gone. You're gone. For now.

It felt a little like when Milena was near her, put her arms around her, kissed her. She stopped being who she was and became someone else for a short time. Except that with Milena, the someone else was still her, was still Louise, the way she might be if things had been good. Milena filled her with possibilities. When the blood flowed, she didn't know who she was becoming. Someone who didn't have a name anymore. Who hurt less, felt less sick. Perhaps no one at all.

She sat for a while like this. Being no one. Being empty, of joy, of pain. Relief. The blood kept coming, soaking her leg, her crotch. She tried not to let it drip on the sheet, but after a while, she slouched, trancelike, and her arm fell to her side.

When she came to, when she had a sense of being again, of coalescing once more into Louise, the bed was smeared with blood.

She went into the bathroom and rinsed the congealed blood off her arm. There it went, a pink stream plunging into the pipes, the sewers, the underground beneath the streets, and then, who knew, the sea, perhaps? How much of her had gone that way, over the years?

Back on her bed, she began the task of bandaging. Her head felt thick, a little like one morning after she'd had too much wine at an opening party at the gallery, but not as unpleasant. There was no nausea, no ache. Just a sense of grogginess. As if her thoughts, even the spiny, painful ones, had been padded, made safe.

She looked at the icon again. There was always the question whether what she did would have appalled Saint Geneviève. She had treated her worldly body with harshness in order to be pure, but was that the same? It was the wrong question to ask, of course. Louise knew she was no saintly figure. She was the demoniac, inhabited by a foul taint. The one in need of a saint's touch, of a cure.

And Saint Geneviève, no doubt, would never have embraced, or even thought of embracing, another woman the way she embraced Milena. Was that a sin as well, another taint? Common sense dictated that the Church would disapprove, to say the least. Men lying with men, there was mention of that in the Bible. Mention, and condemnation. It couldn't be much different for women lying with women, why would it be?

Louise pulled the gauze tight around her forearm and fixed it in place with two bandage clips. She could feel the tiny metal teeth through the cloth, pricking her skin like a miniature cilice.

Something inside her refused to accept that her feelings were an abomination. In the end, wasn't the only sinful act the one you knew to offend God and committed nonetheless? Whereas if, in your heart of hearts, you truly did not hold it to be a sin...

Could one plead ignorance so easily?

It didn't matter. Not to one such as her. Perhaps to someone pure, the risk of offending God further would have been graver. She was a lost cause, even to His grace.

Sometimes, she allowed herself to dream of a day when the only thing that mattered between her and God were her own choices. Not the evil that had been forced on her, sullying her in His eyes, the taint that never truly lifted no matter how many times she dug it out of her flesh like a festering corpse out of unhallowed earth.

Let me choose my own fall from grace, if that is what loving her means. That is all I ask: one choice entirely my own.

Then she could leave the judging to God, like Katarina had done on the ice. If He took her up on it, if He took everything she had in order to punish her, so be it. Everything she had for everything she wanted. It seemed a fair trade.

The bandage was done. It was a little too thick around the joint. She couldn't quite bend her arm. But she couldn't risk bleeding through another coat, either. Who knew what Uncle Claude would do, in his concern for her?

She looked at her clock. Four thirty. Hardly worth going to sleep before heading to the gallery. But she felt calm, almost serene. The memory of her vigil at the grave was already fading. Perhaps it had all been a dream. She blew out the candle on her night table and sank into the blood-stained sheets.

•

She woke up at five o'clock, unable to go back to sleep. For minutes before sitting up, she stared at the stains on her sheet. When had she bled?

She became aware of the stiff bandage around her arm and remembered. Strange. Normally, she slept soundly after her excoriations. Instead, she felt restless.

In the kitchen as she sipped the morning's first cup of tea, she turned on the radio. The taxi driver who had taken her back from Tours in the night had been listening to the news. Reports of brutal confrontations between the students and the CRS near the Jardin du Luxembourg were coming in. Grenades were being used, paving stones hurled, fires started. By the time she got out of the taxi in front of her building, there had still been no end in sight.

That was why she felt so nervous, of course. Milena would have been there, in the thick of it.

The battle was over, the announcer informed his audience. The streets were gutted, lined with demolished cars. Hundreds had been hospitalized, hundreds more injured, among them many policemen. And, naturally, hundreds of arrests had been made.

She had to call Milena. Almost six. She didn't want to wake up the roommate, the tall redhead with the freckles. Pauline. They'd never really met, although Milena had mentioned telling her about Louise now and then. It could hardly have been the whole story. She might wonder why Louise called so early to ask about Milena. But what of it? People worried about friends, didn't they? Besides, from what she remembered of the layout of the apartment, Milena's room was closest to the phone in the hallway. If she was there, she might pick up first. If. The worst that could happen, of course, would be for no one at all to pick up. She would have no way of finding out anything then.

She turned off the radio and dialed the number. With any luck, in a few moments she would be speaking to Milena.

But it was Pauline who answered. At least it hadn't taken more than three rings. Louise was relieved; she hadn't woken her up.

"It's Louise," she said. "Milena's friend."

"Louise, Louise," Pauline murmured. Then, louder, "Louise, yes. Of course. From the gallery."

"I've been listening to the radio. I was worried about Milena."

"Your timing is good. I was just about to leave. Unfortunately, the news I have is not so good."

Louise's heart began to palpitate. "What happened?"

•

Pauline met her by the entrance to the Val-de-Grâce hospital.

"Have you seen her?" Louise asked.

Pauline shook her head. "I just got here. Let's go."

They got out of the elevator, turned a corner, and headed down a corridor. Pauline counted the room numbers, pointed toward the end of the hallway. "There."

The door to the room opened and Jacques stepped into the hallway. He looked pale, with dark rings under his eyes. When he saw them approaching, he nodded a greeting.

"How is she?" Pauline asked.

Jacques shook his head. "Hard to say. They have her on a drip, to prevent swelling inside her head. That's crucial now, they tell me."

"But she's still unconscious?"

He nodded.

"Can we see her?" Louise asked.

"Of course," Jacques said. "I'll go get you some coffee."

•

There was no stopping the tears. Even with Pauline standing at the other side of the bed, watching. But she was crying as well.

"Oh, mon Christ." Louise collapsed on the chair by the bed and took Milena's hand. An IV catheter was taped to her arm, hooked up to a drip. Her head was bandaged, the face underneath swollen, discolored, as if she had been in a boxing match and lost. She was breathing regularly, if flatly. But she didn't stir. Not at Louise's touch, not at the sound of her voice. Her eyes remained closed.

Pauline pulled up another chair. There were three more beds in the room, altogether. One, next to Milena's bed, was empty, one occupied by an older woman with her leg in a hoisted cast. In the fourth, by the door, lay a young man with bandages on his arms and head. Another victim of the previous night's battles, for all they knew. Both were asleep, or unconscious. Louise was suddenly aware of the typical hospital smell: disinfectant with an underlying note of urea.

"I feel like apologizing to Jacques," Pauline whispered.

"For what?"

"I was pretty mad at him, for a while. I thought he was acting like an idiot to Milena ever after that evening. You were there, weren't you?"

Louise nodded.

"As if their friendship hadn't meant anything to him," Pauline went on. "I was ready to dismiss him as just another self-absorbed prick. But he may have saved her life."

"He found her?"

"He saw her collapse, got the medics to her. He's been here with her since before three. The doctors said that if help hadn't gotten to her right away, she might have died."

"Jesus." Louise fumbled blindly inside her purse. It seemed to take her forever before she found a handkerchief. "How did this happen?"

"She was hit by a paving stone," Pauline said. "An accident, no doubt. You must have heard on the news how severe the fighting was."

"How do you know it was a stone?

"Jacques found it lying on the ground next to her. There was blood on it."

For several minutes, they sat in silence. A soft sound of snoring came from the bed by the door, from the woman with the cast. Louise realized that she was still holding Milena's hand. She glanced at Pauline and let go.

"Keep holding it," Pauline said. "She can probably feel it. It'll comfort her."

Louise hesitated. "Maybe you should hold her hand for a while."

Pauline smiled. "Let's not confuse her."

Louise wasn't sure what to make of the remark. But she'd heard it too, that coma patients were aware of what went on around them. Of being touched, spoken to. She took Milena's hand again, squeezed it softly. No reaction.

The door opened, and Jacques entered with two paper cups. He walked across the linoleum floor, handed one cup to Louise, one to Pauline.

"Thank you," Louise said.

"The doctor says there's no telling when she might wake up," Jacques whispered. "Could be hours, could be days. We just have to wait. But she's not deteriorating. That's something."

Louise and Pauline nodded.

After a few minutes, Jacques leaned toward Pauline. "Can I speak to you outside for a moment?"

•

Louise heard her name called. Quietly, almost a whisper, but with insistence. She lifted her head. Her neck was stiff and achy. Where was she?

The hospital, of course. She had fallen asleep with her head on Milena's bed. Still holding her hand.

Cold morning light shone into the room. The woman with the cast on her leg was reading a newspaper. Not surprisingly, the headlines were concerned with the confrontations of the night before. The young man in the third bed had still not woken up, but he had shifted his position. Not comatose, Louise thought.

A wave of panic hit her. What if Milena didn't wake up, not today, not tomorrow? She pushed the thought away, but it kept hovering at a distance.

Jacques stood at the other side of the bed, across from her. "They serve breakfast in the cafeteria in the basement. I'll stay here. Pauline is already down there."

"How long have I been sleeping like this?"

"Not long. Ten, fifteen minutes. Go, eat something."

"I'm not hungry," she said.

"Another cup of coffee, a croissant. Keep your strength."

Louise shook her head.

"Go ahead." He sat down on the second chair. "Besides, Pauline wants to talk to you."

Louise rubbed her aching neck. "I prefer tea."

He smiled a lopsided smile. "They have that, too."

•

Pauline was waiting for her at a table toward the back of the cafeteria, by a wall underneath an oversized and non-descript abstract painting, dipping a piece of pastry into a coffee bowl. When she saw Louise, she gestured emphatically toward the counter. Louise sighed. Everybody seemed to find it imperative to eat and drink constantly. She took a tray and got a sablé and a cup of tea. The line was short; most of the customers at this time of the morning were hospital personnel arriving for their dayshift.

She put her tray down in front of Pauline and checked her watch to time the tea. Pauline observed her. "You're the fastidious type, aren't you?"

"About certain things."

"It's funny," Pauline said. "You and Milena have been friends for a while now. And yet today is the first time I'm talking to you."

Louise broke a piece off the sablé and started slowly picking it apart. "The last time she tried to introduce me to one of her friends was a bit of a disaster."

"Yes, because he confessed his love for her that evening." Pauline chuckled. "It's not what typically happens, I assure you. At least as far as I know."

Louise shrugged. She found it easy to believe that people fell in love with Milena all the time.

"You two seem to have grown quite close, at any rate."

"She's my friend," Louise said.

"Why, yes." Pauline cleared her throat and bit off another piece of pastry soggy with coffee. "Still, it's funny. You don't strike me as her type."

"Her type?"

"Usually, Milena runs with the political crowd," Pauline said. "The kind that have been in the news a lot lately, you know. Students, agitators, whatever you want to call them. You seem a bit more, how shall I put this— haute bourgeoisie?"

"I choose not to think in such terms."

"Maybe not. But those are the terms, nevertheless."

Louise ate one of the sablé fragments. She glanced at her watch again and pulled the tea bag from her cup. Then she proceeded to break the other pieces of the cookie in half, one by one.

"Jesus Christ," Pauline muttered. "Perhaps fastidious isn't the right word. Why are you doing this?"

Louise shrugged. "It calms me."

"I suppose I can see why you'd need that."

"I have this feeling you're about to interrogate me."

"Not really," Pauline said. "But I would like to ask you about a few things."

"Is that what Jacques meant, when he said you'd like to talk to me?"

"Yes."

"What do you want to know?"

"Well, it seems to me that when Milena is with you, she must be in a different environment, so to speak, from the one I usually see her in. I don't know if that makes any sense."

"It doesn't," Louise said.

"You must move in different circles," Pauline said. "Meet different people."

Louise shook her head. "Milena and I never spent time with other people."

"Really?" Pauline raised an eyebrow. "You must be fascinating company."

"Honestly, I don't see how it concerns you, how Milena and I spend our time together."

"Please, there's no need to bristle." Pauline sighed. "Jesus, I don't like questioning you like this, as if I was some sort of flic. But there's something I need to know, something Milena never talked about."

Louise went back to picking apart her sablé. "Like what?"

"I don't know if she mentioned this to you," Pauline said. "If she didn't, I'll be violating her privacy, but under the circumstances…" She finished the last of her coffee and stared into the bowl. "Milena started seeing someone a few months ago. She never told me who he was, and I don't think anyone else knew. None of her friends at the university, anyway."

Louise stopped crumbling the sablé. "Seeing someone?"

"Some mystery man," Pauline said. "I think things were going pretty well, but who knows? She never told me anything specific."

Louise felt a pang of—what? Jealousy? Most likely, Milena had made up the story to account for the many hours they spent together. Except that she had never mentioned making excuses with Pauline. "She didn't say anything to me."

"Really? Too bad. I was hoping you might know who he was."

"I know nothing about that," Louise muttered. "About him." She thought of their first kiss, outside her door, of what Milena had said to her: I can't promise you anything. Had she spoken the same words to someone else? It would only make sense, of course. What did a miserable creature like her have to offer someone like Milena? Sadness, bandages, blood, and doubt. And she didn't even know about the worst part, the revolting defilement she carried. But still, Milena had come to her, had knocked on her door, kissed her. Would she have done that, for someone truly and utterly without worth? And was she even so lacking in worth, that she would have to quietly accept having her heart broken? Something stirred in Louise, a rebellious thought she had not known for nearly as long as she could remember: I don't deserve this.

Pauline frowned. "Is something the matter?"

Louise shook her head. "I'm just so confused."
Honesty. If not love, at least she wanted that.

"I see. Now, you are sure she never mentioned anything?"

"Of course I'm sure," Louise snapped. "Why are you asking me these questions, anyway? Milena is lying upstairs unconscious and you want me to tell you how she spent her private time away from you and your friends?"

Pauline dabbed her lips with a napkin and sat up straight. She took a pack of cigarettes out of her jacket, looked around, and put them back. "What if there is a connection?"

"Between what?"

"Between certain people Milena knew and what happened to her," Pauline said. "Because I don't think it was an accident."

•

Louise closed her eyes. The sudden rush of vertigo only got worse. She opened them again. "You think someone attacked her? On purpose?"

"It's not as far-fetched as it sounds," Pauline said. "Suppose there was a problem between Milena and this man she was seeing."

"What kind of problem?"

"I don't know. A problem. They happen all the time in relationships, you know. Jealousy, suspicions, or maybe one person wants to end it and the other doesn't, who knows? The point is, infatuation can turn to hatred pretty easily."

"A lover's quarrel," Louise murmured. She felt a chill. What if Pauline was right? What if there had been

someone else, someone who knew about Milena and her—
someone who was jealous? An older lover, maybe not
even a man, someone with whom Milena was breaking
things off. Perhaps in order to be with her, with Louise.
The thought briefly made her feel better, but wouldn't that
mean that she was the reason for the jilted lover's anger?
That she was ultimately to blame for what happened to
Milena?

Was God's punishment this swift?

She didn't want to believe it. But the idea lodged
in her mind like a splinter, driving itself deeper and
deeper.

"That makes it sound almost romantic," Pauline
said. "I'm thinking more along the lines of some brutish
son-of-a-bitch who couldn't deal with a woman who has
her own head."

"Why would Milena see someone like that?"

"People are good at hiding their worst sides. At
least as long as they get what they want."

"This is a horrible thought," Louise said. "I don't
want to believe it."

Pauline shrugged. "Not up to us."

"But she was in a street fight. I listened to the
reports on the radio. It was complete chaos. Isn't it much
more likely, in a situation like that, that she was hit by a
stray paving stone?"

"I suppose you imagine those stones were flying
through the air in all directions, like hail," Pauline said.
"That's not exactly what was going on. Let me explain to
you what Jacques said." She fished a pencil out of her
purse. "As you may or may not know, the CRS troopers
started clearing the Rue Gay-Lussac from the north." She
flattened a paper napkin and drew a crude street map on it.
"Here, from this square, the Place Edmond Rostand.
That's about where I was, with a couple of close friends, at
the time Milena was hit by the stone. And she was about

here—" She marked a spot a block and a half down from the square. "Just south of Le Goff. Now, the CRS was trying to come through Le Goff at this point, but they weren't making much headway, and they certainly hadn't reached the Rue Gay-Lussac yet. Of course they also came from the south, but that wasn't until later. Are you with me?"

"What does all this mean?"

"Use your head," Pauline said. "I know you've never been near a street battle, but you don't need to be a seasoned guerilla fighter to figure this out."

Louise stared at the napkin. It seemed silly, but she felt a burning desire to show Pauline that she could take up the challenge of figuring out her puzzle. "Wait." She raised a hand. "If the CRS were attacking here, and here, and farther down toward the south end of the street…"

Pauline nodded. "Now you're thinking."

"There were no troopers near Milena when she was hit."

"At least not near enough for anyone in that area to throw paving stones at them," Pauline said. "First of all, those things are heavy. And even if you're strong enough, you don't hurl rocks from the rear, through clouds of gas and smoke in the dark, over the intervening heads of your own comrades. It's too dangerous. The flics wear helmets to protect them. We don't."

"But in the confusion, isn't it possible for someone to have lost their head, and done it anyway?"

"Sure," Pauline said. "For a complete idiot. We weren't the disorganized rabble those radio reports make us out to be. We all knew that we had a responsibility toward each other, and toward possible non-combatants. We conducted briefings, held meetings, to make sure people knew what kind of stupid maneuvers not to pull. The last thing we wanted was a headline screaming that a

student brained an innocent passerby with a paving stone."
She crumpled the napkin and dropped it on her tray. "I'm
not saying there is no way this could have been an
accident. But there is room for doubt. For suspicion."

"Suspicion? Of what? Or whom?"

"Of someone who had it in for Milena, and who
saw the perfect opportunity to attack her."

"That stone nearly killed her," Louise said. She
felt the sting of tears in her eyes. "Who could hate her so
much?"

"Hell may have no fury like a woman scorned."
Pauline snorted. "But men are far more likely to bash
someone's head in when things don't go their way."

"You don't mean—" Louise swallowed.
"Jacques?"

"Good God, no. But we do know there was
another man."

"Or the random idiot who lost his head," Louise
said.

Pauline sucked the air in through her teeth with a
hiss. "I just wonder if it wasn't an idiot with a motive."

"The whole question will be moot once Milena
wakes up. She must have seen who threw the stone."

"We can't be sure of that," Pauline said. "And it
might be a while before she comes to. I hope it won't be,
but who knows? Why waste time?" She shook her head.
"No, we need to find out who this other guy is. And I will.
Someone has to know him."

•

In the hospital room, Jacques was awake, sitting
by Milena's bed, his back to the door. He looked broken.

He turned around and smiled faintly when he heard Louise and Pauline enter. But his eyes were filled with grief.

They walked quietly up to the bed. Louise studied Milena's silent face. No change. Her right cheek was bruised where it had hit the pavement. Her lips were swollen, encrusted with dried blood.

Had she kissed someone else with them?

And if so, would that change things? Should she want Milena less, care less, feel less pain at the sight of her beaten face?

There was no such decision before her, of course, she knew that now, any more than she would have to face a grand choice to risk perdition. Only a feeling that stood unshakably beyond all reason, beyond jealousy and thoughts of hurt pride, and beyond all her fears about this world and the next. And no matter what happened, at least that belonged entirely to her.

She sat down and took the lifeless hand in hers. She reminded herself that after all, the secret lover might be herself, and the attacker in the Rue Gay-Lussac a random fool, the solitary hothead who had missed all the briefings and meetings Pauline had spoken of.

Wake up. Please, wake up.

She felt selfish for her wish. God forgive me, she thought. I need to talk to her, to hear her voice undoing my uncertainty. To get the assurance craved by every self-centered heart since time began: you, only you. No one else.

"She had a visitor while you were in the cafeteria," Jacques said.

"A visitor?"

"Well, perhaps not in the strict sense of the word," he said. "But some guy came in looking for her."

"Who was it?" Pauline asked.

"I'd never seen him before. I saw him look at the lady with the cast, the sleeping guy by the door. Didn't seem to interest him. He took a few steps toward this bed, then he saw that I'd noticed him. He took one good look at Milena, turned on his heels, and out the door he went."

Pauline frowned. "Strange. What did he look like?"

"About my age, but taller than me, and kind of thin. Full dark hair, no beard. Street clothes. Nothing too nice. On the whole, not particularly distinctive. Could have been anyone."

"Very helpful."

"He was definitely looking for her?" Louise asked.

"I'd say so." Jacques pursed his lips. "If he was looking for one of those other people, why didn't he stay? It's possible that he was altogether in the wrong room, of course."

Louise began to feel ill. "Did he have flowers?"

Jacques chuckled. "Flowers?"

"Did he?"

"No," Jacques said. "What does that matter?"

Louise shook her head. She shaded her eyes with her hand. What did it matter? She hadn't brought any, either.

"It might mean he was just checking on her," Pauline said. "In a hurry to get here. Or he didn't mean to bring or leave anything to begin with."

"Wait a minute," Jacques said. "Who besides us and a few other people, all of whom we know, would have any idea that she's here in the first place?"

Louise dropped the hand from her eyes and sat up straight. "The one that threw the stone."

Pauline nodded. "He wanted to see the damage he did."

"Shit," Jacques whispered. "And I let him go without even asking who he was."

•

Pauline and Jacques stayed for another hour. But Pauline was restless. She wanted to start her search for the unknown man, the possible secret boyfriend, spurned lover, attacker, whichever he was.

"I need to call my uncle," Louise said. "After that, you can go. I'll stay here with her."

"All day?" Jacques asked.

"All day."

She took the elevator to the lobby and found a payphone. Uncle Claude answered immediately, barely letting the first ring finish. "Where on God's earth were you last night? I tried to call you endlessly. I even went to your apartment."

"I was in Tours," she told him.

Silence. "In Tours?"

"I wanted to see the grave. But listen, Uncle Claude—"

"I pleaded with you to come to the funeral, and then you go on your own?"

"I didn't want to go to the funeral," Louise said. "I just wanted to see that it's true. That it's finally over. That he is over."

"For Christ's sake, Louise. That is a terrible thing to say."

"Then it's the right thing to say about him."

"You went there after work? And came back in the night? But how?"

"I took a taxi. Then another taxi back. Does it matter?"

"I can't believe this," he stammered. "Where are you now?"

"I'm in a hospital. Milena had an accident."

"Good God," he said. "Last night, at the protests?"

246

"Yes. She suffered a head injury. She's in a coma."

"Will she be all right? Should I come?"

"There's no need," Louise said. "But I will stay with her. The doctors say she might wake up anytime. I don't want her to be alone."

"Of course not. Very good. I'll manage here, don't worry. Let me know if there's any change. Or if you need anything."

"I will, Uncle Claude."

"And when you come home—I imagine you won't be there the night?"

"I don't think they allow that."

"Come see me in the evening, then. There's something I need to tell you. Something I learned when I was at your parents' house." A long pause. "It concerns Frédéric."

"I'll be too tired tonight," Louise said. "And Frédéric has been dead for so long, uncle. What news can there be that can't wait?"

"The sooner you hear what I found, the better. Please believe me."

When she returned to the room upstairs, Pauline was inspecting Milena's clothes. They had been hung in a closet by the door. "I should have them cleaned," she said. "Look at this. Dirt, blood. Jesus." She lifted a pant leg. "The knee is torn here, too."

"I'll take them tonight," Louise said. "Perhaps you can bring some of her clothes from Levallois tomorrow."

"Right." Pauline placed the hanger back in the closet. "You really want to stay that long?"

Louise nodded. "Until they tell me to leave."

Jacques approached from the hospital bed. He leaned in close. "I wonder if we shouldn't contact the police."

"That's a great idea," Pauline said. "I'm sure they'll be thrilled to investigate the case of a protester who got injured during last night's riots for possible foul play."

He shrugged. "Just a thought."

"I want to have a talk with this guy Milena was involved with. It's the only way for us to find out more."

Jacques sighed. "If only anybody knew who he was."

After that, they left. Louise could hear their voices through the closed door, receding down the hallway.

•

It was a long, silent vigil, interrupted only two times. Once, the old woman with the cast received a visit from her son, who brought her a box of chocolates and an immense bouquet of yellow tulips. But he stayed only briefly, and the room was quiet again except for the occasional rustle each time the woman picked another chocolate from the box. The scent of the tulips mingled with the hospital smells in a sweetly sickening mélange.

At two in the afternoon, a young couple came to see Milena. A girl with smooth black hair reaching down to her hips, who introduced herself as Jeanne and the young man who accompanied her as Marcel. He had a black eye—from a truncheon blow, the girl explained— and several cuts on his hand where he had stumbled into broken glass trying to get away from the flics. Apparently, Pauline had already filled them in on who she was. The black-haired woman told Louise how in spite of the disastrous outcome of the fights with the police, the movement had gained a political victory, that the jailed students were to be released, the Sorbonne soon reopened, and that the government had put itself in the baleful position of a brutal oppressor. After a few seconds of this, the young man told Jeanne to stop talking. He urged Louise to use the opportunity to have lunch in the cafeteria. But she had no appetite.

Some time after the couple left, Louise fell asleep again, with her head next to Milena's arm. When the nurse woke her up, the light in the room had begun to fade. Visiting hours would soon be over, she informed Louise. A few minutes later, the overhead lamps came on.

She got up and took Milena's clothes from the closet. The duffle jacket was covered with dirt, and there were some dark stains on the lapel which had to be blood. She could drop the clothes off at her cleaner's on the way home. She checked the pockets to make sure they were empty. The only thing she found was a crumpled note on which Milena had written down two addresses. The first was that of a Paris law firm. Legal representation in the event of troubles with the police, probably. The second was a street address in Montmorency. No name was included. It was circled twice for emphasis, but there was no telling what its significance might have been to Milena.

Or was there?

Louise hurried down to the payphone in the lobby and dialed Milena's number. After several rings, Pauline answered. "You're still at the hospital?"

"They just told me to leave," Louise said.

"How is Milena?"

"Still not awake."

"Go home and get some rest, Louise. There's nothing more you can do tonight."

"Does Milena know anyone in Montmorency?"

"In Montmorency? Why?"

"I found an address in her jacket," Louise said. "I wonder if it means something."

"That depends. Is there a name?"

"No name, just an address. And it's circled. Twice. It must have been important to her." There was a long silence. "Pauline? Are you still there?"

"I just thought of something," Pauline said. "Last night, when I was at the Rue Gay-Lussac, I tried to call Milena several times. I finally reached her around eleven. She said she'd been out until eight, and after that, asleep. I didn't think it was important at the time, but now I wonder. She must have gone through something exhausting."

"My god, Pauline, what if she was in Montmorency? What if it's his address?"

"Let's not jump to conclusions," Pauline said. "But it might be worth taking a look. I'll come with you."

"When can you meet me?"

"How about tomorrow morning at the hospital? I can be there at ten."

"Tomorrow morning?"

"You weren't seriously thinking about going now?"

Louise hesitated. "No," she said. "No, of course not. Good night, Pauline."

•

The taxi driver leaned toward the open passenger window with a skeptical expression on his face. "You don't seem too happy, Mademoiselle. Are you sure this is where you want to be?"

Louise looked up and down the sidewalk. It was dark. A light wind sighed in the tops of the trees lining the street. In intervals, streetlamps cast their circles of yellow light into the gloom. At the far end of the street, a solitary figure was watching a dog lift its leg under a sign post. She turned back to the driver inside the brightly lit taxi. "It has to be."

"Has to be, huh?" The driver chuckled. "All right."

Louise watched his taillights recede along the street. The dog walker turned a corner and disappeared. She was alone, an explorer deposited on the shores of an unknown island with no certain knowledge if or when another ship would come by to take her home to safety. On another occasion, she might have enjoyed visiting Montmorency. From what she'd heard, it was a pretty enough little town, once a summer resort for wealthy Parisians and home to renowned cherry groves, now largely residential. Aunt Corinne had even owned a house here, many years before she'd married Uncle Claude. The thought made the strange dark streets feel almost familiar.

She turned around and took in the forbidding hedge of arborvitae, with its leafy tunnel leading to the iron gate. The tops of the slender trees reached into the night like spearheads. She couldn't even see a house from the street.

It was time to come up with a plan. Suppose she rang the bell, and the man Jacques had described at the hospital opened the door. Was she to simply ask him if he had gone to the Rue Gay-Lussac the night before and thrown a paving stone at Milena's head? If he had in fact done it, he might not be too pleased to be tracked down. Louise decided she would stand back from the door, poised to make a run for the garden gate at any sign of danger.

But after that, what? Come back with the police?

Not much of a plan. But you had to start somewhere.

He couldn't kill her, could he?

She entered the opening in the hedge and stepped up to the garden gate. She could make out the shadow of a house between two trees. None of the windows were lit. Bad luck already. No one was home. Unless they were already asleep, or in a room toward the back.

Louise brought her face close to the steel bars in an effort to peer into the garden. She wasn't sure what she might be able to see that could prove useful, but it couldn't hurt to know the terrain before ringing the bell. There wasn't much she could discern in the darkness aside from weeds and an ill-kept lawn. In the far right corner, she thought she saw a patch of tall flowers. Foxglove, perhaps.

Something began kicking around wildly in her stomach. She had to gulp for air.

Impossible.

The faun.

She pushed her face against the gate to be able to get a better look. The rusty metal bit into her cheek.

Aunt Corinne's faun. From the photograph in Uncle Claude's foyer.

She grabbed the steel bars. Her knees felt weak.

Aunt Corinne had stood next to the exact same faun, her hand resting on its marble shoulder. In the dark, Louise half imagined she saw a slender silhouette position itself next to the sculpture.

It couldn't be coincidence.

Why did Milena have the address to this house? How could she even have known it?

Uncle Claude. Of course. He had invited Milena to his apartment to talk. Louise had never had a friend, and he would have wanted to get to know her, maybe ask her to tell him if she knew whether anything was wrong with Louise. It was just like him. The old worrier.

But that still didn't explain anything. What interest could Milena have had in Corinne's old house? Uncle Claude himself never talked about it. He probably didn't even know where it was.

Did the mystery man, by some bizarre quirk of fate, live in what had once been Aunt Corinne's house? Except that the place looked as if no one had inhabited it in years. Now that her eyes were getting used to the dark, Louise noticed the signs of decay everywhere. The ragged garden, the broken pantiles on the roof. The cardboard replacing a window pane upstairs.

What kind of person would live in such disrepair?

Louise felt a dull pain burrow into her skull and expand. She closed her eyes and steadied herself against the steel bars, massaging her temple with one hand.

A buzzing sound pulsed through the metal. She started violently.

With a shrill creak, the gate swung open.

She took a step back, looked toward the house.

There was light behind the glass panes of the front door. Yellow light, dim, as if filtered through a curtain.

•

It was simple, of course.

She'd been standing by the gate for minutes, staring into the garden like a fool, and someone had seen her from inside the house.

From behind those dark windows.

Now they meant to see what she wanted. And in the end, if the man she was seeking did indeed live here—absurd as that seemed—she would want to see him, too, and speak to him. She wasn't really sure how she would go about it, what she would say, or what good it would do. But that's what she had come here for.

She set a foot on the slate slabs leading to the door.

Why didn't he come out to get a look at her?

Because he could see her just fine from where he was hiding.

She took a few slow steps toward the house.

No. This was wrong. Dangerous. No normal person acted this way, buzzing a stranger into their garden and then not emerging from behind the door. And it was dark, with all those trees and bushes around. The arborvitae blocked out most of the light from the street. What faint light remained in the sky—quickly turning a rich cobalt blue dotted here and there with stars—was blotted out by the two tall chestnut trees flanking the house.

She felt a sudden panic. Had she already advanced too far into—

She turned around to look at the gate. Ajar, the way she had left it.

She mustered her courage one more time and continued toward the front door. Ridiculous, no one was trying to trap her. Perhaps the inhabitant was an old lady, living alone, distrustful of any stranger outside her door. That also explained the poor state of the house. Perhaps she had no one to fix things for her.

But Louise's body wasn't fooled by such logic. Her legs wanted her to leave. She turned and took a step toward the gate, away from the house.

Something exploded behind her.

She spun around. The front door had flown open. Broken glass hit stone with a bright noise. A figure leapt at her.

She tried to run, but the shock paralyzed her.

Like in a nightmare.

She wanted to scream, but a hand locked roughly over her mouth. Her arms were pinned to her sides.

Perhaps this was a nightmare. It didn't seem real.

She kicked, hit air, lost a shoe.

He was dragging her back to the house. The dreadful old house. Suddenly, his grip relinquished. She had a sense of flying; he was throwing her. A stink rushed at her. Stale food, garbage. Mold. She landed on the floor with a crash that knocked the breath out of her. Her head hit something hard. The pain was bright and sharp. She expected to pass out, but didn't.

I'm going to die, she thought.

The door slammed shut. She heard more glass falling to the floor.

She didn't dare open her eyes. But she knew she had to. How did they say? Look death in the face.

No one who did anything like this to you meant to let you leave. Or live. She thought of Milena and sadness bore down on her like an avalanche. Life wasn't so hard to lose; she wasn't afraid of that. But love was.

She opened her eyes, didn't look up. Her face hurt. She wiped it and her palm came away red. Blood. Only this time, she found no relief in the sight.

Well, she thought. Let's get this over with. She raised her eyes toward her captor. The breath went out of her a second time.

"Maurice?"

"Finally." He stood above her, his eyes wild, unblinking. With that ever-present, senseless smile on his lips. "Finally, you've come back to me."

And he laughed.

•

Louise kicked at the oily carpet underneath her, trying to scramble as far away from him as she could. But she was already backed into a corner.

"Maurice," she stammered. "What are you doing here?"

"What am I doing here?" He took a step toward her, smiling. Behind him, the stained canvas that covered the front door billowed in the wind where the glass panes had shattered. "I live here."

"Jesus Christ." Louise dabbed at her nose with numb fingers. More blood. She looked around. In the sickly light from a naked light bulb—whatever lampshade had once covered it had long broken—she saw more of the hallway. There was filth everywhere. No one had cleaned here in years. "This house—"

"Is a dump?" He nodded. "Maybe. But that's all I got. I wasn't as lucky as you."

"What are you talking about?" She tried to get to her feet, but he grabbed her shoulder and pushed her back to the filthy floor.

He crouched down in front of her. "All this time," he said. "All this time all I could do was look at you."

There was something in his voice. The same thing that was in his eyes. God help me, Louise thought.

"But now you're here." Again the laugh. It frightened her. "After all those years, we're together again, you and me."

"We were never together, Maurice."

He put a hand on her chin, lifted her head. She tried to turn away, but his grip turned rough, holding her face in place. "You just don't remember," he said. "But you will, soon."

"There's nothing to remember," Louise muttered. But she knew they weren't having a conversation. He was having his say, whatever it was that he needed to tell her, and she would have to listen.

"It's funny, really, what brought you here. Or who, I should say. That sullen friend of yours told you, didn't she?"

"Of course," Louise said. He didn't know Milena was still unconscious. Hadn't been able to make sure, because Jacques had been there. A lot depended on not telling him otherwise. Her life, perhaps. "The others are on their way, too."

"Bullshit!" His hand flew up and the back of it struck her in the face, knocking her head to one side. The pain was tolerable—pain always was—but the sudden violence of it stunned her. At least for a moment, she didn't have to look at him. "You think I'm stupid! You all thought I'm stupid!" He hit her again, less hard this time, and laughed. "Nobody's coming!"

"Believe what you want," Louise said. She touched her mouth. Now that was bleeding, too. It was the first day in as long as she could remember that she'd been injured by a hand other than her own.

"I'm smarter than the lot of you," he screamed. "Smarter than you, smarter than your uncle! Smarter than your arrogant cunt friend who was here last night trying to snoop around! And smarter than your piece-of-shit father!"

"My father?" Louise looked up. His face was contorted. Was it rage, or grief? Hard to tell the difference. He might start crying, or hit her again. Maybe both. "You know nothing about my father."

His features went through another transformation. For a moment, his expression relaxed, turned nearly blank. Again he touched her chin and lifted it toward himself. His eyes narrowed. "I know everything about him. He was my father, too, for a time."

"Nonsense." Louise shrank from him. Put the pieces together, a faraway voice screamed inside her head. Somehow, this all makes sense, it has to. Even his ravings. The house. Why would he be here, live here? He would never be able to afford the property, even in its current decrepit state. And why had Milena come here? The faun, that was why. She had known this had been Corinne's

257

house. There was something Milena had found out that she'd never had a chance to tell Louise. And Uncle Claude knew it too. He'd meant to tell her, earlier on the phone.

"Yes, little sister." He laughed again. "My father." It sounded like a wheeze, like a drunk's laughter. "Until one night he wanted to beat me, and I fell into the river. All his fault!" The laughter rose in pitch. "A handkerchief and a boat turned loose. That's all it took to fool him. Now who is slow, little sister? Not me!"

"Mother of God," Louise croaked. In one terrifying instant, the puzzle assembled itself. "Frédéric?"

•

Part of her wanted to throw her arms around him, embrace the long-lost brother, thought dead, his bones covered with mud at the bottom of the Loire for all she'd known.

One look into his eyes, and that part of her died.

He nodded. "Isn't that something? Had them both fooled. The puffed-up ass and his sheep of a wife."

"Why, Frédéric?" The name still resisted Louise's tongue. When she looked at him, all she saw was Maurice. Lanky, awkward, snoopy and clingy, but harmless. "Why did you never tell us? Jesus Christ, all these years I thought father was to blame for your death."

"And he might as well have been," he bellowed. "He wanted me gone!"

"That's not true, Frédéric."

"Shut up!" His hand shot across Louise's face. The pain was sharp and shattered her last memories of Maurice. "You know nothing about it. He wanted to send me away, so I couldn't be near you anymore."

"You're my brother." Louise touched the spot where his knuckles had landed on her cheekbone. She winced. Her entire face was beginning to feel raw. "Why wouldn't you be near me?"

"Exactly!" Frédéric's voice was shrill with pleasure at her agreement. "But he couldn't understand that." The grin reappeared, like a branch pulled briefly out of the way only to snap right back into place. "I heard him talk with mother one time, inside the study. They didn't know I was at the door. He said I was a danger to you. That I wasn't normal."

Something laid itself around Louise's throat and slowly tightened. "A danger to me?" Images rose up from pools of forgotten memories where they had lain drowned for years and years, breaching the surface with black ripples and blossoming like poisonous water lilies. Sometimes he had hurt her. She wasn't sure why, or even how, and she hadn't been able to tell anyone, she had been so little. But she remembered pain, and fear. Just like now.

He nodded vigorously. "Can you believe it? All I did was love you. But he didn't understand. You didn't either, but you were small. You would have understood, in time. I know." He reached out and caressed her face. The touch was more nauseating that any blow he could have dealt her.

With a whimper, Louise recoiled. "What happened that night? Why was father so angry with you?"

"I knew he wanted to have me taken away," he said. "They were supposed to come for me the next day. He wanted to separate us. Mother was against it, of course, she told me so. She said I would have to leave while they slept, and hide. I knew it was my last chance."

Something icy crept up Louise's back with a thousand spiny feet. "Last chance at what?"

"To be with you," he said. "To have my little sister all to myself." His eyes turned liquid with a hideous affection. "So close to me."

"Oh, God." Louise wanted to pick up one of the shards of broken glass from the front door and cut into herself so deeply that the blood never again stopped flowing. "What did you do?"

He leaned forward, his voice almost a whisper now. His breath smelled sour, like spilled vinegar. "You really don't remember?"

There was no more room to retreat from him. A searing eruption burst into Louise's throat. She twisted sideways and retched onto the filthy carpet. "My father," she wheezed. "All these years…"

"He woke up and found us," Frédéric said. "But it was too late. Oh, how furious he was. All his plans had failed. I think he wanted to kill me."

Louise spat the last of her stomach contents into the corner. "He should have. God forgive me, he should have."

Frédéric ignored her. "So I ran to mother. I could always rely on mother. She told me to go hide, like we planned. She came for me later, and took me here, where it was safe. They thought I was dead. We fooled them, mother and I."

"You're mad," Louise said. "Mother never would have helped you, after what you did."

He giggled again. "Eugénie? Of course not. The stupid cow wouldn't take a piss without your father's permission. No, I'm talking about my mother."

"Your mother?" In all the horror and revulsion, a glimmer of hope: that this abomination, this depraved filth crouching before her, was not altogether of her blood. "Who was she?"

"My mother was always there for me," he said. "She was the one person who cared about me. The one person I could trust. And you know what's funny?" He bared his teeth in a savage grin. "All these years, you thought the same things about her."

Comprehension rushed at Louise like a black wave, inexorable and brutal. For a second or two, she went under, unable to breathe. She held on to consciousness with all that was left of her strength. "That's impossible," she whispered.

·

Louise's head started hammering. "It can't be," she muttered. "Aunt Corinne would never have lied to me."

"And why not?" he sneered. "She did everything for me. Why else do you think I have this house?"

"You ran away and hid here. Without her knowledge." But Louise knew he was telling the truth. Corinne had known. She had sheltered him, had even installed him at the gallery, as if in mockery of her unsuspecting husband. Corinne had lied to her, watched her turn against her parents; had she lived, she would have watched as Louise let her father die even as he begged to see her one last time. "How could she have done this?" She groped around blindly on the disgusting carpet. Maybe if she found something sharp. She could ask him to give her a moment, let her do it, let her find some relief. Surely he wasn't averse to the sight of her blood, the way he had hit her. Blood was the one thing that mattered, the only hope she had. "What about your father?"

His smile gave way to a mask of rage. "Who gives a damn who my father was?" he screamed. A spray of sour saliva flew into Louise's face. "I'm sure he was someone more decent than the bastard who raised me."

"My father helped you," Louise rasped. "He took you in and gave you a home as if you were his own, God only knows why." She started sobbing again. He had been capable of so much generosity, so much kindness. And she'd let him die alone and in despair, for nothing. He had been trying to protect her. All this time, trying to protect her from the adder he had nursed at his bosom. How could she have been so blind?

"He was a tyrant," Frédéric howled. "He tried to tear us apart, you and me. He had no right!"

"He had every right. He was my father."

"None of that matters anymore." His voice sounded calmer again. It frightened Louise, she felt safer with his outbursts of rage than with his sickening attempts to be gentle. "We're beyond his reach now, little sister."

"Don't call me that. You're not my brother. You're hardly my blood." She spat on the carpet between his feet. "Thank God for that."

"You're right." He smiled. "Do you see now, how wrong it was of him to step between us? There is nothing wrong with us being together." He reached for her wrist and pulled her toward him.

Louise wrenched herself out of his grip.

"Don't be like that," he growled.

"Go to hell."

He hit her across the face, hard. She fell sideways and had to brace herself against the floor. The pattern of the carpet, barely visible under the grime, squirmed under her eyes.

"See what you've done," he said. "You made me angry. It always made me angry, when you were like that. But I don't want to be angry with you."

Louise felt his hand on her back, stroking her as he kept muttering his apologies. Her stomach convulsed in disgust. Drops of blood fell from her nose and splashed

onto her hands as she heaved. There was nothing left in
her to throw up.

She sank into the corner, still trying to move away
from him. Her vision was blurry. Crouching close to her,
Frédéric was a twisted shadow outlined against the broken
door, his body coiled as if to launch himself at her any
moment. Like the faun on Corinne's urn, Louise thought.
Not held in check by his mother's hand, but protected by
it.

"Don't cry, little sister." He reached out and wiped
the vomit from her mouth with his hand, flicked it away. It
hit a wall, stuck, and slowly descended past a spray of
brown stains made by God knew what. "We're together
now, that's all that matters. This time, no one will come
between us. You'll see."

•

Somehow, she found the strength to kick and
scream. No one could hear her, of course. But she wasn't
crying for help. She was screaming because there was
nothing else to do, no words that would help vent her
despair, her revulsion. Once, her foot hit something hard,
and he grunted.

He slammed her into a wall, and all the breath
went out of her. Then he continued dragging her up the
stairs.

The stink was less thick up here, but no less
appalling. He kicked open a door.

The bedroom.

A horrible mess. Gray sheets, lumpy featherbeds.
A reek of old socks. He slammed the door shut, dropped
her on the bed. It was dark, the window covered by heavy

curtains. He locked the room, dropped the key in his pocket.

He struck a match and lit a lamp sitting on a dusty dresser. It was the twin of a lamp Aunt Corinne had given her years ago, during their week in Saumur. The lamp Louise had dropped one night and of which nothing was left now except for the sliver she kept in the lacquer box on her bedside table. It was so hard to believe. Aunt Corinne had lived here, once, years ago, before she'd concealed her degenerate son in this place. The last quick trip to Montmorency, before their planned departure for England, the trip that had killed her, it had been to him, to see he would be taken care of while she was gone. Corinne had known. Had always known.

He unbuckled his belt, took it off, and threw it into a corner.

He was going to do it again.

I'd rather die, Louise thought. But there was no way to find death here, except at his hands. And he wasn't going to kill her. Not before he did what he meant to do.

She couldn't just lie there and let it happen. She was no helpless five-year old. Not this time. She could at least put up a fight.

He walked around the bed, a bestial silhouette against the pale light seeping through the curtains. "Finally, little sister." He chuckled, reached for the bottom hem of his sweater and pulled it over his head.

Louise acted without thinking.

She swung her legs to the side, pulled them back, and planted her feet in his groin with all the force she could muster.

He let out a high-pitched grunt and folded in half, trying to extricate himself from the sweater.

Louise jumped up on the mattress. The old springs squirmed under her feet and she nearly lost her balance. One of them made a sound like a far-off gong.

She would lose this fight, she knew. Even if she knocked him down for a moment, she'd never be able to get the keys out of his pocket and escape. He would come to, beat her senseless, and rape her. The way he had done nineteen years ago.

But she was determined to deal out what pain she could to him before that.

She threw herself at him, shoulder first, bouncing off the collapsed mattress. She hit him just as he ripped the sweater off his head. In the half-light, she could see his eyes, glittering with rage. Even as he fell backwards, he tried to swing at her.

Carried forward by her momentum, Louise toppled off the bed, to the floor. That was it. He'd be on top of her in a second. She braced herself for his brutal grip, the beating he would give her.

Instead, she heard a crash of glass and a muffled yelp.

She looked up. For a moment, all she saw was that he was entangled in the curtain. He thrashed about and the curtain rod came off. Screws flew into the room, landing somewhere with bright clacks.

She jumped up, across the bed, and tried the door. Against hope. Locked, of course. She turned around, certain she'd see him coming at her.

Something wet and warm sprayed into her face and she gasped.

Louise was used to the sight of blood. But nothing could have prepared her for the fountain spurting from his neck. Like from a garden hose.

A slice of window pane still stuck in his flesh where it had severed the artery. He took one step toward her. A gargle rose from his throat. Sounded vaguely like her name. Then he fell.

It was over quickly. A quiver, a spasm, a sort of sigh. Silence. Within seconds, all of the blood inside his body was on the floor.

Louise felt the door behind her moving upwards, bruising her vertebrae. Only when her tailbone connected with the floorboards did she realize that her legs had given out underneath her.

She sat by the door until the last trickle from the gash in his throat had ceased. Until the edge of the wound stopped glistening and turned dull in the flickering light of the petroleum lamp.

She heaved again, uselessly, until she was spitting blood and mucus.

A strange calm settled over her. She knew she was in shock. Somehow, she managed to crawl over to his corpse and retrieve the key from his pocket.

Before she left the room, she extinguished Corinne's petroleum lamp. Then she picked it up and smashed it into the mirror above the dresser.

Step by step, she made her way down the stairs. A few times she was sure she would fall and break her neck. After an eternity of struggling against weakness and the danger of fainting, she arrived on the first floor. Then, out the door. Dreamlike.

The shriek of the rusty garden gate almost deafened her.

She staggered along the arborvitae, up the street. Had to watch her feet, take care for every step. One shoe still missing.

She had no idea how much time went by like this. Plodding along with one foot ice cold. Eventually, she buckled and sank to her knees next to a fence. She expected to pass out. Please let it happen, God.

Switch me off. But consciousness didn't relent. Her eyes wouldn't close. What could she do, then, but sit like this? Maybe hum a melody. A lullaby. Why not?

Footsteps. Someone was coming, calling out to her. Mademoiselle, Mademoiselle. Not his voice. Of course not.

Later, more voices. Something pricked her arm. And finally, she slept.

4 EPILOGUE

It seemed to Milena as if she had been sitting on the bench for hours. She still drifted sometimes. Perhaps it was the medication. Or perhaps it was simply the way time stood still in cemeteries.

A breeze had sprung up, carrying with it the smell of rain. The first clouds began to dim the morning sun.

A few yards down the gravel path that ran the length of the cemetery, she saw Louise embracing her mother. She'd been introduced briefly, when they met her outside the gates. Eugénie de Benoît was as beautiful as her daughter, with the same sadness in her eyes. It lifted a little every time she looked at Louise.

They had stood at Francois de Benoît's grave together, mother and daughter shedding their silent tears. After a while, Milena had walked off and found a bench under an ancient poplar.

She closed her eyes and listened to the breeze sighing through the leaves. Birds sang. There was peace here.

She heard a crunch of gravel and looked up. Louise came walking toward her. Her mother was leaving in the other direction. She rounded a hedge, and was gone.

Louise sat down next to Milena. "We're invited to lunch," she said. "In about an hour."

Milena nodded. "Are you sure she wants me to come? You must have so much to discuss."

"We had time to talk this morning. And there'll be time to talk in days to come." Louise slipped a hand around Milena's elbow. "I'll be coming back every week. Lord knows I owe him that."

Milena looked around the cemetery—deserted, so close to midday—and put her arm around Louise's shoulders. Louise started crying again. A debt of tears that would take years to repay in full.

"I still can't believe it," Louise said. "All those years, Corinne lied to me. After all father did for her and Frédéric. She destroyed my family, nearly destroyed me."

"You suffered for a long time on her account. But she could never have destroyed you."

"Her son would have. What do you think he would have done, after he was through with me? He couldn't ever have let me leave." Louise made a face as though she was about to spit. "He was evil. An abomination."

"No," Milena said. "What he did was terrible. But he was mentally ill, not evil." She touched Louise's hand, pushed back her sleeve. The scars would never fully fade. But at least there had been no new bandages in a while. She caressed the ravaged skin. "There are no demons, Louise. No taint that would disgust God. Not in you."

"I'm just so ashamed. That I was so easily used. That I turned so blindly against my father, my mother, without giving them a chance."

"You were lied to." Milena opened her purse and found the bottle of painkillers. "It wasn't your fault."

"The migraine again?"

"Yes. But it's getting better." Milena closed her eyes and let Louise massage her forehead. The tender gesture helped more than the medication, when the headaches came. "The doctor says they'll eventually go away. But it'll take time." The throbbing in her skull relented as Louise's fingertips traced the scar tissue that straddled her hairline. The scar was most likely going to be part of her face's landscape forever. It makes you look tough, Pauline had joked, it's a battle scar, after all. But weren't they all? There were always battles, even if one didn't know it at the time. Some were fought side by side with friends, but most of them were fought alone.

"I'm ashamed for distrusting you, too," Louise said.

"If you hadn't, you would never have gone to Montmorency. Who knows, perhaps he would eventually have come for me, to finish the job."

"I still wish there had been another way."

"Of course."

A sudden gust of wind bathed them in cool air. The trunk of the poplar creaked behind them. The sighing of trees, Milena thought.

"I can't tell my mother who you are," Louise said. "I hope you understand that."

"She'd be shocked that you consort with revolutionaries?"

"You know what I mean."

"I don't expect you to tell her," Milena said. "I'm not sure if I'm ready for that. I've told Pauline, but for now, that's enough. I'm in no rush to make announcements to the world. As long as we know who we are, you and I."

Louise nodded. She touched her lips to Milena's temple. "I don't know what could be more important."

Milena felt a raindrop on her nose. Then another. Louise looked up into the sky, shivered, and pressed against her. Milena followed her gaze. More raindrops, light and cool, touched down on her skin. A million gentle fingertips started tapping on the silver leaves above their heads. In the distance, toward the horizon, green treetops shimmered in the sunlight where the clouds had already passed.

Milena drew in the fragrant air and smiled. "Nothing in the world," she whispered.

- THE END -

ABOUT THE AUTHOR

Henning Bauer was born in Germany and has been living in the United States since 1994. In addition to being a writer, he is a linguist, language teacher, and freelance translator/editor. He lives with his wife in San Francisco, California.